Anne Wilson did a Ph.D in socio... became a freelance journalist. S... video scriptwriter. She is marrie... and lives in London.

truth or dare

Anne Wilson

First published by The Women's Press Ltd, 1996
A member of the Namara Group
34 Great Sutton Street, London EC1V 0DX

British Library Cataloguing-in-Publication Data
A catalogue record for this book is available from the British Library

ISBN 0 7043 4461 0

Typeset in 10/13pt Garamond by Contour Typesetters
Printed and bound in Great Britain by
BPC Paperbacks Ltd

*To Mark, who gave me the mornings,
and much more besides*

Acknowledgements

Thanks to my friends who gave encouragement and support, especially Mike, Ros and Andy, and my mother, E P Riley. Special thanks to my agent, Lisanne Radice, for opening the door.

chapter one

My kids don't go to fancy schools. Hannah goes to the local primary which has the advantage of being within spitting distance of Sainsbury's. Jacob is at a state nursery next to the public library, five minutes' walk from the counselling clinic where I work. So when Caroline Blythe phoned up one sweltering summer afternoon, just after I'd collected Hannah from school, to ask for advice on where to send her darling Harriet, I assumed she had something else on her mind.

'I know you don't approve of private education, but do you know anything about Claremont?'

'Only that it's bloody expensive.'

I was tired and distracted. Hannah and Jake were arguing loudly over who should pour the apple juice. After a second's deliberation, I decided I hadn't the energy to threaten them with the violent chopping gesture I use to signal 'I'm on the phone. Put a sock in it, or die.'

'. . . marvellous maths education and it's supposed to be awfully egalitarian, but I'm a bit worried about the creative side. You don't know anyone who has a child there . . .?'

Most of the people I know would be hard pressed to buy the blazer.

'No, I can't say I do. Look, Caroline, I'm a bit busy at the moment, so –'

'Sorry. Of course, I'll let you go. Actually – there was one other thing.'

I allowed the silence to stretch, punctuated at my end by the bump

1

and slosh of a carton of apple juice hitting the deck. I shook my fist silently and pointed to the sink.

'I'm a bit worried about a friend of mine. A problem with a man, sort of – I just wondered if I could come and see you tomorrow . . .?'

I was only half listening – Hannah was climbing on a cupboard door to reach the taps – but I registered with puzzlement that Caroline was using the old therapy cliché: I need to see you, my friend has a problem.

'Wouldn't it be better if your friend came to me herself?'

Caroline hesitated. 'It's . . . she doesn't . . . um . . . acknowledge the problem at the moment. You know . . . I don't think she'd see the point. All I can say is . . . it could be life-threatening.'

Caroline sounded uncharacteristically rattled. I was intrigued – as intrigued as you can be when you're watching two children fighting over a dish cloth. Journalists like Caroline don't usually go in for high emotional drama – but they are persuasive.

'I know how busy you are, Sara, but if you can spare the time . . .'

I cursed inwardly. 'Shall we meet for lunch – or do you want to come to the clinic?' For which read – is this professional, or a free counselling-cum-chat, a favour for a friend.

'At the clinic,' she said firmly. Professional. At least she could afford to pay if she decided to continue sessions, unlike most of our clients.

I scanned my diary. 'What time were you thinking of?'

'Say – two thirty?'

I looked at the dreadful day outlined on the page in front of me, full of difficult clients, with two hours set aside for writing a painful report for social services on a kid who'd died of a heroin overdose. I'd been putting it off for days. I calculated that Caroline's newspaper job meant a lot of late nights, so she probably didn't get up too early, relying on the nanny to get Harriet to school.

'It looks like I've only got a bit of time around nine fifteen . . .'

'Nine fifteen's fine.'

You can have half an hour and no more, I thought, and if I'd got to the end of that assertiveness course I'd tell you so. 'See you then,' I finished lamely, making a mental note to re-read *Saying What You Mean and Meaning It.*

'Thanks, Sara.' Caroline resumed her normal tone. 'And love to Hannah and Jacob.'

As I put down the phone and picked my way across the sticky floor to re-do Hannah's 'clearing up', it struck me as odd that Caroline had turned to me for help, even on behalf of 'a friend'. Journalists from Grove Park don't usually come to community counsellors based in Acton, even if they do have the added bond of having met through the baby mafia. That was our affectionate name for the National Childbirth Trust – the NCT – the middle-class solution to grandma living in Scotland and big sister in Kent. No family around, so you make an artificial one with people who are having a baby at the same time as you. Ante-natal puffing groups become post-natal support networks, through which you make grateful contact with women with whom you may have nothing in common except broken nights and stretch marks. I'd met Caroline at a working mothers' group when I was having Jake and she was having Harriet. I'd pretty much pulled out of the whole scene by then, but they'd asked me to talk to the group 'as a professional and a mother' on the strains of juggling the two roles.

Caroline stood out a mile, even in a group of professional Chiswick mums. She was six months pregnant, but the sharp attention of her expression was about as far from bovine as you could get. Being tall and slim, she managed to look sleek and glamorous despite her growing belly. Her tailored dress was cunningly cut to emphasise slender hips and long, silky legs and she asked astute questions about motherhood which I was hard pushed to answer. But she also showed a humorous and vulnerable side which made her prickly questions seem less aggressive. She wasn't the type of woman I'd have as a bosom buddy – too hard, too single-minded – but she was a hell of a lot more interesting than the nappies and nipple spray brigade. I'd seen her quite a few times since then, at swimming galas, children's parties, places where you know a lot of faces, but have a job remembering all the names. People always remembered Caroline's. She had an aura of strength about her, a sense of importance: I always felt mildly sorry for Harriet, thinking what a hard act she had to follow.

'It wasn't me, Mummy, it was him! He tried to stop me pouring it, but I'm the oldest so I should, shouldn't I?' Hannah interrupted my thoughts with a high-pitched whine, goose-stepping round the kitchen after me and somehow managing to spread the sticky liquid to the place I'd just cleaned. Jake was sulking, a Duplo man hanging out of the corner of his mouth.

'Snot fair!'

I launched into the familiar late-afternoon routine of squabble refereeing, soothing and cajoling, trying simultaneously to listen to the playground woes of a seven-year-old, do my half of a complex fire-engine puzzle and cook for the kids the kind of meal that would reassure us all that I was a proper Jewish mother. There were the inevitable six o'clock phone calls from the clinic. It wasn't until eight o'clock, when Hannah and Jake were both tucked up in bed, well fed, scrubbed and plugged into story cassettes that I remembered the phone call from Caroline. My neighbour, Steve, had come over to make dinner and tell me about the play he was about to start rehearsing. I poured myself a long cool beer.

'What life-threatening problem could her friend possibly have that I could help with?' I mused, mostly to myself. Steve gave me a merry look then reached for the beer can beside my chair and took a long gulp. I stared distractedly at his balding head, stubbly throat and crinkled T-shirt. Actors can be the tattiest people. He finally closed his mouth on the beer, smacked his lips, flung out one arm and intoned in a rich, booming voice.

'Ah, life! Life! How tenuous thou art!'

'Sshh!' I hissed, motioning upstairs where the children were, hopefully, asleep.

As it turned out, Steve's quote couldn't have been more apt.

On the surface, Caroline looked like a fish out of water, sitting on the couch in my consulting room. She was wearing sharp, steel-grey tailored trousers with a short jacket to match, and a swirling silk blouse in muted peach. On her lithe, feline body, the combination seemed to be the perfect marriage of serious power and seductive femininity. I felt an utter frump in comparison, acutely aware of my barely combed mass of frizzy hair, and my usual assortment of clothes-that-missed-the-laundry-basket, grabbed in the frantic interval between breakfast and the school run. I'd put on a skirt in a half-hearted stab at respectability, but the sloppy shirt, low-heeled shoes and big earrings betrayed the fact that I didn't really mean it. Caroline's face was made up subtly to emphasise high cheekbones and penetrating dark blue eyes, set far apart over an aquiline nose. She looked serious and severe with her straight hair scraped back into a low pony tail, held by a slide. Her mouth, lightly covered with lipstick, was wide and determined. She was poised on the edge of her seat like a cat ready to pounce; I expected her to whip out her tape recorder any second. Yet in another way, she was like a typical client coming for the first time. Her eyes darted from my face to different objects in the room; her hands betrayed tension, her fists constantly opening and closing. Beneath the bright, alert manner lurked a nervous, wary woman.

As she told her story, in short, crisp sentences, cold, reporter-style, I found myself torn between two conflicting emotions – fury that she was wasting my time with such a stupid tale and curiosity about what it was she really wanted. When she looked at me for some kind of reaction, I tried to control the impatience in my voice.

'So your friend's got a problem. She's been having an affair with a married man –'

'But it's finished now –'

'Your friend *had* an affair with a married man which is now over,' I repeated flatly, 'And you think –'

'But she still sees him,' added Caroline.

'Right.' I sighed, through gritted teeth.

Caroline fixed me with a cold gaze and her tone became

mechanical and hard. 'My friend was involved with a married man, whom she still sees. I know more about this man than she does. She *has* to stop seeing him.'

'Why? What's the matter with him? A murderer, rapist – bad breath? Give me some help here, Caroline.'

'He . . . I think he's involved in something very shady. I can't say any more.'

'You said on the phone it might be life-threatening.'

'It might. I can't go into detail.'

'I see.'

'My friend's got a problem' is such a tired ruse, I couldn't believe a sophisticated woman like Caroline was using it. But I had to give it a try.

'What's all this to you, Caroline? Why does it bother you so much?'

She looked me straight in the eye.

'I'm not talking about myself if that's what you think. I do have an interest, yes. She's a . . . friend. I want to help her, but I feel . . . helpless.'

'What about the man?'

'What about him?'

'Are you involved with him?'

'No. I hardly know him.' Her downcast eyes told me she was lying, or hiding something.

'So you want me to help you with your feelings of helplessness?' I was floundering. I could do with some help with my own.

'No. Yes. Indirectly.' She felt down towards her bag on the floor and extracted a packet of cigarettes. She looked at me. 'Do you mind?'

I did, but I shook my head. Anything to get to the bottom of this load of bullshit, and get her out of my office. I'm not a psychoanalyst. I'm not into middle-class angst. I'm a counsellor. I see people who know what the problem is – a mortgage they can't repay, kids they can't control, a partner who beats them up – but can't find a way out. I listen, put it back to them a different way, help them to see the options. My job is helping people hack a path through the crap so they can get on with their lives. I just wished Caroline would go and get on with hers. She pursed her wide lips and took a deep drag from the cigarette, blowing a long line of smoke towards my overstuffed bookcase.

'I want you to talk to her.'

'But you said she wouldn't want to –'

'I want you to contact her. She won't listen to me, Sara, in fact she won't even speak to me. But if you could just tell her about this guy, she may see what she's doing to herself.'

I couldn't believe what I was hearing. 'Caroline! I can't do that. Ring up a complete stranger and say "Hey, let me give you the dirt on your lover – a friend of yours tells me you ought to give him up"'

'I know it's unorthodox –'

'Unorthodox! It's ridiculous.'

'Tell her you're my therapist. Tell her I'm in this awful position of knowing this man is, well, a criminal really – and if she keeps bothering him, I don't know what he'll do.'

'Why don't you go to the police?'

Her eyes drifted away. She looked tired. For the first time, it struck me that she may simply be asking for help. Her job was highly stressful. I knew she lived with Harriet's father, but I'd rarely heard her mention him – I wondered if the relationship had turned sour and she had found someone else. Maybe she couldn't cope any more and this was the only way she could tell someone.

'It's a story I've been investigating . . .' She sighed heavily. Then all of a sudden, she seemed to change her mind. She shook her head and gave a short nervous laugh. 'Of course. You couldn't possibly talk to her. I see that.' She stubbed out her cigarette into the lid of the packet and put it back in her bag. 'Look, I must be going. I'm sorry I've wasted your time.'

My head was reeling. What on earth was going on? I motioned her to stay where she was.

'Caroline, we've been sitting here for half an hour and I still feel you haven't got round to what you really wanted to talk about.'

Her face registered nothing. That's unusual. I was rushing it, but I

7

had no option; I had a suicidal adolescent waiting in reception.

'We can talk about what's troubling you now, or we can fix an appointment for, say, the beginning of next week when we've both got more time. Then, when we've sorted out what the problem is, I can refer you to someone who can help. I can't take you on myself because you're a friend, but one of the other counsellors in the clinic –'

'Thanks, but no thanks.'

She stood up and smiled sadly, a smile which made me feel uneasily that I'd failed in some way, missed my cue – that she was disappointed in me. I stood up and laid a hand on her arm.

'Think it over. I can't talk to your friend, but I can talk to you.'

Her face closed and she nodded coldly. She clearly felt that she'd tried to tell me something and I hadn't heard it. I shrugged mentally. It happens. Wrong time, wrong counsellor. We said our goodbyes and she left quickly. As I watched her, from my window, run over the road past the library and get into her smart black Renault, I knew she wouldn't be back.

I was right about that, at least. Three days later, she was dead.

The Acton Counselling Centre started out as three grumpy women bemoaning mental health provision over plastic cups of coffee at a social work conference. Clancy, Mel and I had reached the same conclusion at the same time: there was a huge gap in mental health services which left a whole section of the community no option but to be drugged to the eyeballs by their GPs or shunted from one out-patients clinic to another. Together, we set out to achieve the impossible – a local centre offering practical counselling to individuals and groups in the area. We would cater for ordinary people with ordinary problems ranging from insomnia to obesity to abuse and we would take referrals from GPs, schools or any other agency, or people could refer themselves directly. The clinic would be funded by a mixture of grants from the health authority, social services and a mental health charity, plus fees from clients who could afford to pay. We were all trained counsellors: over several months, we developed a broad set of principles of practical counselling, used all the contacts we'd built up as social workers, fluttered eyelashes and lobbied councillors for local authority grants and, on the stringiest of shoestrings, started the clinic in the basement of a converted wallpaper factory.

That was five years ago. Now we were based in a red brick, semi-detached Victorian house behind the High Street. Funding was still precarious, but our reputation and Mel's patient and continuous PR efforts generally saw us through. Bit by bit, we'd imposed some kind of order on its shabby, dingy rooms. We made the downstairs sitting room into a reception-cum-waiting area. There was a plush, three-seater russet-brown corduroy sofa, a few easy chairs, with cushions, in warm, autumnal colours, and a low pine coffee table with a range of not-too-out-of-date magazines. In one corner of the room, near the net-curtained bay window through which came the muted sounds of traffic and people chatting on the pavement outside, was a low red plastic table stacked with Lego, crayons and paper, a big box of toys and several small plastic chairs. Mel had insisted on a play area – she works a lot with children and single mothers. In the middle of the room was a U-shaped desk, with switchboard, files and computer, presided over by Doreen, the super-efficient receptionist whom luck had delivered to our door in the early days of the clinic.

Doreen was in her late fifties. She lived on the South Acton estate and had three grown-up children. Originally from Northern Ireland, she had come to England when she was fourteen to work in one of the Acton laundries. She was large, brisk and pleasant, and she made it her business to keep all of us – staff and clients – firmly in line. She was a strict time-keeper and wouldn't stand for rudeness. There were no excuses, not even a 'troubled psyche'. But her firmness was tempered with an expansive kindness and flexibility which would put most doctors' receptionists to shame. Doreen had been known to hug violent drug abusers, soothe screaming infants and engage morose adolescents in some semblance of conversation. She used

9

the same techniques on us – her common sense philosophy told her that when it came to having problems, there wasn't much to choose between counsellors and clients. And she was right.

There were five counsellors in the Centre now – three women and two men. Our interests varied, but we were all committed to the idea of a local counselling service, taking up where harassed GPs and overworked social workers left off. Mel tended to specialise in very young children and young single mothers – most of her cases were rejects from the local child guidance clinics. Clancy, Greg, Robin and I did some family counselling, but our caseloads were more varied and included private clients. Clancy also had what we called her 'grey groupies' – small counselling groups for depressed elderly people. The pensioners adored Clancy, with her boundless energy and no-nonsense advice, dispensed with a strong Manchester accent. It was a constant mystery to the rest of us how she got them to come in the first place, though her racy publicity ('Are you getting enough? Sex and the Over Sixties') must have lured a sizeable contingent.

We operated pretty independently as counsellors, but each week we met to talk over our cases and argue about who left the dirty coffee cups in the sink over the weekend.

At the staff meeting the Monday after Caroline's death, I was still reeling from the shock. The friend who had broken the news to me hadn't known I'd seen Caroline recently, and I hadn't realised until I sat in the meeting how upset I really felt. Suicide, she'd said. No one had any idea why.

'You can't blame yourself,' Clancy was saying. 'What more could you have done? You said she could see one of us if she wanted. We'd all have acted the same.'

'I wouldn't.'

Everyone turned to Greg. He was staring at me, poker-faced as usual. Bastard, I thought, bitterly.

'With a story like that,' he intoned in his deadpan voice, 'I'd have booted her out after the first five minutes.'

I laughed gratefully and felt a little better.

'What bothers me more than anything,' I said, trying not to sound as shaky as I felt, 'is that she seemed anything other than suicidal. She was jumpy, scared maybe, but still in control. No hint of self-destruction.'

Mel gave me a gentle searching look. She tucked a strand of wispy hair behind one ear and fixed me with her large grey eyes. 'She wasn't a client of yours, Sara. Just a friendly acquaintance. You say you hardly knew a thing about her.' Her tone was soft and soothing. 'Of course you're upset, but you hardly had time to make a professional judgement.'

The others murmured in agreement.

Their support was comforting, but I still couldn't let it go.

'You have a gut feeling on these things, Mel. I've had scores of patients who've tried to top themselves. You get to be able to spot the ones that are serious and I just wouldn't have put her in that category.'

There was a momentary silence.

'Take a few days off,' Clancy suggested. It sounded more like an order. 'But don't sit around moping.'

I opened my mouth to protest that time off was the last thing I needed, but I suddenly saw the sense of it. I was upset. I'd hardly slept. I was finding it hard to think of anything else. We talked about how best to clear my schedule for the next two days and Greg took on the job of fixing new times with the clients I'd miss.

As I left the meeting, I had a moment's light-heartedness – it had been months since I'd had a whole day to myself – but depression took over as I crawled home through the traffic in my rattly old Vauxhall Chevette. Why on earth would someone like Caroline Blythe want to commit suicide?

I jolted to a stop outside my terraced house. The street was deathly quiet, empty except for a lone mother wearily pushing a pram to the shops. I wondered if Caroline really *had* had a friend who was in trouble. Maybe I'd feel better if I looked into it. If there was a friend, I might be able to help her if it seemed appropriate. I had failed spectacularly to help Caroline when she was alive – perhaps this

11

could make up for it to some extent. It was the least I could do. And it might be good therapy for me.

I got out of the car, opened the front door and walked into the cool, silent house.

I started by ringing the woman who'd told me about Caroline. Alex is an NCT stalwart – she seems to know everyone and everything – and I knew she'd had contact with Caroline through organising the newsletter. In between the slurps and burps of her breastfeeding baby, she told me what she knew.

'It was Harriet who found her, that's the awful part. Apparently, she died of a drug overdose.'

'What sort of drugs?'

'The person who told me wasn't sure, but she thought, knowing Caroline, it would have to be cocaine.'

'You mean Caroline . . .?'

'Well, they do, don't they, that lot? Parties and so on.'

'Oh, right.' Clearly, we led sheltered lives in Acton.

'It was the morning after a party at her sister-in-law's. Sunday morning. Her husband stayed there on the Saturday night because he was playing golf the next morning –' Alex paused to shift the baby on to the other breast, and gave a squeaky 'ouch' as he latched on.

I was still struggling with the thought that Caroline took cocaine. 'So Caroline came home on her own and took an overdose and was found by Harriet on the Sunday?' What an odd time for a mother to choose – a night when she knew her child would be the first to find her.

'Supposedly. Unless she took something at the party and it got to her once she was home. I'm not sure how these things work. But isn't it awful? Lucky the nanny was there. She called the doctor and everything and got the husband back from his sister's. Why did she do it, d'you think? She always seemed so . . . together. So strong.'

Alex sounded upset. She didn't know Caroline much better than I did, but the horror of it had clearly got to her too.

'I was going to ask you the same question.' I was loath to tell Alex

12

about Caroline's visit to the clinic, but I decided it might help prompt her memory about Caroline's friends. 'Look, Alex, between you and me, I saw Caroline a couple of days before she died. She was worried about a friend of hers . . . something about this woman having an affair with a man and the man being a bit dodgy. She wanted me to talk to her friend – do you know who it might be?'

'She doesn't see much of her NCT group any more because she's working.' There was a five-second pause while Alex thought about it. 'I know one of her friends . . . Helen Marchment. She lives in one of those enormous houses in Heathlands Road and she's on the same dinner party circuit as Caroline. I think they shared a nanny at one time and the children go to the same nursery. Yes, Helen's a good friend of hers. Was, I mean.' But she added doubtfully, 'I'm not sure if she's the right one. I think she's happily married.'

After exchanging a bit of local gossip, I rang off and dialled the number Alex had given me. Helen, amazingly, was in, and when I told her Caroline had come to me for counselling, she agreed to see me straight away.

Alex hadn't exaggerated when she'd said the house was enormous. It was one of those elegant, detached 'five bedrooms and a nanny flat' houses in a quiet tree-lined street, a few minutes' walk from Chiswick High Road. I rang the bell, suddenly conscious of my jeans, big trainers and baggy T-shirt. I should've dressed up, I thought, then quickly dismissed the idea. The sight of Helen, immaculately turned out in a silk blouse and a black pleated skirt had changed my mind. I could never have lived up to that. She had fine, light brown hair, swept back into one of those elegant swirls which was somehow held together by pins. Her face was well-proportioned and composed, pretty but un-lived in to my critical eye. Her figure was not unlike Caroline's – she was tall, lithe and leggy – with an enviably flat stomach that belied the idea that she'd ever had a baby. I put my hand on my own stomach, in an involuntary gesture, and found a gentle curve which had never quite disappeared since I'd had Jake. Had Helen changed her clothes because I was coming, or did she dress like this every day? She looked the type who might wear a designer number for playgroup. Unsmilingly, she invited me in, and ushered me into a large, elegant sitting room to the left of the front door. The furnishings were straight out of a Sunday colour supplement – deep, plush sofas in swirling pastel colours, heavy curtains and clever-looking lighting. I tried to make my dirty trainers invisible by tucking them under the valance of the sofa. A disgusted look passed over Helen's face, instantly stifled by a polite half-smile.

'Coffee?'

'Lovely, thanks.'

It was already made, in a glass coffee jug on a low, polished oak table, filling the room with an irresistible aroma. As she poured it, a man in a dark pin-striped suit and sparkling white shirt popped his head round the door. He smiled at Helen, not noticing me trying to blend into the sofa behind the door, blew her a kiss and whispered throatily, 'Bye, darling. See you tonight.'

She smiled back at him, a genuine smile with her eyes, then gave a wave in my direction.

'This is Sara. A friend of Caroline's.'

'Ah!' He saluted me awkwardly and cast a sheepish grin at Helen. Her eyes were adoring. 'Bye-bye, darling,' she oozed. 'Have a good day.'

He blew her another kiss and disappeared. Bloody hell. I didn't feel too hopeful now that I'd found Caroline's hapless friend.

Contemplating the steaming cup of rich, dark liquid on my knee, I was at a loss to know where to start.

'I'm really sorry about Caroline. It must have been a terrible shock. Alex said you knew each other quite well.'

'Very well. We were extremely close!' Her tone was sharp, almost bitter.

I glanced up in surprise.

She smiled uneasily. 'I'm sorry. Yes it *was* a shock. I knew she was unhappy. God knows, she had enough cause to be. But to commit suicide!'

14

I kept still, with my eyes fixed on Helen, saying nothing. Her sharp, angular features had tensed into a frown and her small brown eyes narrowed.

'Stupid man! People think he's so ... jolly amusing ... but I saw the other side of the story.'

'Her husband?'

Helen nodded. 'Dear James.' Her mouth set in a tense line of disapproval.

'Really.' I nodded sympathetically.

'She used to sit here and sob sometimes. Especially just after Harriet was born. He had no idea about new motherhood, being tired – you know.' I nodded. I knew, all right. It was six months after Hannah's birth before I could remember what day of the week it was. 'He just expected her to pick herself up and carry on the way they did before they had children.' Helen shook her head. 'I just can't believe it.' She bit her lip, trying not to cry. Then her face froze hard. 'It's his fault. He drove her to it.'

'What sort of things did he do?'

'It's what he didn't do,' she replied hotly. 'He relied on Caroline for everything. Even when Harriet was a baby, Caroline was supposed to run the house, do her job and still have time to nanny him.' Her mouth curled with contempt. 'Some men can't deal with successful women, can they? Caroline was incredibly bright. She made him look stupid.'

'Did she ever think of leaving him?'

Helen gave a harsh laugh. 'Oh, she thought about it. Many's the time I said to her, "Why don't you just leave him?" She earned a good salary, it wasn't as if she needed his money.' Helen shook her head wonderingly. 'But she seemed to like the little boy in him. She was constantly getting him out of scrapes. Perhaps it all got too much for her in the end.' Helen's eyes suddenly shimmered with tears. I wanted to ask about James' scrapes, but the sad trickle which cut a path through her virgin make-up stopped me. She didn't look the type to cry easily.

'I'm so sorry,' I said.

15

'It's Harriet who'll suffer now,' she sniffed. She reached over to the occasional table, fished a tissue out of a china holder and smoothed round her eye make-up. Then her lapse of control seemed to make her conscious of my presence and register the fact that she didn't know me from Adam. Her manner became more brusque. 'Anyway, what's your interest in Caroline? You said on the phone you wanted to ask me something.'

I told her what I'd told Alex but without going into detail – that Caroline had come to see me because she was worried about a friend, who was in some kind of trouble. I added that I wasn't sure how true the story about the friend was, that sometimes people invented things like that when they needed help themselves.

'I doubt that,' she said brusquely. 'Caroline wasn't the type to go snivelling to a –' She stopped mid-sentence, aware of sounding cross, and added carefully, 'I suppose she did have a lot on her plate.'

'You mean James . . .?' I prompted. 'Or perhaps her work. She mentioned a story she was investigating . . .'

Helen glanced at me suspiciously. 'Both.'

'D'you know what the article was about?'

'No,' she said quickly. 'She was very cagey about it. They have to be, don't they, journalists. She'd just say things like it was a really big story, then, later, that it was getting a bit too close to home, things like that.'

'I wonder what she meant by that? Could it be another of James' scrapes?'

Helen shrugged. Whatever she knew, she wasn't giving it away.

'So you don't know who the friend might be? I'd like to talk to her if I could.'

Helen shook her head. 'Haven't a clue.'

I tried a different tack. 'I'm sorry if this sounds intrusive, but were you and Caroline getting on okay? It doesn't sound as if she had much to time to see her friends.'

Helen was nettled. 'Of course. Even if she didn't have time during the day, I saw her at dinners and parties. We had a wonderful time on Saturday night, that's why it's so hard to believe –'

'You were there?' I asked in surprise.

Helen looked slightly irritated. 'Yes. I was there.'

'How did Caroline seem?'

'I've told you. She seemed fine. As fine as she ever was, given the awful man she lived with.'

'Did anything happen at the party which might have upset her?'

Helen put down her coffee and fixed me with a mildly hostile gaze. 'Look. What is this? I don't know anything about any friend of Caroline's, I don't know what made Caroline do what she did except that her life wasn't a bed of roses. I'd really rather not talk about it if you don't mind.'

She clearly wanted me to go, but I had one more question.

'Of course. I'm sorry to have upset you. But – could I just ask this one thing. Was Caroline having an affair?'

Helen's face stayed stony. 'I really don't know.' But she couldn't resist adding, 'If she was, it would be a jolly good thing. Tit for tat.' Aha. So James' transgressions didn't stop at being an unreconstructed male.

I drained the rest of the delicious coffee, thanked her warmly and left. I swear I could hear the hoover removing my traces before I'd reached the front gate.

It had turned into a beautiful day outside. The early morning chill had given way to a bright, fresh summer's day, the kind we think of as quintessentially English, but don't get too many of in this muggy, polluted city. I sat in the car and wound down the windows, wondering what to do next. The breeze was heavy with the sweet fragrance of summer roses and the leaves shimmered prettily in the sunlight. It was almost like being in a country village. I drank in the tranquillity and thought over what Helen had told me.

So Caroline had problems. Somehow that didn't seem to help much. Did the fact that she had a weak and possibly unfaithful husband explain why she committed suicide? Hardly. Or rather maybe, maybe not. There were always two sides to a story like that and layers and layers of history. Three years ago, I had been in the same situation and I was still here to tell the tale. Could Caroline's suicide have been more related to the story she was investigating? My thoughts kept returning to her manner that morning she came to see me. Why did the idea of her killing herself seem so unlikely? I sifted mentally over the few cases I'd seen where a client diagnosed as suicidal had actually pulled it off. You couldn't generalise; there was no single thing which marked them out. Except . . . one thing perhaps. A sense of purpose. That's what they were lacking and that's what Caroline seemed to have. The image of her walking resolutely towards her car . . . places to go, people to see. Perhaps it was just an illusion, but she had seemed to be pursuing something with a single-mindedness, a zeal which was the opposite of the hope-lessness I'd seen in other depressed people. How much cocaine had she taken? I wondered. That was a sure way of telling if it was a deliberate suicide. Caroline was an intelligent woman – if she'd really meant to do it, she wouldn't have taken too little. That's what I'd try to find out next.

Satisfied for a moment, I closed my eyes and let the warm summer air wash over me. Only the slight swish of the breeze and the merry twitter of birds broke the silence. I started to relax. 'Olive oil,' I thought. 'I must put that on the Sainsbury's list. And crisps for Hannah's lunchbox.'

''ello, 'ello, 'ello – we can't 'ave you parking 'ere!'

I jumped at the voice and my eyes snapped open. A male face was framed by the open passenger-side window, the chin resting on a pair of muscular arms which emanated from a crisp white short-sleeved shirt.

'Barry! Shouldn't you be catching burglars or something?'

'Not many about this morning.'

'Just waiting for a few to confess, are you?'

His lips twisted to an approximation of a smile as he glanced round the car and then at me, with that never-miss-a-thing scrutiny that coppers can't help having.

'What about you – off work? Not enough nutters to keep you going?'

18

I shook my head. 'Compassionate leave.'

He caught my sudden seriousness and raised one eyebrow enquiringly.

'A friend of mine bumped herself off.'

Barry was all ears. 'Anyone I know?'

I shook my head again.

Barry and I are the most unlikely people to be on friendly terms, but we had been for seven years, ever since we'd had to go together to break the news to the mother of a sixteen-year-old boy, that her son had been stabbed to death in a 'queer-bashing' incident the night before. I was the boy's social worker. Barry had known plenty of vicious crimes, had seen, on more than one occasion, the bodies of people who'd been kicked to death, but this had really shaken him. As we'd walked away from the mother's flat I'd suddenly realised why Barry was so upset. I touched his arm in silent sympathy and although he didn't move a muscle I knew then that Barry had understood that I'd realised he was gay. I could only imagine what that must mean for a policeman, especially a detective sergeant. Neither Barry nor I mentioned it explicitly but I urged him to see stress counsellors at the Met about his reaction to the death of the boy. Barry refused, I guess he couldn't risk any hints of his sexuality circulating through the Met.

As Barry shook his head sympathetically, a sudden thought struck me and I got out of the car.

'Actually, Barry, you're just the man I wanted to see. How much cocaine would you need to take for it to be fatal?' Barry knows that kind of thing. He was a beat officer in Soho.

'It depends. Why?'

'This friend. She came to see me a couple of days before she died and – it's hard to tell, but she didn't seem suicidal.'

'Caroline Blythe?'

I gasped. 'You knew her?'

Barry hesitated. 'As a matter of fact, I'm just about to visit a friend of hers.'

It was my turn to look questioning. 'Helen Marchment?'

He nodded.

'Why? You don't normally investigate suicides, do you?'

Barry hesitated again. 'It seemed like a straightforward suicide,' he said, slowly, 'but there are one or two . . . loose ends.'

'Like what?' I searched his face intently and found nothing. I couldn't leave it at that.

'Come on, Barry,' I said impatiently. 'What's the mystery? She was a friend a mine. Sort of.'

Barry hates words like mystery – too much like a telly detective. He sees his job as ninety-nine per cent detail and one per cent deduction.

'No mystery, we just want to save the family any embarrassment.' He stopped.

I nodded encouragement and said softly. 'How exactly did she die?'

He stroked the golden hairs on his arms casually. 'Overdose. By injection.'

I frowned. 'Injection? Surely – she wasn't an injector, was she?'

'Do you think she was?'

'No!' As soon as I said it, I felt unsure. How did I know? I hardly knew her.

He nodded thoughtfully. 'That's what I mean. Just a few loose ends . . .' He threw me a charming smile and tapped the roof of the car.

'Nice motor. Antique, is it?'

I made a face at him.

'I'll be in touch,' he promised and turned back towards Helen's house.

A few loose ends . . . I got back in the car, fired up the engine and headed home.

chapter two

That night I dreamt Caroline was being tortured by the Nazis. She was in a small, dank cell, tied to an iron cot, her legs clamped tightly together. They were sticking thin burning needles into the soles of her feet, taunting her that she would never walk again. She screamed and screamed and I saw the waves of pain shooting through her convulsed body. I kept trying to reach her, to pull them off, but the more I strained towards her, the more unreachable she seemed. When the screaming stopped and Caroline finally passed out they dragged her, limp and pale, into a cold white-tiled shower, where the poison gas slowly started to fill her lungs. I shouted at them to let her go, begged and shouted and struggled . . . and I woke with a start and a stifled scream as a hand touched my face.

'Whatsa matter, Mum?' whispered Hannah. 'You woke me up. You were shouting.' She lifted up the duvet and snuggled in beside me. Her small body felt safe and comforting; she smelt deliciously of warm skin and strawberry flavoured toothpaste. I was still shaking from the dream. I slipped an arm round her and kissed her head.

'Silly Mum had a bad dream,' I murmured. 'Back to bed now. Sorry I woke you up.'

She sighed sleepily and trotted back to her room. I lay awake in the darkness trying to dispel the horror of the nightmare.

I listened to the muted night sounds in the street – the intermittent hum of a car on the main road several streets away, the distant rattle of a train carrying, no doubt, some sinister nuclear cargo under the cover of darkness. I heard Charlie, the neighbourhood insomniac, pass under my window on his customary beat – click-step, click-step, the metal of his stick beating out its slow, painful rhythm. I breathed slowly and deeply and tried to relax. It was times like this when I missed David – the only time, actually. In my limited experience, living with a man had little to recommend it, but there was something to be said for being able to snuggle down after a bad dream and cuddle up to another body sleeping peacefully beside you. I hadn't lived with anyone since David, and I never brought boyfriends home unless the children were away, so sleeping beside another person was a luxury. I hadn't slept with anyone for about three months now, more through inertia than anything, but for the first time I really missed having someone around. Was I getting old? I would be thirty-four next birthday. I pulled a pillow down beside me and wrapped myself around it in a vain attempt to extract some comfort. Pathetic. I sighed and wondered whether I could be bothered to get up and make a hot drink, risking waking both the children. I couldn't.

I threw aside the pillow and tried to empty my mind and sink back into sleep. Suddenly, it that clarity of thought which often comes on the verge of sleep, an odd contradiction struck me: why was Caroline, whose husband, according to Helen, was having an affair, trying so hard to be sympathetic to a friend who was playing the role of Other Woman? I opened my eyes and stared into the darkness, trying to puzzle out her motivation. Before David's affair, I regarded women who got involved with married men as misguided, but benign; afterwards, they became The Enemy, colluding with a man's disloyalty and deceit. Yet here was Caroline pursuing some man's mistress, trying to warn her about some impending doom. Must be quite a friend. Or was there another reason?

Caroline must have wanted to warn her pretty badly to come to me for help. There must have been another woman. And Helen was right. Caroline wasn't the type to come to a counsellor to sort out her personal problems. It seemed likely that the warning was connected to the article she was writing. But why, in the midst of all this activity, would she suddenly decide to commit suicide by shooting herself full of cocaine? It definitely didn't add up. Caroline did not seem disturbed. She looked nervous, driven, a hunter who wanted to find, or do, something before she herself was hunted. I shook myself mentally; it's easy to let imagination embellish reality when you're lying alone in a night-hushed house. But it made me more determined than ever to find the woman involved with a married man. Perhaps she could tell me more about the newspaper story Caroline was pursuing and perhaps that, in turn, would help explain her death.

A thin line of blue-grey light was seeping round the blinds in my bedroom. Soon Jacob would be awake. I tried to banish all thoughts of men and women and death and call up a favourite fantasy: lying face down on a Caribbean beach in the hot sun, with a cool breeze blowing in from the sea. A handsome, muscular surfer, who hasn't a thought in his head and is barely able to string two words together, is lazily rubbing sun-tan lotion into my back and legs with slow, circular movements. 'Up a bit, Brad,' I murmur, directing him to a place where a few grains of sand are disturbing the delicious sensation of the oil. The warmth of the sand creeps into me and the light strokes of his fingers pull me gently into oblivion.

It never fails.

I arrived back at my house after the usual frantic morning rush, feeling exhausted. Getting three people up, dressed, fed and washed; remembering whether today is swimming or ballet; gathering the long list of essential accompanying items – an old toilet roll, cotton wool, a worm ('Miss Jeffreys says we've *got* to, Mum') – always left me reeling, but on a normal day, arriving at work brought instant structured demands which banished the harassment of the first two hours of the day. Usually, I spent a few moments sitting in my consulting room, nursing a cup of strong coffee, staring into space and organising my day. Today, coming back to a quiet empty house was strange and depressing and my weariness hit me like a sledge hammer. I made a cup of coffee, slumped down at the kitchen table and gazed glumly at a cornflake floating in a half-drunk glass of Ribena.

The phone made me jump.

'Hello?'

'You're up then?' Barry's gravelly voice leapt out of the earpiece.

I made a face. 'Noooo. Just sitting here waiting for the maid to bring breakfast.'

'Yeah. How would you like a little visit?'

'Official or friendly?'

'Can't it be both?'

All Barry's visits are official really. He can't ever forget he's a policeman.

'Is it about Caroline?'

'Just wanted to pick your brains,' said Barry evenly. I looked around at the dirty breakfast dishes and the toys littering the kitchen floor and felt an instant desire to get out.

'How about buying me a coffee at the Pigalle?'

'Suits me. Half an hour?'

'Great.' I put the phone down, feeling better, and started running through the questions I wanted to ask Barry. I looked down absently at my T-shirt, flung on at seven that morning, and registered that it had 'Wishbone Ash Tour 1975' in faded letters across the chest. I leapt upstairs and changed into a scoop-necked black top and a pair of beige cotton shorts. I glanced quickly in the mirror as I grabbed my purse. Not bad, I thought. I've learned to live with my large tits and rounded bottom and tell myself my small waist makes up for them. I'd put on a bit of weight on the hips though. I made a mental note to cut out the doughnuts and to start swimming regularly again. As a last-minute gesture, I stabbed vaguely at my mop of hair with an Afro comb, but it was a bit like trying to prune a hedge with a knitting needle. I shook the curls out again and convinced myself it made me look interesting and trendy.

Barry was already there, the only man drinking a cup of PG Tips in a place known for offering a choice of twelve different types of coffee.

The Café Pigalle is Chiswick's attempt at a Bohemian hangout, modelled on a famous Parisian café, but it only manages to attract the right clientele at weekends, very late at night. The rest of the time, it's a slightly pretentious, overpriced coffee shop reluctantly patronised by early shoppers who know there's nowhere else to take the weight off their feet except MacDonald's, two doors down. At this time on a weekday morning, there were only two other customers. To our left, a man in his forties with long hair and John Lennon glasses, alternately staring into space and scribbling intently with a pencil in a spiral notebook. Typical Chiswick poseur. To our right, several tables away, a young bored nanny with close-cropped bleached blond hair, her nose deep in magazine, studiously ignoring the whining one-year-old in the buggy beside her.

I pulled out the chair opposite Barry and ordered a *cappuccino*, made with dark Columbian, from the cool, distant waiter.

Barry gave me a welcoming grimace. 'How are you feeling?'

'Better, thanks.' I eased myself into 'good citizen' mode. 'So how can I help you, officer?'

Barry laid his large arms on the table and fiddled thoughtfully with the sugar bowl. 'Tell me what happened the day Caroline Blythe came to see you.'

I took a deep breath and launched into the familiar story – her phone call, the friend with a problem, a man who was doing her no good. Barry listened carefully, interrupting with questions to clarify each bit of information, making sure he had it right. Half-way through my story, my *cappuccino* arrived. As I paused to spoon the froth and chocolate off the top, Barry pulled out a notebook from the pocket of his jacket, flung round the back of his chair, and jotted down a couple of notes. He watched me lick my spoon for a moment or so – in a mildly disgusted way – and then asked.

'Why did she choose you?'

I leaned one elbow on the table and cupped my chin in my hand. 'Because I'm a wonderful counsellor, Barry. And a warm, caring human being.'

He gave a wry smile. 'Really – how well did you know her?'

'Not that well. Mothers' meetings, that type of thing.'

'So you weren't really a friend?'

I took a couple of sips of coffee and thought about it. 'She knew I was a counsellor – she was quite clear that she wanted to come to the clinic rather than meet socially. Maybe she thought I was a bit unconventional. Out of her normal social circuit. Perhaps she just thought she could trust me.'

Barry nodded. He frowned thoughtfully. 'So she wanted you to contact this friend and tell her . . . what?'

'That the man was bad news, a criminal, whatever. She mentioned a story she was working on. I wondered if she might have got her information while she was researching it.'

'What kind of story?'

'I have no idea.'

Barry made another note. 'This man . . . was he a friend?'

'She said not. Though I'm not sure I believe her.'

'Did she actually say he was a criminal?'

I tried to think back. 'Yes, I think so. And whatever she knew about him was life-threatening to the woman – she definitely used that word.'

'Hmm.' Barry brushed his pen against his lips. Then a sudden idea struck him. 'Maybe you know this woman.'

'Know her? Why should I?'

'It would make sense.'

I thought back to my conversation with Caroline. ' "No," I said to her – "I can't just ring up a total stranger", and she didn't contradict me.'

'Just a thought.' He looked disappointed. Perhaps I was another loose end which was stubbornly refusing to connect up and establish a clear-cut suicide. I was sceptical about knowing the friend. I ran quickly through a list of acquaintances in my head; no one was having an affair with a married man that I knew of. And there was no one who was likely to know Caroline. I shook my head again.

'Never mind,' said Barry. He doodled in his notebook while I took some more sips of coffee.

I felt I had done my bit for the criminal justice system – now it was Barry's turn to give information. I asked Barry to tell me what they knew, aware that I'd only get a highly edited version.

'We don't know that much yet. A smart party out in Surrey – lots of media types, a few local notables – a small amount of drugs, we think, though nothing was found. Mrs Blythe leaves about half past midnight on her own – her husband's staying the night to play golf early the next morning. She gets home about one fifteen – the nanny's a bit hazy about that, but she thinks she heard the door about that time. Some time after that she must have taken a sleeping pill and some time after that –,' Barry paused. I looked at him expectantly. Barry shrugged. 'You know the rest. Gave herself a massive dose of coke and snuffed it between two and three a.m.'

I tried to take it in. 'Let's get this straight. She gets home, takes a sleeping pill, then o/ds, intravenously. Where was the syringe?'

'On the bedside table.'

'How long does cocaine take to work?'

'The amount she took . . . very little time. Unconscious in a matter of minutes . . . could be dead in, oh, half an hour . . .'

I gazed at him, incredulous. 'So why did she take a sleeping pill if she knew she was going to kill herself?'

Barry looked vaguely uncomfortable, but he answered coolly. 'People do strange things . . .'

'Was there a note?' I persisted.

Barry shook his head.

'Any needle tracks on her arm? Legs? Has anyone said she was a junkie?'

'Look. I told you there were loose ends –'

'Loose ends?' I said it louder than I meant to and my voice had gone up a pitch.

The writer, who had buried his head in his hands in search of inspiration, looked up and stared. I stared back angrily – get on with your novel, mate – but I lowered my voice.

'It's bloody suspicious if you ask me. Are you saying that Caroline Blythe decided to kill herself, took a sleeping pill for no reason and then took an overdose with a massive intravenous hit of cocaine? Why didn't she take more sleeping pills? Why, for God's sake, didn't she leave a note, if only to explain things to Harriet? She was a journalist, Barry – as in writer!'

Barry shook his head. 'She was an intravenous drug user – there were more syringes in the bathroom and a small supply of coke. It probably seemed like a good way to go. The sleeping pill? Inexperience. She had never o/d'd before, she didn't know what it felt like and didn't want to know. As for the note – some leave 'em, some don't. I'm not saying it's a textbook suicide, but believe me, very few are. There's always some inconsistency.'

I looked into Barry's clear blue eyes. He made it sound very plausible. But I remained unconvinced. A mother doing that to her child? And I could see that she might indulge in a little social cocaine but to have as much of the stuff as Barry said she had taken? Whatever Barry said, I resolved to contact the newspaper where Caroline worked to try and find out if anyone had suspected her of drug abuse.

Barry was beginning to look impatient. 'What are you thinking?' he asked. 'That someone else injected her?'

'It's possible,' I said defensively.

Barry put his hands behind his head.

'What would you expect to find on the sides of the syringe, Sara?'

'Why, fingerprints, I suppose, Detective Sergeant.'

'Exactly.'

'And there weren't any?'

'Only Caroline's.'

I wasn't impressed. 'I'm still suspicious.'

Barry raised his hands, palms up, maddeningly calm. 'As I said, it isn't a textbook case.'

We fell silent. I couldn't stop thinking about Harriet finding her mother dead. I tried not to picture the scene, but I couldn't help substituting Jacob's face for Harriet's. He'd stand by the bed at first, and give my cheek a wet, puckered kiss, then he'd yell 'Time to wake up!' in my ear and climb on to my chest. When I didn't respond he'd shake my shoulder, chuckling, sure I was only playing. Then his smile would fade, his shaking become more urgent: 'Wake up, Mummy, wake up, wake up!' His voice would leap to a higher pitch, disbelieving, anxious, then rise to a cry, a wail, hysteria . . .

'Are you sure she did it, Barry?' It came out sounding more urgent than I meant it to.

Barry thought carefully before answering. He shook his head slowly. 'No, I'm not sure. We're still making enquiries.'

I looked him straight in the eye. He knew I expected more.

He sighed and leaned forward again, resting his elbows on the table. 'All right, I'm not happy about the sleeping pill. And I haven't found much yet to suggest that she used drugs regularly. But it's still early days. We haven't got enough to justify a murder inquiry.'

'What about the fact that she didn't seem suicidal?'

Barry looked sceptical. 'Hard evidence, Sara, that's what you need. She was depressed, under stress. Husband was having an affair – that's enough for most coroners. Mind you . . .' Barry hesitated; I sensed he'd started to say something and immediately regretted it. He was on the edge of being as indiscreet as a conscientious DS ever can be.

'Yes?' I prompted, trying not to sound too eager.

He couldn't back out now, but he chose his words carefully. 'The family's got some fairly impressive connections.'

I didn't quite get it. 'What about it?'

Barry glanced at the writer at the other table, now scribbling madly in his notebook to avoid catching the eye of the waiter collecting his empty cup. Barry lowered his voice. 'They're, shall we say, not being as forthcoming about Mrs Blythe as they might. That's normal in a case like this – sweep it under the carpet, anything to avoid a scandal – but something tells me there's more to it than that . . . I get the impression strings are being pulled higher up.'

'Your Chief Superintendent?'

Barry stared impassively. I took it as a yes.

'Could it be the cocaine at the party?' I asked.

'Could be.' Barry drained the rest of his tea, almost cold by now, and waved to the waiter for the bill. He had said more than he intended and I could see he wouldn't be drawn any more.

'So what will you do now?' I asked quickly.

'I've still got a few more people to talk to. Then I'll put in my report and it's up to the boss what happens next.'

We stood up and walked towards the door. I put my hand on his arm.

'Promise me one thing, Barry.' He stopped and turned towards me, raising his eyebrows, questioningly.

'Tell me if you find that friend of Caroline's. I really would like to talk to her.'

He gave my hand a friendly pat.

'I can't promise, but if I can, I will.'

I nodded. 'Thanks.'

We stepped out into the muggy air and said our goodbyes.

As I started walking back down the High Road, thronging with the usual Chiswick blend of shoppers, howling babies, media types and 'resting' actors, I got a sudden rush of irrational anger. How could everyone go about their daily business as if nothing had happened? A woman who walked down this very street, who bought her microwave dinners in the same Marks and Spencer's, who tut-tutted, just as they did, about the terrible lack of parking in the region of the High Road – she was dead, apparently by her own hand, and they were alive, but indifferent. And her family seemed more interested in saving face than in finding out what had actually happened.

Who was looking out for Harriet in all this? Who would explain to her, in five or ten years' time, why her mummy had seen fit to take her own life without a word of explanation, or even a goodbye? I shoved my hands into the pockets of my shorts and frowned at a few passers-by. I felt restless and annoyed. Barry's attitude irritated me too. I certainly didn't expect him to give me any more information than he already had, but I did expect him to take my questions seriously and give more credence to my professional judgement. The fact that Caroline did not display any suicidal tendencies *was* evidence of sorts and Barry should know that. I turned off the High Road and clomped down the side street where the Chevette was parked. Why were detectives, even friendly detectives, so sure of their unique ability to penetrate the human mind? So dismissive of other people's need to know? Were the pure professional motives of the police as likely to do Caroline justice as my raw desire to find out the truth?

Stuff you, Barry, I thought. Stuff you and your Chief Superintendent.

I got in the car and started the engine with an angry roar.

I must have been the last person James Blythe expected to see that morning. He seemed so surprised that anyone would have the temerity to call at his house at such a delicate time that he invited me in. He led me through the wide, high-ceilinged hallway towards a room at the back. The house was in Bedford Park, one of those fantastically expensive red-brick jobs with Adam fireplaces which I'd often drooled over from the outside, but never actually been inside. It was the type of place to give estate agents multiple orgasms – moulded ceilings, elegant archways and a polished oak floor. The walls were hung with antique architectural prints, expensively framed. As we passed the large, pine-panelled kitchen, I glimpsed Harriet playing with her dolls' house under the watchful eye of a young nanny and an elderly woman, presumably her grandmother. Harriet was talking to her dolls in a shrill voice; the women were hunched over steaming cups, looking pale and tense.

James strode briskly down the corridor and opened the door to a large, light, airy office, drenched in sunlight. It was bigger, probably, than the whole of the downstairs of my terraced house, with two french windows opening out onto the patio, patterned with small Italian tiles. Beyond the patio I could see narrow, well-tended borders and a velvet smooth patch of lawn, remarkable in a house with a child (where were the sandpit, the climbing frame, the paddling pool?) The walls on each side of the french windows were lined with bookshelves filled with fat and glossy textbooks. Against the third wall, there were sleek black filing cabinets and a power desk with a high-backed, black leather chair. I guessed James had been sitting at the elaborate drawing board – all rulers and guy ropes – on which lay a half-finished plan of some building or other. The plan was completely incomprehensible to a mind like mine, which can't even read a street map; all I could make out was that it had lots of rooms and stairs and I'd stake my life it wasn't sheltered accommodation for the hard of hearing.

To one side of the room, there was a meeting area, which looked like it had been carefully arranged for a photo session for an avant-garde design magazine. Low 'designer' chairs (black and white deckchair covers, stretched over a couple of wire coat hangers) posed self-consciously beside a three-cornered glass and metal coffee table. Comfort was clearly not an issue. On the wall near by, I noticed a calendar of modern paintings, with 'James Blythe, Architect' printed tastefully across the top.

James must have been in his early forties, handsome in a bland, English way, with fair hair which he constantly combed back through his fingers into a deliberate wind-swept look. He had the kind of pink-cheeked boyish face which stays for ever public schoolboy even into middle age – chubby and eager-looking – and a bright-eyed, hearty manner, intensified by stress. Twenty years ago, when his face was hewn in the bony relief of adolescence, his short, receding chin might have looked artistic, but now, closely shaven and filled out by too many business lunches, it looked weak and complacent. He was dressed in a sporty, golfing outfit – beige gabardine slacks, navy blue Lacoste shirt, white socks and loafers, his only concession to bereavement being a black arm-band worn over the left sleeve of the shirt. (How do people manage to dig out

32

these things at such short notice? Where does one buy a black arm-band?)

'I appreciate your seeing me, Mr Blythe –'

'James – please.' He waved me towards one of the wire and canvas chairs and sank heavily into the one opposite.

'I know this is a terrible time for you.'

He nodded absently.

'If there's anything I can do . . .?'

He stared at me blankly for a moment, floundering. 'Ah. Right. Yes. Don't think I caught who . . . your –'

'Sara Kingsley. Caroline's therapist.' Therapist was a word I knew he'd understand. It registered on his face like a bombshell.

He flushed scarlet. 'Therapist? Sort of shrink, you mean? Good God. Didn't even know she –'

'She'd only just started.' I countered smoothly. 'Her first session was last Thursday.' It never fails to alarm me what a good liar I am.

'I see.' Emotions swept across his features in succession – annoyance and anxiety becoming paramount. I glimpsed a photo of Caroline in her wedding dress on the wall behind the drawing board, smiling and radiant. I carried on before I lost my nerve.

'I just wanted to say how sorry I am . . . what a tragedy . . .'

'Yes.' He ran his fingers through his hair and stood up. He walked over to a small fridge at the side of the room, opened it and pulled out a bottle of Perrier. He was seriously rattled. He seemed to be thinking through some of the implications of Caroline having a therapist.

He turned back to where I was sitting. 'Aitch two oh? Fruit juice?'

I shook my head. 'Nothing thanks.'

He took a glass from the shelf above and poured some water. I took a gamble and made as if to stand up. 'Look, I think I'll go. I just wanted to –'

'No!' He held up his hand. He swallowed a mouthful of water.

'I don't want to intrude.'

'Not at all. It's . . . interesting.' He scanned my appearance furtively, noting large breasts and bare legs, then took a sip of water and sat down again.

I stayed where I was and waited for him to make the next move.

'Any idea . . . why she came to see you?' He didn't look at me, or wait for an answer. 'Down in the dumps, I suppose – was that it?'

I met his eyes, saying nothing. He took it as assent.

'Always getting depressed, my wife. Stressed up – you know. It was the work. Worked awfully hard, all hours.' He searched my face for a reaction and found none. Just bland acceptance of anything he might choose to say.

I am a cipher. You can tell me anything James.

'We certainly had our ups and downs,' he said with a false heartiness. 'I don't know what she said to you, but we were happy. Married ten years. Happiest ten years of my life.' His desperate cheerfulness dropped between us like a dead weight. He watched it fall and relaxed a little. 'Can't expect a marriage to work if the other person's never there, can you?' he asked dolefully. 'Chap plans a romantic weekend away with his wife and what happens? "Something's come up, darling – got to go to the office." So I stopped bothering. Work always came first. Before her family, even.'

You mean before you, I thought cynically.

'It was Hattie – Harriet – that kept us together. I wanted another one, y'know – come from a large family – but Caroline . . .' He shook his head. 'Had her career to think of.' He shot me another anxious glance. Being a counsellor gives you daily practice at presenting an encouraging, but non-reactive mask. If he was wondering how much I knew, he wouldn't find the answers in my face.

'Things had been . . . choppy lately, I suppose she told you that. To be honest with you, I think there was someone else in her life. I'm quite sure about it actually.' He said it plaintively, with an edge of self-righteousness, raising his face and jutting out his chin. I had a sudden vision of James as a little boy in short trousers, telling tales on his sister – 'Guess what she did! Isn't she naughty?' Even from a stranger, he wanted approval for himself, censure for Caroline. He lowered his eyes and gave a short incredulous laugh.

'Ridiculous thing was, she was the jealous one! Always imagining things about me and other women. She was paranoid really. That's the word – paranoid.'

Oh, come on James, I thought. You can do better than that. He paused – I let him.

'It had got particularly bad lately,' he continued, 'I did notice that. She seemed upset, always wanting to know where I was going and so on. She was spending less and less time at home. Bad for the child, I thought, and I told her so. I think I might have even suggested that she talk to someone about her . . . problems. Yes, I'm sure I suggested it.'

I bet you did, Jim lad, I bet you did.

Infidelity – tell me about it. Even when David's affair was out in the open between us, he told all our friends how suspicious I was, how paranoid, how jealous. And how bad it was for the children that I seemed irritable and depressed. The powers of projection never cease to amaze me. Now, too late to help myself, I can detect a man who wants his wife to be his mother at fifty paces, through bullet proof glass, blindfold – the wide-eyed innocence, the desire to blame, the heart-rending appeal to anyone who'll listen. A weak ego in need of continual massage. The man who, once he is sure of you, becomes petulant about every moment that takes you away from him. They see it as the perfect justification for infidelity. If my mummy isn't here, I have to get my cuddles somewhere, don't I? Shocked at my own vehemence, I checked myself. Was I being too hasty in my judgements? I scanned this petulant face – no, his manner was all too familiar. This was a man who would always see himself as the injured party, even if he'd been screwing other women since his wedding night.

James didn't seem to detect that my bullshit monitor was flashing. He gazed at me with mournful eyes.

'She wanted us to go to one of these marriage guidance things, but – I don't know – I wasn't keen – we never did, somehow.'

No time, I suppose. Too busy bonking the mistress.

'I wish we had now.' He looked at me and his chin started to tremble. He raised his hand to his forehead in a weary gesture. His voice cracked.

'I bloody wish we had!'

I struggled not to be touched by his emotion. His hand moved up and swept his hair back again. He stifled a rising sob with a cough and took another sip of water. He coughed again, pulled out a handkerchief from his pocket with the long fingers of his right hand, blew his nose, then stared into his glass. I scrutinised him silently. I wanted to see it as Mills and Boon heroism – self-conscious grief – but even I had to admit that beneath the posing and defensiveness there was genuine distress. Bewilderment.

'You must be terribly shocked,' I ventured, with false gentleness. Permission to be sad. It seemed to get to him. He swallowed hard several times in the silence that followed. When he finally looked at me his eyes were filled with tears.

'How could she do it?' he whispered hoarsely. 'How could she do this to Harriet?' He looked away again. I chose my next words carefully.

'Are you sure there's no possibility of . . . anyone else being involved in this?'

He started visibly. 'What do you mean?' He said it sharply.

I tiptoed over the eggshells. 'I mean, you're quite sure in your own mind that Caroline meant to take her own life?'

'Of course! That's what the police said, and there's no reason to suspect –' He frowned and his chin trembled. 'What exactly are you trying to say?'

I stroked my chin thoughtfully. It's times like this that I wish I wore glasses so I could take them off and suck the ends meditatively. 'I saw Caroline on Thursday and she didn't seem suicidal. She didn't even seem particularly depressed. Agitated, perhaps, and anxious. Obviously I'm concerned that I might have made an error of professional judgement, but I'm also suspicious. Did something happen between Thursday and Saturday which made life suddenly not worth living? And the way she died – forgive me, I know this must be distressing for you – but did you know she had a drug problem? That she actually injected drugs?'

James looked uncomfortable and it wasn't just the coat-hanger chairs. He shifted in his seat and his eyes darted from one part of the room to another.

'You're asking the same questions as the police and my answer is the same. I don't know. You live with someone, you think you know them –' He sighed. 'I knew she took things from time to time. At parties, or when she had to work all night – who knows? Yes, she may have started injecting.' He finally looked me in the eye. 'We led very separate lives.'

The phone rang – a discreet, modern whirr. James sprang up to answer it. 'James Blythe speaking.' His tone resumed its former heartiness. He paused, listening.

'Lady Parrish, hello!' He glanced at me and shrugged self-consciously. 'Yes, indeed. A great shock. One just doesn't expect . . . oh, bearing up, thanks, bearing up.' He was all doleful smugness, a forlorn puppy, slavering at the feet of titled sympathy. I looked away to hide my disgust and gazed down idly at the pile of papers beside my chair – today's post, some back numbers of architectural journals, an open filofax. A telephone number caught my eye: it looked familiar. 'L. at work' then the number, 0171-722 3333. The kind of number you remember. I looked away, not wanting to snoop. Where had I seen that number before? I couldn't think. 'L. at work.' Perhaps it was a company I used for something. James was finally managing to get off the phone.

'Many thanks, Lady Parrish. Very kind. Perhaps see you next weekend then. Most kind – goodbye.' He put the phone down and turned his attention back to me. Now, where were we? Ah, yes, milking another female sympathiser.

'Did up her Suffolk place,' he explained, gesturing towards the phone. 'Been a good friend ever since.' He sighed and glanced distractedly at his watch. He was clearly losing interest. Even so, I risked one more tack.

'Do you know anything about the story Caroline was working on?'

'Did she mention that?' he asked quickly. 'In therapy?'

'Not really,' I hedged. 'Do you know what it was about?'

He waved one arm dismissively. 'Completely out of my depth, I'm afraid. Didn't tell me a thing about her work. I even read a different paper. Not a clue. She'd get all worked up about it . . . bloody paparazzi, I used to say, easy money feeding off other people's misfortune.' He gave a hollow chuckle, and looked at me for appreciation, but when he found none, the laugh stopped abruptly and hung on the air, leaving a vague tension. James shuffled in his chair uneasily.

I took it as the cue to leave, and stood up. 'I'd better let you get on.'

He seemed relieved. He stood up and held out a hand. 'Glad to have met you.'

I fished a card out of my bag and handed it to him. 'If I can be of any help at all . . .'

He glanced at it and put it on his desk. 'Right.'

'And if you feel Harriet needs any support or help, I can give you the name of a very good child psychotherapist. Very experienced with bereaved children.'

He looked seriously underwhelmed with the idea. 'Well. Good to know. If we run into problems I'll give you a buzz.' He opened the door and started to follow me down the hallway, but I stopped him.

'Please don't bother. I'll see myself out.'

'Right oh.'

'Goodbye.'

'Bye for now.' I felt his eyes on me until I reached the front door. I turned back and he gave a slight wave. He looked weak and pathetic standing there in the doorway, his shoulders slumped.

'I expect we'll meet again,' he said, too heartily.

I tried not to think that it sounded like a prophesy of doom.

chapter three

The girl hunched on the sofa of my office was sobbing noisily, her straight stringy hair flopping like wet spaghetti round her bony, black clad knees. I leaned forward and gently touched her shoulder.

'I think this sadness is very important, Tracey.'

Her head shot up and she glared at me through red, puffy eyes, her face smeared with cheap mascara. 'My fucking mother fucks me around an' all you can say is the fucking sadness is important. Well fuck you!' She shook my hand off her shoulder, returned her head to her hands and howled bitterly.

I moved my chair nearer. 'Shall I tell you why? C'mon Tracey, look at me. Because it's the first time you've realised that inside, you feel like a little girl. You're a little girl who needs looking after. That's the truth and it's important you know it.' The crying intensified. Sixteen years old, as streetwise a kid as you'll ever come across, dressed like a tart in a skin-tight, strappy black top and bottom hugging black Lycra shorts and yet she reminded me so much of my seven year old daughter. I rubbed her shoulder rhythmically and made soothing noises while she cried herself out. Eventually, she started to sniff and hiccup. I put my arm round her.

'That's it. It's all out, now.' I gave her a cheery squeeze. 'Hey, the girl done good Tracey! Takes some people months to cry in counselling and you've managed it in seven weeks.' She squirmed in her chair, unused to praise, trying not to look pleased, and wiped her skinny arm across her nose. I stood up and fetched a box of tissues from my desk.

'This is what I want you to think about for next week – this feeling of being your mum's little girl, wanting to be looked after, but not knowing how to show it.' I pulled out a few tissues and passed them to her.

'Here. Tidy yourself up or you won't look like Madonna.'

She gave a long blow, threw her hair back with one hand and scowled at me.

'I hate fucking Madonna,' she growled.

I grinned. 'She's sexy.'

She rolled her eyes dramatically. 'She's old.' She looked up at me for the first time, regaining some of her characteristic bravado. 'Like you. You're a real wanker you are.'

'I take that as a compliment.' I glanced at my watch. 'Time's up.' I smiled. 'Go.'

She spat on to a tissue and, thrusting her face close to the glass of my bookcase, wiped carefully round her black-smeared eyes. Then, tossing the tissue in the direction of the waste paper basket (it missed), she smirked cheekily, got up off the sofa and made for the door. I folded my arms and refused to look irritated.

'See you next week,' I reminded her.

'You might,' she shrugged, and made what she hoped was a dramatic exit, somewhere between a flounce and a wiggle, leaving the door wide open. I chuckled silently, picked up the stray tissue and shut the door. Another triumph for adolescent counselling.

Not all my clients have Tracey's charm. I mean that. Tracey was dragged screaming through the door seven weeks ago by her mum who said she was a moody, unmanageable little whore on the brink of a criminal career – only in slightly stronger language. The epithet seemed to belong more to the mother than the daughter, but that was another story. Clancy took on the mother and Tracey came to me. For the first two sessions, she mostly sat in hostile silence, picking her nose and flicking the contents on to my carpet. The third time, I shot her a few home truths which triggered a temper tantrum worthy of a two-year-old. It loosened her tongue and Tracey proved over the next few sessions that she had a pretty good idea why she felt the need to nick everything in sight in every shop in Acton High Street. She was intelligent, startlingly clear-headed and, though she hid it remarkably well, sensitive and well-meaning. After seven weeks she was still moody and unmanageable, but she was beginning to understand why, and see what she could do about it. After a few more sessions, Clancy and I were going to put mother and daughter together for a joint fireworks party – I just hoped I didn't end up as the catherine wheel.

Having two days off meant two days of back-to-back client sessions with hardly a second to scratch myself. I liked being busy, but not this busy. On the Friday, I was glad to take a breather and grab a quick lunch out with Clancy at The Horse and Plough. Acton's full of dark, dingy pubs with about as much charm as a wrestler's armpit – The Horse is no exception. But at lunchtime, it attracts a loyal clientele of loud, cheery pensioners by serving a huge, cheap two-course dinner of meat and two veg and a stodgy pudding. Clancy likes the geriatric ambiance; I love the stodgy pudding.

'So how's the lady with the guilt complex?' asked Clancy, loudly. She dumped her lager on the table so hard that an inch of it slopped on to the beer mat. She dragged her chair round the table with a ear-splitting scrape – Clancy likes to have a good view of the action – then sat down, finally with a thud. The tight-lipped, mousy woman at the next table stared.

I frowned at Clancy, but it went right past her. 'I don't really feel guilty,' I murmured defensively, 'I just want to know why she did it. And if I could've done anything to prevent it.' Clancy opened a packet of cheese and onion crisps with unnecessary force and started to crunch them meditatively.

'Like what?' she said.

'Like – I don't know. Talked to this friend of hers. Taken a bit more notice.'

'Crap. You're not psychic.' She reached into the bag for another handful of crisps.

'The whole thing is odd,' I persisted in an undertone. 'The way she's supposed to have died . . . If she was an intravenous drug user, she was a pretty unlikely one. And who would take a sleeping pill, knowing they were about to kill themselves with an overdose?'

Clancy stopped munching and looked at me. 'What do the police say?'

I shrugged. 'Not a lot.'

'Ha! Typical.'

'Why?' I tackled my roast lamb with roast potatoes and gravy whilst Clancy poked the air to count off the reasons.

'One – because that MP was at the party. Two, because she was a woman. And three, because someone's told them they got to find a suicide, not a murder.'

'Murder?' I muttered with my mouth full.

'Yeah, murder.'

Of course that was what had been on my mind but I was still shocked to hear the word out loud. Then the rest of her spiel registered. 'Hey, wait a minute. Which MP?'

Clancy's rich brown face clouded. 'The guy who defended that cut in pensions two years ago. What's his name?'

'Hunt. Sir Edward Hunt.'

'That's him.'

I grunted my surprise and polished off the last of my peas, potatoes and gravy, one eye firmly fixed on the jam sponge and custard. A large pensioner, a pasty-skinned woman with an enormous flower print dress stretched across her stomach, squeezed past our table on her way to the bar. Noticing Clancy, she uttered a loud inarticulate greeting and clapped her on the back. Clancy started, then, recognising the flushed face, grinned and gave her arm a tap that sent the white flesh wobbling. The woman looked at me and jerked her thumb at Clancy.

'She's a cheeky one,' she rasped.

'Certainly is,' I agreed.

The woman started laughing and shaking her head and she cuffed Clancy on the shoulder. 'Told the vicar to piss off. Piss off!' She threw back her head and let out a throaty howl which degenerated into a cough. Her breath must have been eighty proof. She moved off, lurching her way to the bar.

'See you Monday, Gwen,' smiled Clancy.

'Nothing like being well known locally,' I said primly.

'She's depressed,' said Clancy, anxiety creeping into her black eyes as they followed the woman's huge backside.

'I see it,' I assured her.

I hauled Clancy back to our conversation by asking her to tell me about Sir Edward Hunt. Clancy's like a walking Who's Who in local politics – she devours political news like chocolate bars. She said he was MP for Hounslow East, young rising star of Major's government; thirty-five years old and already a junior minister. She said she didn't know much about him except that he was reputed to be highly ambitious, was popular with local businessmen and came from an absurdly rich family, who made it big in Argentina. He lived outside the constituency and rarely appeared at local functions.

'So what was he doing at a party frequented by half the Chiswick NCT?' I mused.

'Hey, Nancy Drew, didn't you know?' asked Clancy in surprise. 'He's married to James Blythe's sister.'

'What?'

'Yeah. Caroline's brother-in-law, Harriet's good old Uncle Edward –'

'Okay, okay. I didn't know.'

'You don't read the right newspapers.'

I don't read any newspapers. Clancy promised to dig out the free local rag which carried all the gory details. Hunt was said to be 'very shocked' at the death of his sister-in-law, describing it as a 'terrible tragedy'. I wondered how Caroline had got on with him and with James' sister. I had no idea of Caroline's politics but I guessed the paper she worked for would be too left wing for Hunt.

As I waded womanfully through the jam sponge, I wondered

aloud whether being at a party where drugs were around was such a good move for a young, ambitious junior minister.

'No mention of coke in the article,' said Clancy. 'But that's not surprising. Hunt as good as owns those newspapers.'

'Does he?'

'Sara,' said Clancy sternly. 'Don't you take any interest in local politics?'

'I screwed a member of Ealing Council once.' I love winding up Clancy when she's on her soap box.

She blinked, glared, then carried on. 'He's got a finger in every local pie you can think of – small businesses, newspapers, local radio . . .'

'I take it you don't like him.'

Clancy snorted derisively.

Clancy may take herself too seriously, but she does always seem to have the inside story. Hunt, she said, was well in with everyone that mattered in the borough of Hounslow. He didn't do a lot of baby kissing among ordinary mortals, but he had friends in the police, the Council and in several big firms in the borough. He was also a member of the government's Family Welfare Group – a group pressing for a return to 'traditional' values. Clancy had even met him, or at least, scowled at him, in the flesh. In the last election, when he was canvassing for his seat, he visited an old people's home where Clancy ran a group. She recalled with glee how Hunt had smarmed up to a frail white-haired old lady and said 'Here's a lady with a nice face. What's your name, dear?' and the sweet old lady had replied 'Bugger off. I'm Labour' to the discomfiture of the aspiring MP. Clancy hooted at the memory. 'He's got charm, though,' she admitted reluctantly. 'He's quite good-looking.' Praise indeed from Clancy, who usually insists that white men remind her of stick insects.

I went back to work with a mental list of people I'd like to talk to about Caroline – Edward Hunt for one.

44

Also, with chronic indigestion.

I was still working through the appointments Greg had set up for me during my two days off. I'd hardly had time to look through the list of afternoon clients, but when I did I was surprised to see Lyn Hargreaves as the first name on it. She was a patient of mine for several months about a year ago. I remembered her as single, over-dressed and about as secure as a child's piggy bank. I tried to think how she'd been when I last saw her. She worked in PR and, for much of the time she was with me, lived in fear of losing her job. But by the time she stopped coming, things had picked up a bit. She'd finished with her lousy, long-term lover, a married man who was stinking rich, had a mean left hook when he'd been on the Bolinger and was into weird sexual games. She'd more or less stopped taking uppers to help her through the day. She'd been referred by her GP, who'd been seeing her on and off for sleep problems. I wondered what brought her back this time.

I dug out her file and it all came back to me. Twenty-eight years old – she'd be twenty-nine now. Only child of an Essex-boy-made-good father and a weak, manipulative mother, packed off to boarding school at the age of eight. Lyn was still very much a daddy's girl, attention-seeking and brittle, who chose men she could manipulate superficially, but somehow they always ended up using and abusing her. She also had a psychological problem with money. We'd spent several sessions talking about practical things like buying a flat, asking for a pay rise, saving money. Lyn was objectively in a fairly good financial position, but she was terrified of being hard up – partly the influence of her father and partly, I thought, the consequence of having a materially privileged but emotionally deprived childhood. Money equalled love – an equation which helped explain her penchant for unhappy relationships with rich, selfish and usually attached men.

When she appeared in my office, she looked slightly older than I remembered her, but her dark curly hair, wide eyes and full lips still reminded me of a little doll whose pouting lips or dimpled smile could melt her daddy's heart. Her figure was shapely, but not plump and she dressed to accentuate the curves; clinging cream silky top and close-fitting black pencil skirt, high-heeled pumps, reminiscent of Marilyn Monroe. But her manner was twitchy rather than alluring; her eyes flicked nervously around the room and she patted her hair and smoothed her clothes continuously as if trying to reassure herself that she was still all there. She didn't mention being on the pills again, but I could tell from the size of her pupils she was back on something. She chose to sit on the sofa rather than the chair, and wanted to get straight down to talking about her current relationship. It didn't take an expert to realise, within the first few seconds, that it was part of the same old pattern – a rich, married man with a neat line in emotional deprivation.

'Honestly, he was sweet at first. Really sweet. I thought "This is it." At last! He took me out, we went to some super places. Physically it was – God! – I can hardly find the words – fab! Out of this world! I know I've said this before, I know – but he said as soon as he got free of his wife, we'd buy a place together. He just wanted to leave it a few months. And I was awfully, awfully happy. I really was, Sara, you've got to believe that, we were, well we are just so much in love.' She caught her breath, panting anxiously; I noted the beginnings of a panic attack and told her softly to relax and take her time.

The familiar story unfolded. After a few weeks, the snatched evenings and occasional weekends seemed miserable rather than romantic. She resented the time he spent with his family. She wondered if he'd ever tell his wife the marriage was over. She begged, he demurred. She begged more, he threatened to end it. But he didn't – because, as usual, Lyn was being Daddy's little helper. She handled publicity for his business, gave him useful contacts, set up lunches with trade journalists. Despite his emotional withdrawal and her increasing hunger for affection, they carried on seeing each other. He bought her expensive presents, she bought his line that if only he could be free of his wife, they could live happily ever after. Then suddenly, very recently, he'd become a free man – free to be with her all the time. But he was already acting strangely, not wanting to talk to her. She could understand it up to a point, but it had made her wonder what on earth she would do without him. She was anxious, she wasn't sleeping, she was scared. What if he wouldn't agree to live with her? (Even worse, I added mentally, what if he would?) She wanted to settle down, have kids, a home. This felt like her last chance – what could she do to persuade him to give it a try? An interesting development in her history, I thought. The first time she'd ever had to face her fantasy being fulfilled – the forbidden man suddenly available. I understood why she had come back.

She'd talked so long, the hour was nearly up by the time she stopped to draw breath. I told her I thought that we had more than enough to be going on with and perhaps, in the next session, we should go back to talking about her father and her previous lover and how the current man related to that pattern. I agreed to see her once a week, but told her I'd have to get back to her about the exact time because I had a fairly tight schedule and she could only manage early mornings or late evenings.

When she realised the time was up she stood up and smoothed invisible creases in her hip-hugging skirt. She fussed around with her bag, fished out her diary and checked where she'd be the next day.

'Could you give me a ring at work tomorrow,' she asked, 'To tell me the time you've set? I should be in the office all day.'

'Fine,' I agreed.

'You've got my number, haven't you? It's still the same one.'

I glanced down at the open file. The number was there all right, a note in my handwriting. It said: 'Lyn Hargreaves at work: 0171-722-3333.'

The kind of number you remember.

I made time between my four o'clock and five o'clock appointments to make a phone call I'd been meaning to make for a while. Jane Marks is a journalist friend of mine, a features editor at the left-of-centre *NewsPost*, the Sunday edition of the same quality broadsheet

Caroline worked for. I met her when we were both undergraduates at the LSE in the mid seventies, the worst time to be at that particular institution. We spent our days there sitting around wondering what had happened to the excitement of the late sixties – actually most of it had joined the Faculty by then and was preaching Marxist philosophy from the comfort of a bijou house in Hampstead.

Jane was a bright, cynical spark from Wolverhampton, who probably made LSE history by getting a First Class Honours in sociology without writing a single essay. We just about stayed in touch through years of bumming round Europe and Asia; then, while I was playing loyal wife and dedicated social worker in London, she did a stint as loyal wife and hack on a local rag in the Midlands. We'd both ended up in London, single and doing jobs we really enjoyed; we didn't see each other often, but when we did, the sense of having a shared history made it easy to catch up.

Late afternoon was a good time to catch her. She sounded not too rushed, like it was a good time to talk.

'Long time no hear,' she said cheerily. 'What've you been up to?'

'Not a lot. Still poking my nose into other people's lives. You know me.'

'We ought to swap jobs some time. We'd hardly know the difference.'

'Jane – I rang to ask a favour.'

'Fire away.'

'Did you know Caroline Blythe?'

'Home Politics pages. The one who died recently?'

'Mmm.'

'No, not really. Why? Did you?'

'She lived near me. I knew her through the children.'

'Oh dear,' she sympathised. 'And she was only young, wasn't she?'

'Yes. Look, I wondered if you could possibly find out anything about the story she was working on before she died.' I could feel her reluctance down the wires.

'I could try,' she said slowly. 'But I might not get far. It's probably been passed to someone else by now and you know what it's like with current stories.'

I leapt in with gratitude before she thought too much. 'Thanks. I'd appreciate it. Can I ring you in a few days?'

She wasn't fooled. 'Why d'you want to know?'

'Partly personal, partly professional.'

'Was Caroline a good friend of yours? Was she having counselling?'

'Er . . .' I stalled.

'Does that mean you're not telling me?'

'I can't break a confidence. You know how it is.'

'Okay,' she said, resigned. 'I'll see what I can do. But you owe me a dinner, right?'

'Right.'

'I'll get back to you.'

'You're a pal.'

Almost as soon as I put the phone down, it rang. I hesitated, knowing my next patient was waiting in reception, then grabbed the receiver, after realising Doreen wouldn't have put it through if it wasn't important. It was Barry.

'This is a quickie.'

'It'll have be, Barry. I've got someone waiting.'

'Quid pro quo. I think I've found that friend Mrs Blythe wanted you to see.'

'Have you?' I said. My stomach lurched, I wasn't quite sure why.

'And Barry the Brain was right. Apparently you do know her. Want to guess?'

I was on the brink of snapping at him to just get on with it, when light dawned.

'Lyn Hargreaves,' I said, with sudden certainty.

Barry sighed. 'I sometimes wonder why I bother,' he said. 'Guess who the man is?'

'James Blythe.'

Barry was peeved. 'If you knew, why didn't you tell me?'

'I didn't. I only just made the connection.'

After a short pause in deference to Barry's wounded ego, I reminded him of my waiting client.

'Thanks anyway, Barry.'

He signed off wearily, 'Keep in touch.'

I replaced the receiver. So Lyn Hargreaves was having an affair with James Blythe. I shook my head and looked at the empty couch where, first Caroline, then Lyn, had sat. Why didn't you tell me, Caroline? Not a friend at all. But my ex-patient. And your own husband's lover.

chapter four

A fresh breeze off the River Thames whipped back my hair. I breathed deeply, tasting the damp river air, savouring that unique mix of countryside, traffic fumes and the promise of the sea that you get on a boat in the middle of the city. I love the river. I love its sense of history and the way it detaches you from the city's frantic grip. Everything looks different – Battersea Power Station, Big Ben, Tower Bridge . . . the river removes you from the bustle of the streets, shows you a new angle, reminds you that although the city changes constantly, the River Thames is timeless. The bright sun sparkled on the gentle waves, chopping out in the wake of the noisy putt-putting engine. I leaned on the railings of the boat, feeling sensuous and romantic in a thin Indian cotton sundress and reflected lazily that my arms were tanning nicely. On our left, St Paul's glided past, its glorious onion dome gleaming amongst the shimmering glass of the new City buildings. The sound of bells ringing in perfect rounds drifted faintly across the river.

I had been promising to take the children on this trip for weeks – a pleasure boat from Chelsea Wharf to Greenwich. Now, they were dashing from one side of the boat to the other, squealing with delight and waving at everyone and everything in sight. Steve was following them, equally excited, his wide trousers flapping in the breeze, squatting beside them to point out the boats and barges. I smiled fondly at their backs. My children are my greatest pleasure and Steve is my dearest friend. He's the kindest person I know. A bit of a kid himself in some ways. Playful as a puppy. Steve's my sounding board, my mentor. We're close, but not intimate.

After David left me, I looked up all the men I'd passed up in favour of happy coupledom and, with a cursory nod to the AIDS era which had arrived in the meantime (they all wore condoms) I notched up every available one on the bedhead. I'd like to say it didn't make me feel better, but it did. I felt liberated, renewed, revenged. As the humiliation receded, so did the need to prove that I could still attract a man. I settled down to a series of relationships, each one of which ran its course like a predestined life-cycle. Ecstatic beginnings, full of promise, waned to humdrum predictability, then ground to a halt. The relationships died a natural death, leaving only a sense of missed opportunities. (Counsellor, heal thyself.)

Steve and I are both shy of commitment. Our friendship is the one constant in both our lives and we guard it closely. It's lucky that sex doesn't feature. We respect each other's privacy. Although we're neighbours, we always phone, never just 'pop in'. When neither of us is involved with anyone, we eat takeaways together, assassinate characters, rent videos, go to the theatre and lament the fact that we aren't involved with anyone.

Steve is quite a bit older than me – forty-two last birthday. He lives alone in a small flat on the opposite side of the street, his last long-term affair having ended three years ago. I met him when David and I first moved to Acton and we had an instant rapport. David was jealous at first and insisted on chaperoning us wherever we went. But, after a while, he got bored with the endless banter and personality analysis and decided Steve wasn't a threat. He was right in a way. Except that Steve was the one who gently forced me to face up to David's infidelity. And it was he who gave me the courage to end the marriage so I could find the kind of life I wanted. All David saw was a small, balding, slightly plump man with an oversized laugh. Yet Steve has everything I admire in a person, man or woman – intelligence, a zest for life, a sense of humour, incisive judgement about people and, above all, unfailing kindness.

Being an actor, Steve's away a lot. His love life is impetuous and stormy. He veers alarmingly from strong, passionate women – with whom he usually argues violently – to charmless bimbos, who beguile, then bore him. When the relationship becomes serious, he panics that he's loved either too much or not enough. His real problem is he finds it hard to trust women. The love of his life was a French woman called Nicole, with whom he lived for seven years. I never met her, but the way Steve describes her suggests to me that she was exactly the kind of woman he needs – calm, self-sufficient and loving. He was young, full of plans and dreams, and completely involved in his work, so he didn't read the warning signs of the relationship foundering. They had a child together when they were both in their mid-twenties; at the same time, he was offered a part in a film, part of which was to be shot on location in Israel. He felt he couldn't refuse it, so Nicole was left for weeks at a time with a young baby, trying to find the time and energy to pursue her own career as a graphic artist. Not surprisingly, during the months he was away, she met someone else. Steve came back one day to find that she had taken the child and gone back to France. He followed her, but she persuaded him that a clean break was the only answer. He came back to England in a deep depression. A friend pushed him into seeing a therapist and, over several months, he sorted out where the relationship went wrong. He got in touch with his son again and Nicole agreed to let him have access. Eric is a gangly seventeen-year-old now and visits every summer. Nicole is still married to the same man for whom she left Steve. I berate Steve for living in the past, but he still believes he could have made it with Nicole had he been older and less ambitious. It stops him wanting to commit himself to anyone. It's easier to have short affairs when he's away on tour, with women who are as different as possible from Nicole.

As I gazed out at the converted warehouses and gleaming office blocks which make up Docklands' ragged skyline, I found myself wondering what attracted Caroline to James. Smug, weak and insincere, with the looks of a podgy English choir boy . . . Then I reminded myself of my bias – perhaps I was a little harsh. I just found it hard to appreciate his charm. The kind of charm that can attract two women as different as Caroline and Lyn. I wondered if he had some unusual sexual gift, then rejected the idea as too revolting to pursue. The ugliness of some of the newer buildings on the river bank and the chaotic mish-mash of styles – symbols of eighties greed and cynicism – began to depress me. Deep down, I knew what attracted both women to James, but I found it hard to accept for reasons of my own. He appealed to their maternal feelings. Caroline – slim, powerful and intelligent – was his emotional mother and his anchor. Lyn, with her soft white body and large breasts, was his physical comforter. With her, he could hide behind the role of big man and sugar daddy, while feasting on her physical tenderness. Caroline was the important one. No wonder he seemed cast adrift now that she was gone, a little boy lost at sea. Lyn was a temptation he couldn't resist – Caroline was a necessity. True to form, he hadn't seen any reason not to have both.

Suddenly, Steve was at my side, eyes bright and out of breath. He draped himself over the boat rail.

'I'm not a well man,' he puffed. I snorted unsympathetically. Steve's a notorious hypochondriac – if he hasn't actually got something, he's convinced he's 'fighting something off'. I tell him his body had seen more battles than the Scottish Borders.

'Over excitement,' I said firmly. 'Stay still for five seconds and you'll feel fine.'

'Jake!' he called suddenly in his huge, vibrant voice. 'Look at the helicopter!' Half a dozen tourists looked skywards – Steve commands an audience without even trying.

'What do you make of it, Steve?' I asked, keeping half an eye on my son who was climbing onto a seat so as to stand a better chance of falling headfirst into the churning river. 'Caroline comes to me with this story about a friend, who turns out not to be her friend, but her husband's lover. The woman also happens to be one of my clients. Caroline wants me to warn her – of some danger which has to do with keeping away from her husband. What's it about?'

Steve looked up lazily at the sky where a lone seagull was dipping towards the mudflats left by the tide. 'Simple,' he shrugged. 'The wife wanted you to get the lover away from her husband. The danger's a red herring. Okkam's Razor.' Steve is fond of Okkam's Razor. He hates complexity – cut the crap, keep it simple.

'Mmmm.' I frowned, unconvinced.

'I don't know why you're becoming obsessed with this,' Steve commented, leaning casually on the railing. He made an open gesture with his hands. 'It's obvious. Caroline wants to get the other woman away from her man. She knows you are, or were, her counsellor –'

'How?' I interrupted.

'Christ, I don't know. Through James?'

'He'd never heard of me.'

'So she'd been watching Lyn's movements.'

'Lyn hadn't been to see me for months.'

Steve waved his hand impatiently. 'Okay, by telepathy, she knew you were Lyn's counsellor, came to you and spun you a line about Lyn being in danger. Went to a party, was finally sickened by hubby's infidelity and decided to end it all.'

I gave him a withering look. 'By taking a sleeping pill *and* an overdose?'

Steve was unabashed. 'Details, details. The point is, you're making a big conspiracy out of it for some reason of your own. It's none of your business.'

'Of course it's my business!' Why was everyone so bloody indifferent about this?

Steve turned away to wave at Jacob, who was pointing out a police patrol boat. I tapped his arm and retrieved his attention, impatiently.

'Caroline came to see me three days before she died. Lyn is my patient and she's also Caroline's husband's mistress. Caroline's dead. Isn't it worth making a few connections?'

'The police are dealing with it.'

'Barry Monks was dealing with it, but he seems to have become distinctly less hot on the trail since last Thursday.'

'Oh?' Steve, at last, seemed interested. He's not too keen on Barry –

55

I think he's slightly jealous of our friendship. Barry had sounded maddeningly sure that Caroline had killed herself when I last spoke to him. I'd asked him how he knew Lyn was James' lover, but all he'd say was that he'd discovered it 'in the course of his inquiries.' He'd interviewed Lyn and, pursuing his hunch, asked her if she knew me. I turned my back to the view and frowned distractedly at Jacob, who was balancing on one leg.

'He said he'd filed his report and things seemed to tie up. I tried to pump him about whether the Chief Superintendent had vetoed a murder inquiry, but he just wouldn't talk.'

'Perhaps he can't dig up enough evidence.'

I chewed my lip thoughtfully. 'Perhaps.' Or perhaps someone was using leverage to stop him making waves. I wondered if Barry would bow to pressure like that – most people would.

Steve looked down at me, bemused and concerned, and rubbed my arm with his hand. 'What's the matter with you? Haven't you got enough excitement in your life with all those spotty teenagers and barking mad women?' Steve takes my work pretty seriously.

I shook my head, refusing to be joked out of it. Somehow, I had to get Steve to see it my way. I value Steve's judgement – his common sense may border on the prosaic at times, but he's also got unfailing instinct. He has a talent for bypassing intellectual analysis and getting straight to the point. If I couldn't convince him there was something suspicious about Caroline's death, I knew I wouldn't have the heart to pursue it. I was like a dog worrying a bone.

'Okay, let's look at it your way. Caroline came to me simply to try and talk me into getting Lyn away from James. I don't believe she'd be that stupid, but let's say that was her motivation – that still leaves the fact that she said James was no good for Lyn because he's involved in something criminal. Three days later, Caroline dies in – at best – unusual circumstances. James' sister is married to Edward Hunt, MP, who is a big mate of the Chief Superintendent. Suddenly, despite all kinds of suspicious evidence, the police think it's a straight suicide. I'm sorry, Steve, I can't let it go at that.'

'Then don't.'

'What?'

'Don't.'

I had his full attention now and his eyes were locked on mine. 'What do *you* think happened?'

I hesitated, caught slightly unawares by his sudden change of tack. I hadn't convinced myself of any theory yet. 'I suppose James could have slipped back home from the party and given her the overdose. After she was already asleep. Then put her fingerprints on the syringe.' It sounded a bit lame.

'Why would he do that?' asked Steve. 'So he could live with Lyn?'

I shook my head, sure at least of this. 'No. He's not interested in Lyn. He might kill Caroline because she was on the brink of exposing something illegal he's involved in. Some deal, drugs perhaps.'

'Her own husband?'

'Why not? And Hunt didn't want a scandal,' I continued, 'so he used his influence to get the police to treat it as suicide.'

Steve gave me a long hard look. 'You're serious about this, aren't you?'

'A woman died, Steve. If James killed her, he shouldn't just walk free. Don't you think James could have done it?'

At that moment a loud cry went up over the other side of the boat. Jake had fallen off the seat and landed bottom first on the deck. Hannah came rushing over. 'I didn't push him!' she protested, pre-empting the accusation. I glanced over at Jake and decided he wasn't hurt, told Hannah to wait one second and looked at Steve. He switched automatically to 'Hannah' code to avoid questions like: 'What's "murder" Steve?'

'I think you're right that someone gave Caroline a hand,' he said carefully. 'But if that's true, the person has a lot to lose. He won't be too happy to have you poking around, so I'd say you should think twice before getting involved.'

Jake ran over weeping copiously and exclaiming with a three-year-old's sense of drama, 'I did fall! Fall off the seat and bump my head bloody awful, Mummy.' He threw himself into my arms. I kissed his head better and stroked his hair while simultaneously assuring a strident Hannah that I was sure she wouldn't do anything so awful as to push her brother off a chair. Amongst the bedlam, I caught Steve's eye. 'I've thought twice,' I said. He met my gaze.

'Then go for it,' he said simply.

Later that night, when the children were in bed, in the semi-darkness of my living room, I finally got round to checking the messages on my answering machine. There was one from Mel telling me to ring in to the machine at the clinic. I dialled the number and pressed the number to play it back. It took me a few seconds to place the voice. It sounded shaky.

'Sara ... I – I just wanted to tell you. I – I – I've been ... kind of ... attacked ... It's Lyn here – Lyn Hargreaves. Two men attacked me ... (a long pause) ... I need to talk to you. It's um, Sunday morning, ten thirty. Could you get back to me please on my home number. Thanks.' My pulse was racing in sympathy by the time the message finished. Poor Lyn. She sounded as if she was still in shock. I wondered what could have happened. Probably a Saturday night mugging. I hoped fervently that they didn't do more than take her money. I checked the time – ten fifteen. I ought to call her at home straight away.

'Yes?' Her voice was shrill with tension.

'Lyn, it's Sara. I just got your message – I'm so sorry. Do you want to tell me what happened?' Initially, silence. I could hear her drawing breath in small, nervous gasps.

'It was last night. I'd been out with Jim.' (Jim! James. She'd said his name before in her session but of course I hadn't made a connection.) 'I – I got back to the house – I have a flat, one of four in the house, you see . . .'

I murmured encouragingly.

'I opened the front door – it's a Chubb lock, with a buzzer system – there's no light inside, it's on a timer and there were two men waiting

for me behind the door, in the entrance hall. They grabbed me and –'
I held my breath, '– threatened me. They hit me, sort of slapped my
face and knocked me down. Oh, Sara, I was so frightened.' She was
sobbing now.

'Did they take anything?' I asked gently. 'Or do anything else?'

'No, nothing.'

I let out a quiet sigh of relief, but I was also puzzled. No loot, no
sexual kick. What was the point?

'Did anyone try to help you – your neighbours . . .?'

'The ground floor's empty. I did scream, but there was no one to
hear.'

'Did the men say anything?'

She hesitated. 'They said it was a warning.'

I waited for her to go on. She didn't. 'What kind of warning?'

'Just a warning.'

'What exactly did they say?' This was becoming like *Mastermind*
with a reluctant contestant: Lyn Hargreaves, specialist subject
motiveless mugging.

'They said if I didn't behave myself it would be worse next time.'

'Behave yourself?'

'Yes.'

If she knew what it meant it was going to take Magnus Magnusson
to get it out of her. 'Are you hurt? Have you seen a doctor?'

'I phoned a friend and she took me to Casualty.' Not James, I
noticed – a friend. Useless bastard.

'They fractured my collarbone but apart from that it's just bruises.
And shock. It was mainly the shock.'

'What did the police say?' There was a silence. 'You have told the
police?' A pause.

'No.' Her voice had taken on a defensive edge.

'Why not?'

'They told me not to,' she replied limply. 'I'm too scared.'

'That's ridiculous, Lyn, you have to –'

'No!' She was vehement.

Then suddenly I got the picture. 'It's drugs, isn't it? What are you taking?'

'Nothing. I don't know what you mean.'

I sighed and glanced at the clock. I'm a harassed mother, Lyn, don't do this to me. 'Come on, Lyn. Isn't that why you don't want to go to the police? These men – do you know them? Are they dealers?'

'N-no. At least – no, I don't know them. And I don't think they're dealers. But –'

'Yes?'

'They said they'd make sure everyone knew . . . that I take things now and then . . .' More now than then, I thought cynically.

'I'd lose my job,' she said shrilly, 'And I'd never get another one. I've got a huge mortgage –'

'What do you take?' I interrupted. 'Heroin? Cocaine? Ecstasy? What?' Silence. Trust me or hang up, I told her telepathically.

'Heroin,' she said quietly. 'Sometimes.'

Oh, God, I thought, no one takes heroin sometimes. I tried to think quickly. I'd have to try and get her to see a friend of mine who specialises in drug abuse. But first, one more try:

'What's this warning about? What do they mean by "behave yourself"?'

'I haven't a clue. It's awfully strange. Bizarre.'

Yeah, weird. Good girls make bad liars. 'I think we should meet tomorrow,' I said firmly. 'Can you make early morning? Say, eight o'clock?' I silently blessed Yasmeen, my childminder, for being so flexible.

'Eight o'clock,' she said doubtfully. 'I – I think so.'

'I think so too. I can't help you if you don't come. It's up to you.'

'You won't go to the police? Promise?' A wheedling, little girl voice. Irritating in a child, intensely so in a grown woman.

'Not between now and eight o'clock in the morning,' I said sharply. Then more sympathetically. 'Go to bed and try to get some sleep. I'll see you at eight at my office.' Her goodbye was almost inaudible.

I put down the phone, stared at the wall for a second, then went into the kitchen to pour myself a drink. I should go to bed, but the shock of Lyn's story had jolted me wide awake. I took down my favourite crystal wine glass and filled it with a rich smooth Chianti I had opened the day before. The glass was one of a set of six a friend had given us as a wedding present – emblems of a perfect marriage. One by one, they had smashed with a ping and a thud, like tiny bells tolling each stage of our disillusionment. Sentimentality made me carefully preserve the last one, almost to prove to myself that something of value had survived.

I opened the back door and leaned against the door frame, savouring each sip of the musky wine. The warm air was heavily scented with night jasmin and honeysuckle which clung tenaciously to the trellis on one side of our tiny garden. On nights like this, David and I used to fetch two chairs from the kitchen, turn off the lights and sit outside, each with a drink in hand, silently listening to the sounds of a summer night. Once a fox came, nosing gently through the hedge, picking a delicate path across our small patch of grass. As a slight breeze shook the trees, he lifted his nose and detected our scent. A flash of eyes, swish of tail and he was off again, stalking his prey in the miniature woodland gardens of Acton.

Caroline had said Lyn was in danger and now she had been attacked. But why? And by whom? If James wanted to get tough with Lyn, he could do it himself. He didn't need to go to get a couple of heavies to do it for him. Yet according to Caroline, Lyn was in danger because of her involvement with James. Perhaps someone was after James too. I shook my head, confused. I started to think about how to tackle Lyn in the morning. She needed help and I didn't want to scare her off. My guess was that she'd started using heroin relatively recently – it had to be in the last year. I conjured up a mental picture of her and realised that she still looked relatively well – a bit jumpy, but her skin was clear and healthy-looking. She'd kept her job so far and she was obviously looking after herself, so perhaps she was, as she claimed, only using the drug occasionally. If Jo, my drug-abuse friend, agreed to take her on we could see her alternate weeks and –

then doubt struck. I was appalled I hadn't thought of it before. How could I possibly carry on seeing Lyn as a client now that I knew of her connection to James Blythe? I tried to imagine claiming at the next staff meeting to be a disinterested counsellor for Caroline's rival and couldn't. I cursed silently. I would have to try and turn her over to Mel or maybe Greg. In some ways a man might be better. I wondered if Lyn would agree. At least it left me free to ask her what she knew about Caroline.

My thoughts were interrupted by the loud jangle of the telephone. I smiled wryly – Lyn cancelling her appointment, no doubt. I took my wine, shut the kitchen door and headed for the living room. But it wasn't Lyn, it was Steve.

'Are you awake?'

'Obviously.'

'D'you know there are two men lurking outside your front door?'

'What?!' I threw down the receiver on the sofa, turned off the table lamp and crept to the window. The curtains were open a crack – I peered through. At first I saw nothing, but just as my eyes were adjusting to the gloom I glimpsed the figure of a tall raincoated man disappearing out of the front gate. I ran upstairs to my bedroom window to try and get a better view, but by the time I got upstairs he had disappeared. I came back to the phone feeling a little shaky.

'They've just scarpered.'

'Yeah, I saw them.'

'What were they doing?'

'Nothing as far as I could see. Just lurking. Probably a couple of drunks.'

'Right. Well, thanks for telling me.'

'Don't worry about it. I'm sure they were harmless.'

'Yes.' I hesitated for a second, then told him about Lyn.

He was reassuring. 'It's just a coincidence. You said yourself no one knows anything about you seeing her.'

'Yes.' I sighed and relaxed again.

'Okay, I'm off to bed.'

'See ya.' I finished off my Chianti, went back to the kitchen and carefully washed and dried the glass. The crystal gleamed and sparkled and I gave it a little flick with my finger just to hear the friendly resonance. I switched off the downstairs lights and went upstairs. I always go to the children's rooms before I go to bed to check on them. I gazed down at Hannah, her face half-smiling and cherubic in sleep, arms akimbo, one leg flung on top of the duvet. She looked so small and vulnerable. Jake was curled in a foetal position across his bed, his head resting on Derek, the enormous velveteen hippo I gave him last Christmas. Gently, I picked him up, laid his head on the pillow and tucked his body under the bedclothes. How could I protect them from a world where men and women lied and cheated, threatened each other with violence and sometimes used it?

Restless and full of foreboding, I went downstairs again and looked out of the window, scanned the hedge for human shapes and strained to hear footsteps in the empty street. Nothing. Steve was probably right – it was a couple of drunks. But just to be sure, I shut all the windows and double locked the front door before trudging upstairs to bed.

chapter five

'You can't trust anyone these days, can you?' Lyn formed her swollen lips into a petulant pout that may have given Jimbo a hard on, but didn't cut any ice with me. She was sitting up on the couch in my office with her feet up – a sorry sight with her red puffy eyes, already turning purple, a split lip and an arm hanging limply in a sling. I wasn't sure who she was referring to – me, Caroline, or the thugs she'd been hanging around with. Perhaps all three. She seemed to think we were three of a kind. I'd told her I couldn't see her professionally any more, but that I was recommending two colleagues who together could help tackle the drugs and her emotional problems. She wasn't impressed. I was abandoning her just as her friend Caroline had abandoned her. Yes, Caroline had been her friend. Everyone was having a good time beating her up either physically or emotionally.

When she stopped feeling so sorry for herself, I tried to tease the story out of her bit by bit. It came out as a tangled mess which I tried to unravel, as she went off at long self-justifying tangents. According to Lyn, she and Caroline had been bosom buddies. Then Caroline asked Lyn to help James with marketing his business after telling her he was 'hopeless at that kind of thing'. As James' 'little boy lost' act started to work on Lyn, things turned sour between the two women. The affair gained pace, Caroline began to suspect, and was less than pleased. Doubly deceived, she confronted Lyn with her disloyalty and demanded that she stop seeing James. Lyn denied it. It ended in a blazing row, which sounded like it had all the sophistication of an Acton pub brawl. Caroline and Lyn hadn't spoken since – except once. Caroline tried to contact Lyn about a week before she died. Lyn, assuming she wanted to open up another round of fighting over James, didn't return her call, but the two women met by chance at a press conference

'She was in a state. I'd never seen her like that before. She said she had to tell me something important, but she couldn't talk about it there. I was dying to know what it was, but then when it came to actually seeing her – I thought it was just to get me interested. Jimmy said I'd be mad to fall for it –'

'Jimmy? James told you not to talk to her?'

'Not in so many words –'

'But he wasn't keen?'

'Nor was I. Anyway, I didn't turn up. I couldn't face it.'

I mulled over what she had said. 'So Caroline came to see me instead.' I added.

Lyn's eyes started to widen in curiosity, but the swelling stopped her. 'Did she?'

I told Lyn what had happened – that Caroline somehow knew that she'd been a patient of mine and, assuming she still was, wanted me to warn her to keep away from James.

'There you are!' said Lyn triumphantly. 'She was going to start it all again. That was the whole trouble with Caroline, she had to have everything her own way. She didn't want him, but she didn't want anyone else to have him either. She couldn't bear to see him happy.'

'Wait a minute. She said it was for your safety. That he was involved in something criminal. Don't you think it might have something to do with this attack?'

'No. That's someone else.' It was an instant response. She had said it without thinking and immediately regretted it. 'Not exactly someone else,' she said hastily. 'I mean I'm sure it's nothing to do with James.'

'Who then?' I sought her eyes, but she looked away.

'How should I know?' After a second or so, she looked at me again, but her gaze was unsteady. 'I think it was a bungled burglary actually.

I could see they'd been in my flat. They must have seen the stuff I had there and put two and two together. And when I surprised them by coming home, they used the drugs to stop me going to the police.'

I looked at her for a moment, trying to guess whether she was telling the truth or not. I thought about it for a moment. 'Did they take anything?'

'Some jewellery.' A lie. Too pat.

'Anything else? Video? Credit cards?'

She hesitated. 'I'm not sure. You often discover these things later, don't you?'

I leaned forward and looked into her face. Her dark eyes darted from side to side, taking on a hunted look. Her skin was pale against the stark colours of her bruises. 'Lyn, you have to trust me. Whatever else Caroline was, she wasn't melodramatic. She was working on an investigative story just before she died –'

'I know. Jim said she was hardly ever at home.'

I gave a dismissive wave. 'I think she may have discovered something. About Jim.' I could see her pulling up the drawbridge. Jim could do no wrong – he said so himself. I carried on regardless. 'I think what happened to you is connected to that. Either because you know something – or they think you do.' She stayed mute, closed and resentful. 'I think you should go to the police.'

'I think you should mind your own business,' she snapped.

I felt a surge of irritation. 'Face facts, Lyn. He didn't exactly rush to help you on Saturday night, did he?'

'I don't know why you've got it in for James!' she said with sudden vehemence. 'It's that bastard Hunt you ought to be blaming.'

My stomach lurched. 'Edward Hunt? Do you know him?'

She donned a guarded look. 'Only through Jim.'

'So what do you know about him?'

'Well, he's . . . corrupt!' she said eagerly.

'In what way?'

She frowned. Nothing seemed to spring to mind. 'Practically everything he does is shady.' Not exactly hard evidence, as Barry would say.

66

'For example . . .?'

She leaned forward and crossed her legs. 'Oh, property deals, local government contracts – you name it. Like when that new swimming pool was going to be built in Isleworth, Hunt got the contract awarded to a company where he's on the board. He stands to make thousands out of that.'

'Does he take cocaine?' I asked.

Lyn looked surprised. 'Only at parties,' she replied candidly.

I laughed. Of course. Silly me.

For some reason, instinct told me that Lyn held an important clue to why Caroline died. Despite her drug-taking, I was sure Lyn lacked the deceit and cunning of a hardened addict. Her evasions were transparent and I knew from experience of counselling her that her doll-like act wasn't just an act; she had a kernel of real innocence. But she scared easily. I would have to take it gently. I felt like I was creeping stealthily towards a bird that might fly the coop at any moment.

'What about Caroline?' I asked as casually as I could muster. 'I know she took cocaine sometimes. But did she ever inject?'

Lyn shook her head. 'Oh no!' she replied immediately. 'She was much too "naice" for that.' Lyn adopted a didactic tone. 'There's a big difference between injecting and sniffing you know, Sara. You have to be fairly desperate to want to inject it.' She looked doleful. 'Like me.' Oh, stop whining, I thought unsympathetically.

I fixed my eyes on Lyn's arm, hanging grey and limp.

'I still think you're in danger, Lyn. And I still think you should go to the police.' I noted critically that an edge of panic had crept into my voice. I closed my eyes for an instant. I felt an unaccountable sense of urgency. This was what Caroline had wanted me to do. But I was doing it for more than that reason alone. I was lamely hoping that if I could get Lyn to take the warning seriously, the compulsion I had felt since Caroline's death would be lifted. Suddenly, sitting in my office opposite Lyn disfigured by the gruesome badges of brutality, I was overcome by revulsion. I really didn't want to be mixed up in all this.

My life is complicated enough, my job puts me in touch with more than enough blood and guts and misery. And the men lurking near my house last night had unsettled me more than I realised. I don't like getting hurt, don't like putting my children in more danger than they face every day living in the city. I'm an armchair heroine. I only know one way to get physical and that usually involves snuggling up under a duvet. I looked over at Lyn and tried to stop myself pleading with her.

'Caroline asked me to –' I began.

'Caroline didn't give a toss about me!' Lyn interrupted fiercely. 'She was a jealous cow. So if that's all that's bothering you, forget it. You've done your bit.' She began to gather up her things. 'You obviously didn't know Caroline,' she added.

I sighed despairingly. She was right.

With her bag on her knee and a tissue clutched in her only functioning hand, Lyn looked small and pathetic.

'Now who's this therapist person I'm supposed to be seeing?' she asked peevishly.

I went over to the couch and helped her up. Her hand felt hot and trembling.

'Greg Martin,' I said. 'He's very good.'

'He'll need to be,' she said, sighing droopily as we made our way to the door.

The noise in the small hall, cramped with people, was becoming deafening. Despite the furious heckling and interruptions, the man on the platform continued to talk in a clear, rich voice, stressing each point with emphatic gestures.

'This government, ladies and gentlemen –' (Loud shouts and jeers from the back of the room), 'this government has done more in real terms for its elderly than any government in the last three decades.' (More shouts and sneers from the back.) 'In the last two years, pensions have increased by eight per cent more than the rate of

68

inflation, a bigger increase than that made by any Labour government.'

Sir Edward Hunt's fine angular features faced his restive audience with majestic calm. From his triumphant manner, you'd think he was giving a post-election speech to a crowd of thousands rather than an AGM address to a roomful of charity workers and a handful of rowdy pensioners. His extraordinarily clear blue eyes ranged penetratingly round the hall, leaving no part of it untouched. His voice rose and fell as he expounded on how much the Conservatives had done for the elderly; he reeled off the statistics with enviable ease, slotting them deftly into neatly reasoned arguments. The logic was faultless, the arguments stank. I stopped listening to the words and sat back to admire his voice. It swelled and receded, hit galvanising high notes, then dropped down to a sweet, low caress. He was very persuasive. It was easy to see how he'd got so far so young, and classic good looks added to the charisma. Tall, straight and slim, with wide shoulders, he looked every inch the English gentleman in his pristine white shirt, expensively tailored suit and sombre silk tie. His hair was black and wiry, slightly freckled with grey which gave him a gravitas beyond his years; high cheekbones and arched eyebrows, one slightly higher than the other, which seemed to set his whole face in a permanent expression of surprise or arrogance, depending on whose side you were on. He had that confidence and certainty that goes with an English public school education, but it was tinged with a cosmo- politan stylishness which tamed it, softened it and used it to good effect.

Clancy had told me about the meeting that morning: the MP had been invited to speak at the AGM of a charity for the elderly. A small, vociferous pressure group consisting mainly of elderly women (no doubt coached in assertiveness skills by Clancy) had come to try and disrupt the meeting to draw attention to the closure of an old people's luncheon club in Hounslow. Clancy was there to lend support with raucous heckling. Being white, middle class and a coward, I arrived alone and elected to sit anonymously in the middle of a row.

Hunt's elegant oration moved on to the role of charities in improving the lot of the elderly. This particular charity, he said, was involved in the excellent work of helping people in their own homes on a day-to-day basis, so they could look after themselves for as long as possible. He praised the field workers and talked about some of the people who had benefited in the past year. Then he eased his way back to Conservative achievements for the elderly, to the expected economic recovery and how everyone would benefit from it, especially those on fixed incomes. If you stripped away the verbiage, the message was a simple one and Hunt made it sound completely natural and right: local authorities are businesses which have to stay in the black; charities are there to help the miniority who can't help themselves. I was star struck. However much you disagreed with the arguments, his delivery was faultless – clear, well-argued and passionate.

At the end of the speech the chairwoman – a mousy woman of about forty in a baggy cardigan – offered thanks to Hunt who had managed, she said, to put the charity's work in context, 'in spite of the efforts of certain disruptive elements in the audience' (sniggering and snorting from the rebellious seniors at the back). Hunt thanked her graciously and said he hoped that the controversy his presence had created would not obscure the essential message that this was a highly successful charity which deserved and needed our support. The audience was charmed and the loud applause drowned out the heckling from the back.

The chairwoman called for questions and Clancy's hand shot up. When she stood up, her gawky frame towered above the sea of white hair around her. She threw back her mane of plaits and flared her nostrils dangerously. She looked like an African queen appearing surreally out of a grey and white cloud.

'Chair!' she intoned in a ringing voice. 'I'd like to ask our politician friend here why it is that services for senior citizens in one of the boroughs of his constituency have been cut by *thirty per cent* in the last eighteen months –' Chair opened her mouth to ask Hunt the question, but was silenced by a regal wave from Clancy, '– and why, if his party is so caring of elderly people, these cuts include the only place that the over-sixties in Hounslow can go to for their *one decent meal* a day!' Cheers, yells and applause greeted the question as Clancy sank back into the ranks of white and grey. I felt proud that we were colleagues, even if I didn't have the guts to yell my support. Hunt lifted his face like a thoroughbred horse ready for the off, his expression thoughtful and keen.

'If I may be allowed to answer the question –' His voice rose above the din. Then, softly but authoritatively: 'This is a matter for this lady's local authority. The Government simply provides adequate –' a ripple of dissent rumbled round the room '– *adequate* funding, but decisions about how those funds are to be spent lies with the local authority. I agree wholeheartedly that the Friary Drop-In Centre provides an excellent service, but it's up to the local authority whether or not they can support it.' He even knew the name of the place.

'I didn't vote for them!' shouted one irate old lady.

'That's democracy for you, madam,' he replied lightly, beaming her a smile. There was a smattering of laughter. There were no more challenging questions – most of the other people seemed awed by Hunt's presence – just a few easy ones about pensions and tax allowances for carers. One woman stood up and gave a rambling tribute to the charity's meals-on-wheels service. She launched into a day by day account of a typical meals-on-wheels menu and got up to Thursday before the chairwoman managed to stop her. The final speaker rounded off the meeting by informing us that a good percentage of us would either be senile or incontinent by the time we reached the age of seventy-five – and on that uplifting note, the irate factions left in disgust and the rest started milling around and queuing for tea and biscuits.

Standing alone to one side, I found myself staring at Hunt. There was no doubt about it, the man had style. I watched admiringly as he glided effortlessly from group to group – bending an attentive ear to an elderly couple for a few minutes, then extricating himself with a few well-chosen words and a charming inclination of the head. On to the next potential elector: same treatment, same timescale. A quick handshake, total attention for two minutes then polite, regretful extrication. What a diplomat! I looked round for Clancy to see if she wanted to go somewhere and sound off about the meeting, but she was over to my right, arguing with the chairwoman of the charity. Clancy seemed to be moving nearer and nearer the woman as she got more energetically into her argument; correspondingly, Chair, hands dug firmly into the pockets of her cardigan, was cowering further and further back towards the wall. I smiled grimly. Go for it Clancy. Just don't be tempted to hit her.

Suddenly, I noticed that Hunt was alone. Without thinking what I was going to say, I started moving across the room towards him. I was curious to discover his attitude to Caroline. Was her death simply a nuisance for him, a potential embarrassment to his brilliant career? Or did he know her and even care about her? In a brief moment of solitude, thinking himself unscrutinised, Hunt glanced restlessly at his watch, clearly wanting to be gone. As he looked up, he caught my eye and resumed his smile. My stomach did a somersault as I walked up to him, but I was determined not to be intimidated.

I cut in just as he was being approached by a short, fat man with glasses. Hunt had a moment's indecision about whom to favour with his attention, but I placed myself right in front of his nose so there was no contest.

'Sir Edward?' I said in a clear firm voice. He flashed me a winning smile.

'Yes?'

'I just wanted to say how sorry I was about your sister-in-law – Caroline.'

He hesitated for a moment and became very still. 'Thank you,' he said slowly. He looked at me as if seeing me for the first time. 'Did you know her?'

I offered him my hand. 'Sara Kingsley. I'm a counsellor – sort of therapist. Caroline came to see me before she died.'

'Really.' If he was surprised he didn't show it. His hand was warm, with a firm grip. He looked me in the eye and I withered slightly. His accent, in conversation, was precise, but not plummy.

I smiled sympathetically. 'It must have been a great shock.'

'Yes, indeed. Especially for the immediate family.'

'Rather came out of the blue, didn't it?'

He seemed reluctant to discuss it. 'I suppose it did.'

'I must confess, she didn't seem depressed when she came to see me. I was shocked that she . . . I felt it was out of character.'

He inclined his head and regarded me for a moment. 'Surely one can't always judge these things?'

'That's true, but in my experience, it was unusual.'

'How long had she been seeing you?' asked Hunt.

'She'd only just started. She knew about me through a friend of hers – Lyn Hargreaves.'

Hunt's face betrayed no recognition of the name. 'I see.'

'I wonder if I could ask you something,' I ventured. I looked at him. Did I dare? His steel-blue eyes were locked on mine, intelligent and penetrating. I could see I had aroused his curiosity, but his aura of power was daunting.

'Of course. Fire away.'

'Well – there are one or two things that bother me about the circumstances of Caroline's death.' Several people were hovering in the background waiting to speak to Hunt, but he chose not to notice them.

'What do you mean?'

'I mean – I had no idea that she took drugs intravenously.'

Hunt nodded slowly. 'I think that surprised us all,' he agreed.

Encouraged, I went on. 'And it's strange that she took a sleeping pill beforehand.' I let that sink in for a moment and looked at Hunt.

'How do you know that?'

'I asked the police to tell me how she died. I wanted to know because if she did commit suicide, I feel I've let her down.' He was listening attentively, jaw set, lips slightly pursed. It was hard to tell, but I felt his interest was genuine. I carried on, feeling that I was gabbling, but unable to play it cool.

'It's not that I feel responsible, it's just that it seems so odd. She must have known Harriet would be the first person to find her. Then there's this story she was working on . . .'

Hunt raised the high eyebrow even higher, calm and questioning. 'A story?'

'Yes. She was obviously worried about it and I think it had something to do with James Blythe.'

'Did she tell you what it was?'

'No. But I'd like to find out. I know it sounds far fetched, but I feel it may help to explain why she died.'

Hunt was silent for a moment. 'What exactly are you driving at?'

I fixed him with a steady gaze. It was a terrible thing to say to a brother-in-law, but I had to say it. 'I'm not entirely convinced that Caroline committed suicide.'

He frowned. 'Have you said this to the police?'

'I've told them, but they seem reluctant to take it seriously.'

Hunt nodded thoughtfully. 'You think Caroline's death may be linked to a newspaper story she was writing?'

'Yes. Have you any idea what it might have been? Something she mentioned to you in passing . . .?'

Hunt shook his head. 'Nothing springs to mind. I might ask my wife, though – she saw more of Caroline than I did.'

'That would be helpful.'

'I understand your concern,' he said quietly. 'And I'm sure James appreciates it.' I guffawed inwardly – I wouldn't bank on it. 'Have you spoken with him?'

'Briefly,' I acknowledged, trying to play it straight.

'Good.' He moved back a little and I realised with surprise that he was bringing the interview to a close. 'I'm glad you've brought this to my attention,' he said with a slight formal bow. 'I shall talk to James about what you've said. Then of course, it's up to him whether or not he wants to take it further.'

I stared at him, taken aback at his change in manner. I lowered my voice so that we couldn't be overheard. 'I don't think you understand. I believe Caroline may have been murdered. James is not the best person –'

Hunt voice was soft but it brooked no argument. 'Ms Kingsley, your conscientiousness is admirable, but this is entirely a matter for the police and Caroline's family. You have quite rightly expressed your doubts to the police and they, presumably, have noted them. But it's up to James to press for an inquiry if he feels it's justified.'

'But –'

'You'll be coming to the memorial service, of course . . .?'

'I'd like to,' I said lamely. 'When is it?'

'Thursday. St Mary's-on-the-Green, two o'clock.'

'I'll be there.'

'No flowers. James has asked for donations – to the Masterton Centre.' A drug re-hab unit. How sensitive. 'We'll be having a small do afterwards – just friends and close family. I'm sure you'll get an invitation – we have your address, I suppose?' It was a cue. I heeded it meekly. He took my card between a long, perfectly manicured index finger and thumb and glanced at it. Then he pocketed it carefully, and held out his hand.

'Nice to talk you, Ms Kingsley. I look forward to seeing you again.'

I felt a chill run down my neck. How could I let myself be dismissed like this? 'Me too,' I said limply.

He turned his back and left the meeting quickly. Stunned, I stood for a moment feeling angry with myself for handling the interview so badly.

I realised with a sinking heart how much I had said, and how little I'd found out.

chapter six

I had fifteen minutes before my first appointment of the day and I used it to try and get hold of Jane at the offices of the *Sunday NewsPost*. She sounded rushed.

'I'm sorry I haven't got back to you, but we've been so busy and I didn't have that much to report.'

I tried to keep the disappointment out of my voice. 'Did you manage to find out what the story was about?'

'I spoke to Harry Leadbitter, one of Caroline's colleagues, and he said it was charities. Corruption in small charities, something like that. Charities being set up as tax shields for businesses.'

'Oh.' I frowned. Charities, not drugs.

'Helpful?'

'Yes, very helpful. Thanks.'

'Sorry Sara, gotta go –'

I spoke hurriedly. 'Jane, just one more thing. D'you happen to know if Caroline left any notes at the office, a draft of the article or something . . .?'

'That's an odd thing. A few days after she died there was a break-in at the *Daily NewsPost* and Harry says they must have disappeared in the mayhem. Her name file on the network was erased too, but Harry knew that she kept some of her stuff in a file coded with her maiden name, so he had a look.'

'And?' I tried not to sound too eager.

Jane sounded unsure. 'He said it was just a list of charities. Why don't you give him a ring if you want to know more? I said you might.' I quickly took down his name and number and promised to ring her when she was less busy to fix a date for dinner.

'Cheers.' She rang off. I dialled the number she gave me straight away. A brusque female voice said Leadbitter wouldn't be in the office until the next day, so I left my name and number and a message asking him to call. I put down the phone and tried to make some connection between James and charity corruption. Did either James Blythe or Edward Hunt have a bogus charity to help preserve the family funds which Caroline found out about? Not impossible. But would Caroline deliberately set out to expose it? Surely not.

At four o'clock that afternoon, Mel and I were drinking a well-earned cup of tea together in her office. I had my feet up on the couch and was inhaling the sweet fumes of apple and cinnamon tea out of one of her matching china mugs. I always feel relaxed in Mel's room. The walls are a pale shade of green with a darker green carpet; the curtains are swirls of soft browns and beige with cream sun shades and the tidy, book-lined walls are restful and unfussy. Mel herself is calm and gentle, slow moving, reflective, but with a razor-sharp mind which cuts through the psychological crap with the efficiency of a chain saw. She is small built, slight and dresses in an off-beat whimsical style all of her own. No bright colours, power suits or shoulder pads – just pretty Indian blouses, delicate print skirts, a stylish, well-placed scarf and her favourite, flat, tan lace-up ankle boots. Her hair is a mass of fine wispy light brown curls which she scoops up behind her head and fixes with a comb. She sits, incongruously, in a high-backed brown leather chair which looks as though it came from the office of J Edgar Hoover in his heyday. I think it was her father's. The massive arms and back should dwarf her, but instead they frame her neat form quite dramatically, as if to showcase her placid self-sufficiency. I never underestimate Mel, especially when she's sitting in that chair.

I was expounding my theories on Caroline Blythe's death to Mel's gently inclined ear when Clancy burst in, all jangling earrings and heavy sighs. She headed without ceremony for the kettle and teabags.

'Prostate trouble – I've had it up to here!' She tapped her forehead with one hand and poured boiling water into a mug with the other. Mel greeted Clancy briskly, then nodded at me to continue.

'That's it really,' I shrugged in reply. 'I suppose Hunt could be in on it as well as James, but he's so controlled it's impossible to tell.' I took a gulp of tea and waited for Mel's reaction. She looked at me and put her head on one side meditatively. I could hear her brain cells clicking into gear.

'Disloyal men,' she said slowly. 'It's something of a theme of yours, isn't it Sara?'

I looked up in surprise. Whatever I expected her to say, it wasn't that.

She sought eye contact and her brow wrinkled into a slight frown. 'Unfaithful men. Deceiving husbands, hostile to the point of murder. Are you sure you're not projecting yourself on to Caroline?'

I looked at her, aghast. 'You think I'm making all this up?'

She calmly scrutinised my face. 'I think you may be seeing what you need to see rather than what's there.'

I pressed my lips together and drummed my fingers on the couch. Clancy's ears pricked up and she jangled one earring with her fingers. Mel ignored both of us. 'It worries me that you seem to be making a martyr of Caroline – the spurned wife. You hardly knew her.' Mel sipped her tea, taking time to consider. Despite my irritation, I marvelled at the dainty gestures.

'Perhaps,' continued Mel slowly, 'Perhaps Caroline was mud-raking with this article of hers. Perhaps she was trying to get Lyn away from James by discrediting him.' She pursed her lips as she thought. 'Perhaps she had a lover herself.'

'So what?' I asked testily. 'Is any of that an excuse to kill her?'

'Was she killed?' asked Mel carefully. I found her scepticism infuriating.

'You mean I've made that up too,' I said acidly.

Mel stiffened slightly. 'I mean you're leaping into the sexual politics of this without getting the basic facts,' she said crisply.

I was stung, but I rose to the challenge. 'Caroline is supposed to have killed herself by injecting cocaine, but she took a sleeping tablet first and left no suicide note. Yet Blythe hasn't even questioned the idea that it was suicide! Those are facts. Where's the projection?' Mel looked thoughtful, but said nothing. I felt as defensive as a guilty shoplifter. 'I may not know anything about what Caroline had on James yet, but I'm looking into it. As to Caroline having a lover – well, she probably did, but what of it?'

'I guess Mel means he'd be a chief suspect,' put in Clancy. I shot her a nasty look. *Et tu*, Clancy.

'All I'm saying,' said Mel softly, 'is that if you have to carry on with this, lower your profile until you know more. Calling someone a murderer – even among your friends – is a terrible accusation And if it gets any further and you're proved wrong –'

'You surely don't think I'm going round Acton saying Blythe murdered his wife!' I exclaimed indignantly. I was beginning to wish I hadn't told Mel. Her cautious common sense was getting right up my nose.

'Things have a way of getting around,' said Mel severely. 'Lyn knows you suspect James, doesn't she? Someone is angry enough with Lyn to attack her. I think you're being rash. You have two children. You've very vulnerable.'

'Oh, for God's sake!' I said exasperated. I looked to Clancy for support, but she wouldn't play.

'She's right,' nodded Clancy. 'You should be more careful.' I opened my mouth to protest again, but Clancy interrupted with a thought of her own. 'What were you saying to Edward Hunt the other night? You two looked like old friends.'

I frowned crossly. Was I being got at here? I started a non commital answer, but Clancy was off on another tack. She has a mind like a flea.

'She's such a chicken!' she said to Mel, jerking her thumb in my direction. 'You should've seen her at this meeting, hiding with the woolly cardigans pretending she didn't know me.'

I shrugged. 'Didn't notice you were there, Clancy.'

Clancy laughed loudly. I smiled and glanced awkwardly at Mel. I was grateful to Clancy for defusing the tension. You never know if she does it deliberately or not.

There was an expectant pause as the two waited to see if I'd concede Mel's point. Sod women, I thought grumpily. Sod counsellors and their bloody confrontations. I was damned if I'd be manipulated. They could wait all day as far as I was concerned. After a moment's pause I drained my tea, set the mug on the table and stood up.

'There are too many mothers in this place if you ask me,' I announced airily.

Mel smiled. 'I'm sorry, Sara. You asked me what I thought and I told you.'

I grunted. Clancy, sitting on a chair with her feet on Mel's coffee table, blew me a kiss and opened her arms.

'It's just cause we love you, baby. How 'bout a hug?'

I stuck my tongue out at her – she does that touchy feely stuff just to wind me up. I looked over at Mel; she was still smiling, but her grey eyes were full of concern. I acknowledged her silently. Okay, Mel, I listened, I just don't agree. With a nonchalant flick of the ankle, I knocked a startled Clancy's feet off the table and went back to my office.

Doodling sulkily on a message pad, I mused reluctantly on Mel's accusation that I was projecting my feelings about David on to Caroline. 'Crap' was my initial reaction. We couldn't have been more different. Caroline was tall, glamorous, fast living, a writer; I'm small, Jewish, no-nonsense – a counsellor who dispenses ordinary advice to ordinary people. We were both married to shits, that's all. With a guilty jolt, I realised the vehemence of my disgust for James. Where did that come from? Ten minutes' chat at a time when the man was still in shock? Stubbornly, I pushed circumspection aside. It's my job to sum up people quickly. James was a bastard. I knew how Caroline felt – was that projection? She was a proud woman. She must have been sick with humiliation at his deception, doubly sick in that the other woman was her friend. Spirals were appearing all over my message pad, more and more complex, round and round and round.

I was trying in vain to resist a familiar memory springing to mind – a party, given by Kate, an old school friend of mine. It was a picture I had played and replayed since David left three years ago. Kate and I had kept in touch, and when she first met David I was delighted that they seemed to get on so well. Then at the party, after I already suspected David of having an affair, I detected knowing looks between them – conspiratorial glances, raw passion, full of longing. Sitting in my office doodling more and more spirals, the horror of that moment of revelation came back to me more vividly than it had done for a long time. At the party, when I saw what had surely been obvious to all our friends long before, I rushed to the bathroom and was violently sick (even as I remembered it, I felt the bile coming into my throat). As I heaved over the toilet bowl, hot tears coursed down my face. I groaned with the sheer pain of the humiliation. I didn't know whom I hated most at that moment, him or her. Feeling depths of anger I never experienced before or since, I crawled on the floor of that suburban bathroom like a mad woman, clawing at the carpet and stifling my furious sobbing with a towel stuffed into my mouth.

David came to the door, his voice full of concern. 'Are you all right, love?' The duplicity in his tone hit me like a crowbar and I crouched down further, rocking back and forth to try and ease the searing pain somewhere inside me. Inside my head was screaming. All the lies! All the false words and filthy embraces! As I clutched at my retching guts and murmured 'Yes, I'm fine' through the door, I knew my life could never be the same again. I could never trust anyone the way I had trusted David. If he'd only told me, face to face. I would have ranted and raved just as I did that night when we got home, but I would at least have been spared the numbing sense of outrage that I wasn't worth the truth. I didn't deserve to be told that his feelings towards me had changed. We'd always despised people who claimed to have an 'open' marriage. We'd always said our commitment to each other was total until one of us decided otherwise. All that meant nothing to him. He really was having an affair. With my friend. My good friend Kate. I prided myself on my insights into other people's relationships. Shouldn't I have seen it? Shouldn't I have known?

I looked at the pad in front of me, ripped with the force of my angry spirals and felt a painful stab as the truth hit me. You win, Mel. I gave a wry smile of recognition. Of course – Caroline was me, killed stone dead by a man. Dead feelings that could never be recaptured, wounds that could never be healed. I looked at my watch and realised with a jolt that I was keeping a client waiting. My head was clearer now. In some obscure way, Mel's insight seemed to have given me more, not less, reason to find out why Caroline died. I was doing this for me, not for Caroline. I wanted to unravel the layers of duplicity, pursue the quest she had started, even if it just turned out to be the blind alley of revenge. I needed to see justice served – not against men generally or errant husbands or disloyal friends, but against deceivers, liars, cowards. Against people not respecting each other enough to know when to dare to tell the truth.

I had passed the small grey stone church many times, but had never been inside. In a hushed, leafy street out of sight and sound of Chiswick High Road, it was set back from the road in a shady cemetery like a church in a country village. I'm no good at guessing the age of churches, but even I could tell that this one had been around a while. The grey stone walls were mossy and black in places and pitted by the rain and wind of at least two hundred years. Its low, crooked spire was topped by a motionless weathercock, which peered sightlessly into the middle distance. Tentatively, I pushed open the gate and stood for a moment on the edge of the tunnel of trees leading up to the door. Apart from the sound of the odd car, all I could hear was birds chirruping and bees humming their path from one patch of sunlight to another. The weather had been muggy and cloudy for several days, but now the sun was bright, the air fresh and the sky a brilliant blue. Soon it would be the summer holidays and the churchyard would resound with the voices of children playing in the park opposite; but for now, its summer glory was muted with the hushed reverence of death.

I'd been delayed by a client and I was late. Caroline's memorial service must have already begun. I hurried up the path and pushed the outer door, which creaked embarrassingly, and paused for a second just inside to allow my eyes to get used to the gloom. A keen young usher in black suit and tie opened the inner door to let me in. I felt like a schoolgirl late for assembly. He handed me a hymn sheet and asked me my name in a whisper so he could write it on a list on the trestle table in front of him. Then, walking on tiptoe, he showed me to a seat on the right aisle, near the back. The church was nearly full and the service was in full swing – though 'swinging' isn't quite the right word.

I hate Christian funerals. All that repressed grief and misery and anguish seems to hang on the air like polluting fog. There's no distinction between those who truly loved the dead person and those who are there out of duty. The sight of all those pale, stony faces made me want to do something outrageous like rip off all my clothes, jump up on a pew and yell 'Okay, hands up anyone who cares a monkey's fart about Caroline Blythe?' Why wasn't anyone wailing?

In response to the vicar's lead, a murmured prayer broke out and spread like a choppy wave across the congregation. No one seemed to know it and by the time we'd all located it on the service sheets, the vicar had moved to the pulpit. He started his address in an echoing drone – a series of platitudes about death and loss and meeting again in the next life. The hypocrisy of the whole affair hit me right in the chest. I wondered what all this had to do with Caroline – an attractive woman, a mother, a talented journalist whose life had been violently and inexplicably cut short. Wasn't everyone thirsting for some explanation, some way of making sense of it? Was this all he could offer? I shifted uncomfortably on the hard seat and looked around for familiar faces. James and Harriet (if she was there) must be at the front near the altar, out of my line of view. To my left, there was a contingent of Chiswick NCT women – Alex, who had told me about Caroline, Helen, several women from the working mothers' group, one or two of whom, keeping discreetly near the back, had brought small babies with them. Helen, clutching on to her husband's arm, looked pinched and red eyed, but was managing to keep her upper lip as stiff as the rest of them. I scanned the pews over the other side of the church and realised I was looking for Lyn. I felt sure she'd be there, but I couldn't see her.

Edward Hunt read the lesson. 'For everything there is a season, and a time for every activity under heaven . . .' His beautiful voice invested a heart rending poignancy in the words, the only uplifting moment in the whole sad affair. He cut a charismatic figure in his black suit, white shirt and black tie. Caroline, I felt, would appreciate his sense of occasion, whatever her view of his politics. 'A time to live and a time to die . . .' intoned Hunt, amplified by the hollow acoustics of the church. I reflected grimly that death had come unseasonably early for Caroline. But for the English middle class, suicide is the ultimate embarrassment, the epitome of bad show. They see it as letting the side down – giving in. No one cared to question Caroline's death too closely in case they found out why she did it – and discovered an emotional despair not too different from their own.

When the service ended, there was an almost audible, collective sigh of relief. By the time I'd managed to squeeze past the throng and emerge into the sunlight, blinking like a mole, the immediate family had already disappeared. The NCT women hugged each other and marched to their cars in stoic silence; most people seemed only too glad to get away. I hung around for a while, but there was still no sign of Lyn. I was surprised she was able to resist the drama of the occasion, but perhaps I'd misjudged her and she just couldn't face it.

'Sara Kingsley? Do come in.' The woman who motioned me into

James Blythe's house was tall and big boned, with a loud voice and a fearsomely organised manner. She was dressed in an ugly black linen suit, with a short-sleeved jacket, pearls at her neck and more pearls, even larger, at her ears. Her fair permed hair, going grey at the edges, was slightly dishevelled – she had obviously been wearing a hat. I could see a resemblance to James Blythe in her colouring, but that was all. Her face was stronger, more astute, with a prominent nose and a pursed, thin-lipped mouth. She took my proffered hand and held on to it.

'Belinda Hunt.' She looked me in the eye. 'I believe you were Caroline's therapist?'

'Counsellor,' I corrected her. 'That's right.' I wished she would let go of my hand. I was slightly shocked at her appearance. I guessed she must be at least ten years older than Edward Hunt and she looked like a grotesque caricature of the Tory woman – Margaret Thatcher on steroids. No glamour, no hint of sex appeal. I'd been feeling a bit frumpy myself, having put on the only dark-coloured dress I owned – a deep maroon shirt waister – but I felt like a fashion model by comparison. I wondered what Hunt saw in her.

'We must have a chat later,' she said imperiously, as if she was ready with a sawn-off shotgun if I showed any reluctance. 'Would you like a drink?' She finally let go of my hand and ushered me down the hall.

There were more people at the house than I'd expected. The 'few friends and close family' was more like fifty or sixty people, all milling around making small talk. It was better than the church, but only just. Belinda showed me into the kitchen, where a knot of people had gathered, and poured me a glass of cold white wine.

'I expect you recognise a few faces,' she said brusquely. Looking around for someone to dump me on, she decided on a man who was standing alone, a few feet away.

'John!' she summoned him. 'Come and meet Sara Kingsley.' He took a few steps towards us, looked me over shyly and held out a hand.

'Pleased to meet you.'

'John is an accountant,' said Belinda, as if that explained everything. She promised to come back to me later – I fought the desire to tell her not to bother – and then she left us in order to 'mingle'.

I'd already decided to seek out Caroline's family, pay my respects and then leave. I didn't want to stand around talking platitudes. I savoured my first sip of wine – it was delicious. Cheers, Caroline, I thought sadly, wherever you are.

John, as if reading my thoughts, lifted his glass. 'To Caroline,' he said, with a friendly smile. He'd actually mentioned her name in a roomful of people who were studiously avoiding it.

I smiled back. 'Yes, indeed. To Caroline.' I looked him over – about six feet tall, built like a soccer player, dressed by Next Directory. Behind his designer framed glasses was a pair of sparkling grey-green eyes, with crinkled laughter lines at the edges. He had that kind of half-smiling mouth that marks out an optimist and a guy with a sense of humour. I felt a faint stirring of the hormones and wondered, fleetingly, if he was attached.

'How did you know Caroline?' I asked him.

'I didn't really. I'm a friend of James.' Ah. Lose two points. 'How about you?'

'I have a child the same age as Harriet.' But I added hastily, 'I knew Caroline professionally too.' I hate making motherhood my primary identity.

A flash of interest leapt into his eyes. 'Are you a journalist?'

I shook my head. 'A therapist – counsellor, actually. But our paths crossed sometimes.'

We each asked a few strategic questions. I established that he was divorced with one small son, with whom he spent every other weekend, and that he knew James in a non-intimate, masculine way – they played golf together and went out for the odd drink. He found out that I was single and worked at the Acton Counselling Centre. I also risked adding that I found gatherings like this hypocritical. He looked quizzical.

'Were you and Caroline close?'

'No. I just hate the way we all pretend no one has died.' I said it more vehemently than I'd intended. I half expected John to decide I was certifiable and move on to someone else, but he stayed put. I folded my arms and watched Belinda playing hostess. She was being oppressively hearty, handing round plates and flashing her large teeth.

'Would you rather James threw himself on the funeral pyre?' John enquired.

I replied without looking at him. 'Belinda would be better.' It was a tactless remark. He threw back his head and laughed. A few heads turned. I felt a bit sheepish – but only a bit.

'I'm sorry,' I said. 'It's just that dos like this bring out the teenager in me.'

'Don't apologise,' he smiled. 'It's better than getting pissed and throwing up over a relative.' I turned to look at him.

'An old friend of mine died of AIDS. I got totally rat-arsed – couldn't cope with it.'

I grinned at him. Like co-conspirators, we sipped our wine in a companionable silence. I wondered how a man like John came to be friends with a pompous bore like James Blythe – a close enough friend to be invited to his wife's funeral after she was supposed to have committed suicide. I found myself wishing he wasn't a golfer (it's a little prejudice of mine) so I could casually invite him out for a drink.

James appeared in the kitchen for a moment, looking pale and drawn. His face lit up when he spotted John, then dimmed slightly when he saw me beside him, but he came over anyway and gave us each a bright, breezy greeting. I saw I wasn't wanted, so I murmured my excuses and left the two of them together, promising to say goodbye to John before I left. I walked back towards the sitting room in search of Caroline's parents. I'd never met them before, but I had no trouble recognising them. They stuck out like sore thumbs from the thirtyish London crowd – a bewildered, elderly couple sitting alone on the edge of a sofa in the high-ceilinged sitting room. The mother was tall and slim like Caroline, with the same fine features and high cheekbones, but she had an air of quiet resignation, whereas Caroline had exuded confidence. The father, tall and gangly, sat with his hands dangling awkwardly between his knees, as if unsure what to do with them. The couple were sitting close together, looking wide-eyed and shocked. Beside each of them was a cold forgotten cup of tea. Their pain was palpable and my heart contracted when I saw them.

I introduced myself as a friend of Caroline's and said briefly how much I admired her. They drank in every word with quiet dignity.

'It was . . . quite a shock to us,' said the father with a strong West Country accent. He took his wife's hand and squeezed it. 'We had no idea . . .' His voice trailed off and I nodded, feeling a lump in my throat as I watched him fight back the tears. He cleared his throat.

'She was coming down for her birthday,' whispered Caroline's mother. 'She was looking forward to it.'

'When was her birthday?' I asked gently.

'Today,' she said hoarsely. 'Today is her thirty-second birthday.'

I felt the tears well up in my own eyes. Life's not fair, I thought angrily. As we sat, Harriet suddenly appeared at the door, looking for her grandparents. She walked slowly and sombrely towards the elderly lady and climbed into her lap. The two clung together, silent and uncomprehending. I asked the couple if I could fetch them another cup of tea, but they both shook their heads. I shook each of their hands and turned to go.

As I headed back to the kitchen to say goodbye to John, I walked straight into Belinda. She refilled my glass with the bottle of wine she was holding and repeated that we ought to have a chat. This time, she said it in a way that brooked no argument.

'We'll go and sit by the window,' she said. I hoped she had something to tell me about Caroline's investigative story or, at the very least, how she had seemed in those last few days. Somehow, I couldn't imagine Caroline confiding in Belinda, but I was willing to bet Belinda's hawk-like eyes didn't miss much. I followed her into the sitting room, past Caroline's parents and Harriet, through the archway to the other end of room, where there were very few people.

Belinda sat down on the floral-cushioned window seat and patted the seat beside her. Obediently, I sat beside her. The window looked out onto a pocket-handkerchief front garden, hidden from the street by a mass of pink and white roses in full bloom. The heady scent wafted through the open window.

'Lovely, aren't they?' she said, following my gaze.

'Lovely,' I agreed.

'Caroline adored them.' She scrutinised my face for a reaction, but I gave none. After a moment, she said: 'Edward told me about your doubts.'

'Not doubts really,' I back-tracked, mindful of Mel. 'I'm just trying to understand.' Her fixed smile grated on my nerves. I got straight to the point. 'Did Caroline tell you anything about the story she was working on?'

Belinda was surprisingly candid. 'Her work had nothing to do with it,' she asserted. 'Caroline was simply going through a bad patch.'

'In what way?'

Her smile seemed to be cast in concrete. 'I'm sure you know the answer to that.'

'So you think she was generally depressed rather than upset about one particular thing?'

Belinda raised her chin and looked down her nose at me. She seemed to be weighing up how much I knew.

'You know Lyn Hargreaves?'

'Yes.'

'You know she and James –' Belinda flapped a hand with expressive disdain. I nodded to show I understood.

'The woman had been hounding them for weeks. James finished their liaison some time ago, but she would not accept it. She made threats, asked for money.' She turned towards me with a steely calm. 'I believe that's what pushed Caroline over the edge.'

Her confidence was compelling, but my instinct told me she was wrong. Caroline was a survivor – it would take more than Lyn's scheming and James' petulant infidelity to bring her down. I murmured something non-committal, hoping she would tell me more about Caroline's state of mind, but Belinda wasn't satisfied. She wanted her statement to be an end to the matter.

'I'm quite sure it was harassment by the Hargreaves girl that made her life unbearable.'

I marvelled at her arrogance. 'So Caroline didn't tell you anything about the charities –'

'She used to be Caroline's friend, you know,' Belinda interrupted. Her mouth retracted into a tight ball of disapproval, the rigid smile taking a well-deserved rest.

'I know.'

'James was a fool to get mixed up with her. I find it extraordinary that two women so different could be friends,' she added. 'Don't you?'

I shrugged non-committally. Actually, no. Women are so good at compartmentalising their lives, they form the most improbable friendships. Caroline had an androgynous quality about her which would be the perfect foil for Lyn's femininity and charm. Caroline was cool, well-organised, rational; Lyn was more fluffy and excitable. I imagined gossipy lunches, phone calls at work and the occasional shopping trip. Belinda clearly didn't agree.

'Caroline – bright, glittering career, marvellous cook.' (Belinda licked her lips, as if remembering successful dishes.) 'A bit neurotic, yes, but you expect that from writers. The Hargreaves woman is a complete lightweight from what I've heard. Obsessed with money. What on earth did they find to talk about?'

'Your brother?' I ventured.

Belinda seemed to be short on humour. 'They had nothing in common,' she proclaimed heavily. I nodded, but didn't speak. I put my hand out of the window into the warm air. The sun was still quite hot, but the light was less bright and the shadows of the bushes on the grass were deepening.

'How's poor Harriet coping?' I asked, to get us on to neutral ground.

Belinda glanced at the small figure over the other side of the room, still crumpled on her grandmother's knee. 'Oh – bearing up.'

I repeated what I said to James about where to go for help if they needed it.

Belinda interrupted with an impatient gesture. 'I don't think that will be necessary,' she said curtly. 'She'll be well looked after.'

Her stern expression told me not to press it. Here was a face that had launched a thousand fêtes, organised a multitude of meetings, sorted the good causes from the bad. If Edward Hunt had ambitions to be prime minister, he couldn't have chosen a better wife. We sat in silence for a minute or so, then Belinda said firmly:

'Believe me, Miss Kingsley, if you are looking for a motive for Caroline's suicide, you need look no further than Lyn Hargreaves. She is a desperate, greedy woman.'

'You know her well, then?'

'I have seen the kind of havoc she wreaks. You see her professionally – you must know how disturbed she is.'

'How do you know that?' I gaped.

Belinda waved the question aside. 'It's irrelevant. Caroline is dead. I think we should let her rest in peace now, don't you?' Her eyes were boring into me.

I met her gaze – don't try your head girl tactics on me, darling. 'I think that depends, Lady Hunt.'

'On what?'

'On whether everyone is telling the truth.'

Her mouth opened to reply, but I stood up. There was no point in staying. Whatever she knew she wasn't telling. 'If you happen to remember anything about the charities story Caroline was working on, I'd be interested to hear it. Your husband has my number.'

'I know nothing about any article on charities.'

She stood up. She had a good six inches on me, so it was an effective move. She enunciated her next words carefully. 'My husband is an extremely powerful man, Ms Kingsley. I want you to remember that.'

'I'm sure you won't let me forget it.'

She frowned her displeasure. At least I'd got rid of the smile.

'Excuse me.' She swept past me and by the time I had turned round she had left the room.

I assumed that meant I was dismissed.

I wanted to get out. The conversation with Belinda troubled me far more than I cared to admit. Anxious to be gone, I made my way back to the hall and spotted John coming out of the kitchen. I still rather fancied him, but somehow talking to Belinda had put me off the idea of making a move. I reached out to shake his hand as he approached.

'I was just leaving. Nice to have met you.'

His handshake was short and firm. 'I really enjoyed talking to you.'

'Me too.' I turned to go, but he touched my arm.

'Look, I hope you don't mind, but I wondered if we might . . . you know, get together for a drink or something.'

I was pleased to see he was embarrassed – I can't bear smooth men who risk rejection without a qualm. I smiled in what I hoped was an encouraging, but not over-enthusiastic way. 'Okay. When did you have in mind?'

'How about dinner tonight?'

Keen, or what? 'Well, I don't think I could get a baby-sitter at such short –'

He grimaced. 'Of course. Sorry. What about Saturday?'

I considered for a moment. The children were leaving that day for two weeks' summer holiday with David and his girlfriend. It would be nice to have something to look forward to in the evening.

'Saturday's fine.' We arranged to meet at eight in a pub in Chiswick. My stomach gave a flip of excitement which I tried to quell because of the circumstances. I don't make a habit of picking up men at funerals. But I couldn't quite repress it and the air seemed sweet with newly mown grass as I drove back to the clinic with all the windows down.

Doreen gave me two messages as I breezed into reception, after registering amazement that I was wearing such a sober-looking dress. One was from Greg saying he needed to speak to me urgently. The other was Harry Leadbitter of the *Daily NewsPost*, returning my call. I raced up the stairs two at a time (nothing like the prospect of a

92

new man to send my fitness soaring). Greg, who had a patient, signalled five minutes, so I tried Leadbitter again while I waited. This time I was lucky.

'Leadbitter,' growled a granite voice.

'Mr Leadbitter, it's Sara Kingsley. Jane Marks gave me your name. I'm a friend of Caroline Blythe. I'm trying to find out a bit more about the story she was working on just before she died.'

'You an' 'alf London.'

'Sorry?'

'Lot of interest in that story.'

'Is there?'

'What's it all about then?'

'That's what I'd like to know.'

'Why d'you want it?'

Journalists – I love the way they beat about the bush. 'I was her therapist. I'm just interested.'

His disbelief seemed to crackle down the line. 'All I got's a list of charities.'

'Then maybe you could send it to me.'

'Come down 'ere and we'll 'ave a chat,' he offered. I said I'd stop by the next day and rang off.

Greg appeared at my door just as I put down the phone. He looked flustered.

'Hi Greg! What's the matter?' He came and sat down beside my desk and looked at me for a second. Then said in his flat Northern voice.

'I've got some bad news, Sara.'

My stomach lurched with dread and I instantly thought of the children. 'What?'

'I'm afraid – it's that client you gave me – Lyn Hargreaves.'

I felt a sudden chill. 'What about her?'

He looked down, clearly reluctant. 'The police called about two o'clock. She's dead.'

I looked at him in horror. He met my eyes. 'Someone pushed her under a train.'

chapter seven

I talk to my mother and I feel depressed for a week. 'Remember Mrs Grover from number 46? Bowel cancer. Poor Mr Grover!' Then the inevitable line, 'Of course, your sister went to pay her respects.' Of course. Judy's the perfect daughter. She married her childhood sweetheart, bought a dinky house three streets away from my parents in Hendon and had two perfect children, one boy, one girl, who both go to Jewish schools. She goes shopping with my mother, twice a week and they sit in the coffee shop mulling over all the miserable happenings in the neighbourhood. 'How are the children?' asks my mother. (Subtext: still without a father?) I mouth platitudes between gritted teeth and make childish faces into the mouthpiece, then put the phone down with a mixture of rage and resignation which I'm reliably told will get better as I get older. I wish I could believe it.

It was Saturday morning. I wandered round the house wishing it wasn't so quiet. I always feel like this after the children go to David's, particularly if they're going to be away longer than just a weekend. At first I breathe a sigh of relief and gleefully plan what to do with my free time; but then I sink into a deep gloom, yearning to hear that plaintive cry Mu-um! echoing round the house. People who don't have kids can't imagine why you miss them so much. But children are a window through which you glimpse a whole different world. Take Hannah – her mind is awash with pirates, buried treasure, enchanted castles and tooth fairies, the sort of thing toy manufacturers would have you believe went out with the ark. She sits in a plastic laundry basket in the middle of the kitchen murmuring unselfconsciously: 'The lost girl knew she would be lost for ever if she couldn't find the magic island . . .' It's like background music, you take it for granted. And Jacob is always talking to inanimate objects – persistently – until they answer: 'Chair? Chair? Chair?' Speaking for the chair is as natural to me as answering the phone.

I sighed and glanced at the clock – eleven thirty. The children had been gone two hours and all I'd done was wander round the house picking up the odd Sticklebrick. I ran a bath, as hot as I could stand it and tried to soak luxuriously, but every time I closed my eyes, I saw Lyn's face – drawn, hunted, with eyes flicking nervously from side to side. And a Tube train hurtling into a station – a bloodcurdling scream – panic – people turning their faces away, shocked and nauseous . . . I'd been trying very hard not to think about her, but without the children to distract me, the hideous way she died descended like a cloud which couldn't be pushed away. Who hasn't stood at the edge of an underground platform, in the dirty rush of wind from an oncoming train, and imagined themselves, or the person next to them, a mess of crushed bones and blood under the cutting wheels? What Londoner hasn't been sickened by the gory nightmare which lies behind those anonymous blackboard signs at Tube stations: 'Delays possible: person under train'?

I stepped out of the bath and wrapped myself in a large bath towel, shivering despite the fact that it was a beautiful day outside. I padded into the bathroom, sat down on the bed and sighed audibly. The sound dropped like a stone in snow. I listened to the silent house and felt dread seep into me through the cold, damp towel. Was Lyn pushed by the same hand that squeezed the fatal dose from a syringe into Caroline's arm? I shivered again. Come on, woman, don't be morbid. I roused myself and wandered over to the mirror. It was the first time that week I'd had time to look at myself – I often go for days without looking in a mirror. Now, with the hushed house closing in around me, I took a good look at my face – dark eyes, olive skin, a big nose, a face framed by a mass of black curls. I looked tense and unsmiling. I moved a bit nearer and looked straight into my own eyes. What I saw in them made my stomach lurch – it was fear. What I'd been trying to avoid since the children left was a voice inside me saying: leave Caroline's death alone, Sara, you don't know what you're getting into. I felt sad and shocked by Lyn's death, but, selfishly, I also felt nervous and vulnerable. I scrutinised the lines around my eyes. I definitely looked older. I swept back my hair and searched my temples for solitary grey hairs.

A sudden sound downstairs made me freeze mid-gesture. I strained my ears to listen – nothing. I grabbed a long T-shirt from the chair and yanked it over my head, walked to the top of the stairs and stood by the banister. Nothing. Then I heard it again – a clatter – like someone trying the back door. A resounding crash brought an involuntary cry from my lips – then a flash of black and white fur thundered past me up the stairs. The cat flap. With my heart pounding, I sat weakly down on the top step and told myself that this, *this* was why I hated fucking cats and why I should never have been swayed by Hannah's tears when she heard of the probable fate of Caitlin's kittens. I picked up a shoe of Jake's which was lying on the stairs and threw it at the bedroom door through which the cat had retreated, taking grim pleasure in the loud crash it made as it hit the wood.

Half an hour later, dressed and finishing my second restorative cup of coffee, I heard the doorbell ring. I peeped through the fisheye and saw the large form of Barry standing in the doorway. I found his appearance absurdly reassuring. I opened the door, trying to quell my eagerness to invite him in.

'Hello Barry – what brings you here?'

'I would've phoned, but I was just passing . . .'

'Nice to see you. Come in.'

'Just a quick chat.' He stepped in and paused awkwardly. 'You've heard about the Hargreaves girl?'

Girl. For once, I didn't have the heart to correct him. 'Yes.' I led him into the kitchen and flipped on the kettle. 'Well,' I said, in a steady voice, 'another suicide?'

Barry paused for a moment. 'No. Several witnesses say she was pushed.'

I started to feel shaky again. I made Barry's tea and we both sat down at the small table. I tried to organise my thoughts, sift the melodramatic from the rational.

I looked Barry in the eye. 'Have you found anyone willing to say that Caroline injected drugs?'

'Forget Caroline – tell me about Lyn.'

'Forget Caroline!' I countered, angrily. 'You may be able to forget her, Barry, but I can't. I'm disappointed in you. I thought you had more integrity than to be bought off by –'

Barry's eyes flashed. 'Bought off?'

'You know what I mean. One word in the Chief Superintendent's ear from some jumped-up MP and you're running to heel like a poodle.' I stood up and paced the kitchen, frowning. 'Why didn't you recommend a murder investigation? What's the matter with you?' I watched his face carefully, not sure how to frame my next question. 'Is someone putting the bite on you?'

Barry's wide jaw twitched. 'There may've been a bit of talk.'

'Ha!'

Barry laid his hands face down on the table and leaned forward. 'Never mind your "Ha!", I'll level with you. Hunt's putting pressure on the Chief Superintendent not to instigate a murder inquiry. At the same time, there's been a few comments on the Division about my living arrangements. That may be a coincidence or it may not. At the moment, there's nothing concrete to suggest that Caroline was murdered –' Barry put up a hand to pre-empt my objections: 'All suicides are a bit odd – it takes more than that to call it murder. But the Hargreaves case has worried me enough to do a bit of investigation off-duty. If I can find anything to link this murder with Caroline Blythe's death, I'm confident the Chief Super will order an inquiry whether Hunt wants one or not.' He softened his tone. 'I'm doing my best, Sara. What was she like the last time you saw her?'

'She was in a bad way. Two men attacked her last week, after she'd been out with James Blythe.'

He flipped open his notebook. 'When? Where?'

'Last Saturday, in the entrance hall of her flat.'

'Did she report it?'

'No.'

'Did you?'

I folded my arms. 'D'you want to hear this or not?'

He gestured me to go on.

'They cut her up fairly badly. It was supposed to be a warning, but she wouldn't tell me what for. They also threatened to tell people she took drugs.'

Barry nodded. 'And you saw her – when?'

'Monday morning. She looked terrible. She told me all about the affair with James, the break-up of her friendship with Caroline.' I got a vivid mental picture of Lyn's disfigured face, the purple tinged eyes and swollen lips. She was like a broken doll. I shook my head. 'I tried to get her to report the attack.' I felt tears pricking my eyes.

'We couldn't have watched her twenty four hours a day,' said Barry softly. I knew it was true.

I sat down and drained the last of my coffee.

'Did Lyn ever mention that James gave her money?' asked Barry.

I thought for a moment then shook my head. 'No. Why?'

Barry had clearly decided to trust me this time. 'We found bank statements when we searched her flat – she was getting regular payments of fairly large sums of money. Any idea where they might have come from?'

'Can't you trace them?'

He shook his head. 'Swiss bank account.'

I pondered the idea of James giving Lyn a regular allowance, but I felt sure she would have referred to it in a session, however obscurely. 'Belinda Hunt said Lyn asked James for money,' I said doubtfully. 'But Lyn just talked about presents and the odd handout. Do you have a theory?'

Barry nodded. 'Either she sold drugs or she was blackmailing someone – maybe both.'

'Blackmail? Who – James Blythe?'

'Blythe – or a former boyfriend. Any thoughts?'

I tried to think back to her sessions the previous year and her descriptions of the man she was seeing. She saw other men too, but he was the main one. I knew he was like James in that he was affluent and married, but I couldn't remember much else, except that he was into violent sexual games.

'I'll look in my notes,' I promised. I found myself thinking about my conversation with Belinda Hunt and her description of Lyn as 'a desperate, greedy woman'. Did she get that idea from James or Caroline, or did she know Lyn better than she made out? Barry interrupted my thoughts.

'What do you know about Robert Winter?'

'Who?'

'Caroline's lover – the art dealer. She met him at one of Hunt's parties. He's got a gallery in Kensington.' Barry hesitated. 'In fact . . .'

'Yes?'

'According to the pathologist's report, she probably had sex with him on the night she died.'

I made a vaguely surprised noise and hoped he would tell me more. It obviously went against the grain with him to speculate with someone outside the Force, but I guessed he wasn't getting much interest inside it.

'The affair had been going on for about six months. He's a young chap. Tall, good looking. He was sitting near you at the funeral. End of the row just to your left.'

I looked at him, surprised. 'I didn't see you there.'

'I saw you.'

I grunted and tried to recall the man's face. I have a good memory for faces. Mentally, I scanned the rows until light dawned. Artily dressed and conspicuous.

'Was he wearing dark glasses?' I asked Barry.

'You should be a copper,' Barry smiled. 'Tell me more about this attack on Lyn.'

I frowned. 'I don't know any more. She didn't seem to know the guys and she said they weren't dealers . . .'

'A warning, eh . . .' Barry mused. 'The payments into her account started just under a year ago, but they'd been getting bigger over the past few months. There should've been one this Friday, but it didn't come – so whoever was paying out knew she wouldn't be around to chase it. Perhaps she got greedy –'

'And they killed her to shut her up,' I finished. 'But why? What did she know?'

Barry drained his tea.

'That, Mizz Kingsley, is what I intend to find out.'

'I have every faith in you, Barry.' I smiled with a lightness I didn't feel.

I had no difficulty getting Steve to come with me to Robert Winter's Gallery. The problem was persuading him to limit his role.

'I could be a buyer for an American dealer and you could be a Jewish princess showing me the London modern art scene.'

'No!' I swung round Shepherd's Bush roundabout and pounded my fist on the horn as a white BMW cut in without warning. The driver hooted back and made a V sign.

'Yeah! Yeah! You too, you rude bastard!'

Steve, looking terminally trendy in a plain black T-shirt, black jeans and boots, was slumped in the passenger's seat, reading *Time Out*. I was all in black, too, except for my huge tropical fish earrings, which gave a splash of colour to the outfit.

'Just tell me what it says about the exhibition.'

'You'll love it. "Alfredo Tuscon has mounted (pardon the pun) a witty critique of phallogocentricity and nuclear war by filling wild, oddly-shaped prophylactics with wax and casting them in bronze. Bristling with bulges, bobbles and prongs, these lethal instruments are presented, fully erect, on launching pads, as if ready for nuclear attack . . ."'

'Oh, God.'

'Um . . . "lethal dildos" . . . blah, blah, blah, "Robert Winter has a taste for the wacky, but he also has a sure eye for unusual work by talented artists – this Colombian sculptor is surely one to watch.' We sat in awed silence.

'Bristling with bulges . . .' I cringed, shifting uncomfortably on my seat.

'I don't know much about art,' quipped Steve, 'but I know what I like.' We both laughed.

'Where's the gallery?'

'Abingdon Road.' I swung left into Kensington High Street and weaved through the traffic and jay-walking shoppers. Steve picked up the tattered *A-Z* from the floor and directed me off to the right, behind Barkers, through the maze of streets of red mansion blocks. Miraculously, we found a free meter a few yards down from the gallery.

Inside, it was surreal. Row upon row of black plinths, topped with metal phallus missiles pointing in different directions, raised to eye level for maximum impact, and balanced on testicularly shaped launch pads. Each one had some ghastly embellishment – sharp prongs on the tip, cone-shaped eruptions on the shaft, ridges, vicious-looking hooks. Seen in their original soft rubber form, they might be amusing, but cast in metal they looked terrifying – violent instruments of gynaecological torture. They took their titles from the condoms – 'Ribbed Sensation', 'Black Shadow', 'Feather Tickler'. Steve and I strolled self-consciously through the first few, dumb-struck, trying to fight the desire to giggle. You had to admire the way they had been set out, each phallus-topped pillar standing out against the rose-white walls of the gallery and the shiny, grey vinyl of the floor. Every step we took made a loud, embarrassing clack.

At first, when the wide-eyed waif at the door had given us a catalogue, I thought we were the only people in the gallery, but after a minute or so I noticed three people in the far corner of the room – a couple and another man. The couple looked forty-ish and affluent – she was wearing a strange turban hat and was loaded down by chunky gold jewelry. The man was more conventionally dressed in an expensive-looking suit, blue shirt and pale pink tie. From the back view, I thought the other man could be Robert Winter. As Steve lingered over 'Deep Delight' – twelve inches of smooth metal, topped by four curled prongs – I moved over to one side to get a better look.

I remembered his face from Caroline's funeral. He was in his late twenties, very tanned, with high cheek bones, and a full, handsome mouth. His dark hair was slicked back from his face – if someone had told him it was flattering to his bone structure, they were right. He wore small round wire sunglasses and a gold stud in one ear. His white, collarless cambric shirt was tucked into black leather trousers, and the big boots gave height to his slight frame. His manner was graceful without being camp. I pictured him with Caroline. He would look rather small beside her, but they would still make a striking couple. Heads would turn in fashionable restaurants, at private views. She couldn't have found a greater contrast to James' golfy, good-scout chubbiness.

The couple were clearly interested in one of the pieces. Winter kept one hand on it as he spoke, gently stroking the metal with his fingers. The woman was doing most of the talking, smiling and gesturing. I could hear the rise and fall of her voice – she sounded American – but they were talking too softly for me to catch the words. Winter said very little, but the woman, particularly, seemed to hang on his every word. I wondered how Caroline would have behaved had she been there. Did she take on a different identity with her lover – more arty, less driven? I felt sure she would have made a point of being seen with him at chic venues. After all, getting back at James was half the idea. They would look beautiful together, do wonderful things, meet interesting people. Yet I had a strong sense that Caroline would not be totally at home in Robert Winter's world. He would be the focus of attention, which she wouldn't like. She was also too cynical to be convincingly pretentious.

Winter was clearly well on the way to selling one of his willies, but was managing to contain his enthusiasm. If his body language was anything to go by, selling art consisted of making vague sweeping gestures and looking as if you'd rather be absolutely anywhere than

102

in this poxy gallery. As the three drifted past me on their way back to the door, the man was asking about shipping the piece to New York and the woman was wondering about the height of the stand and whether it would fit 'naturally into the space'. Winter answered unsmilingly, in monosyllables. He finally saw them out and, to my horror, Steve immediately walked up to him and tried to engage him in conversation. I ambled over as casually as possible, before Steve got carried away.

'. . . and it's such a fascinating idea.' Whatever Steve's opening gambit was, Winter wasn't impressed. His lips were slightly parted – it may have been an attempt at a smile. Close to, his features were even more perfect. His skin was flawless – smooth and golden – and he had the kind of chiselled features a razor commercial model would kill for.

'Do you collect?' He was facing Steve, but his eyes were hidden behind the cool designer shades.

'Only ideas,' drawled Steve. I felt like gagging. 'I'm looking for inspiration really. The character I'm playing at the moment has a latent, power-hungry machismo. It's rather hard to capture . . .' He gazed moodily at the metal knob nearest to him.

'You're an actor?' said Winter, only marginally interested.

'*State of the Art* at the Albery – have you seen it?'

'No.'

'You should.'

Before they both keeled over with the effort of being unimpressed with each other, I slid a conversational spoke in the wheel. Looking quizzically at Winter, I said nonchalantly, 'Haven't I seen you somewhere before?'

He lifted one shoulder.

'Of course!' I pretended to wish I hadn't mentioned it. It was the best I could do – subtlety has never been my forte. He raised one eyebrow in curiosity.

'You were a friend of Caroline Blythe,' I explained. 'I saw you at the funeral.'

'Yes.' He ran one slender finger down his nose and then placed it on his lips and said nothing. I waited, but he didn't add anything.

'I knew her too.'

'Are you a journalist?' he said it sharply.

'No, we just have children the same age,' I said. 'How did you know her?'

'We met at a party.'

'Oh.' We lapsed into silence. Steve came to the rescue.

'Lovely lady, wasn't she? Terrible shame.' I'd never heard him use such a plummy accent. It was perfect, not over done.

'Terrible,' I agreed gratefully. Then to Winter. 'She was awfully down, though, wasn't she?' No reaction. All I could see was myself reflected in his glasses. I had addressed the remark to Winter, but Steve cut in again.

'She was depressed about some story, wasn't she – an article she was writing?'

'I told you, darling. It was an exposé of a charity.' I turned to Winter. 'It was all rather intriguing. Did she tell you about it?'

He deigned to part his lips at last. 'I didn't know her that well.'

Oh, really? That's not what I heard, pal. I left a pause in case he wanted to fill it. He didn't.

'Sad, though, wasn't it?'

'Yes.' There was a heavy silence. Not a big talker, Robert Winter. His mother had clearly overdone the warnings about not talking to strangers.

'Did you sign the book?' He asked finally.

'Not yet,' answered Steve brightly. I sensed he was all ready to continue the scene, but I caught his arm.

'We'll do it on the way out.' I offered my hand to Winter. 'Sara Kingsley.' He took it gingerly. His hand was warm and soft. Fleetingly, I wondered whether he was a good lover. I decided he was more the type who would want to make love in front of a mirror so he could keep a constant check on his appearance. As Steve and I turned our backs and clattered our way back towards the desk, I felt his eyes staring at our backs. We signed our names, but didn't put an address. If Winter's next exhibition was anything like this one, I didn't want to be notified.

We stopped off for lunch at a cheap Chinese noodle bar in Kensington High Street. Unleashed, Steve played the scene more as he would have liked it, improvising frivolously on the theme of art, inspiration, life, creativity and the meaning of metal phalluses. On a more serious note, we agreed that Robert Winter was hard to fathom. His reluctance to talk about Caroline seemed strange to me, but, as Steve so flatteringly put it, 'Anyone who doesn't weep openly in the first five minutes is repressed in your book.' I still felt a vague sense of disappointment. I hadn't had any real plan in going to see Robert Winter and I didn't expect to be welcomed with open arms, but most people who have lost a loved one are desperate to talk about them. Winter betayed not even a flicker of interest at the mention of Caroline's name. Steve proclaimed Winter to be a red herring, which gave me the perfect opening to call him a cold fish. Steve made a face, slurped his soup and changed the subject, asking me what I'd found out from my visit to the *NewsPost*.

'Not a lot.' I said, with a sigh.

It had all been vaguely disappointing. Leadbitter turned out to be exactly the gruff, boozy hack he'd sounded like on the phone. I wished I'd managed to catch him before his long lunch and I also bitterly regretted wearing a T-shirt. He breathed alcoholic fumes all over me and addressed most of his remarks to my tits. Three people had enquired about Caroline's notes for her story – James, the police and a man who wouldn't give his name. The first draft of the piece – if she'd done one – had disappeared in the mayhem of the burglary just after she died. Only Leadbitter knew about the file she kept on the computer in her maiden name. He'd shown it to the police, but no one else, just in case it turned out to be significant. But he found my charms irresistible (big leer) so he'd decided to trust me. Anyway, all it contained was a list of charities.

The list seemed to have been culled from a charities' directory –

Caroline had set up her own database of several hundred small charities. Each entry gave the names of trustees, a summary of main activities and an outline of income and expenditure for the previous year. Leadbitter guessed she'd been given a tip-off about a particular scam – like charities being set up as tax shields – and was in the process of scouring a charities' directory for likely charities. Leadbitter quickly flicked through the first ten or so, but each one was the same format – name of the charity, list of trustees, area of activity, income and expenditure. I felt daunted both by the technology – I pretend to be computer literate, but I'm not – and by the length of the list. Phones were ringing all around us and Leadbitter was yelling intermittently to a journalist working at a VDU over the other side of the room:

'Kev? Put China on three and shift the Mafia thing to two.'

'Aw, Harry, I've just –'

'Fuck off, just do it.'

I asked him what Caroline would have done with the list.

'Depends what she was looking for,' he barked. 'I'll jus' show you 'ow it works, then you'll 'ave to work it out for yourself.' Accompanied by a series of slurred mumbling and grunts, he stabbed at the keys with his stubby fingers. He seemed to be asking the computer to pull charities out of the list according to particular criteria – all those concerned with mental handicap, for instance, or all those with an income of more than £50,000.

'There you are then,' he said, jumping up and indicating the chair he'd just been occupying. He lit up a cigarette, blew smoke in my face, said I was welcome to stay and run a few checks, and to give him a shout if I came up with anything. His charm was beginning to underwhelm me. I said I couldn't stay – I had no idea what I was looking for and, secretly, I didn't feel able to run the checks without a bit of help. I told him I needed to take the list away with me. I was disappointed. I'd naïvely expected a list of one or two pieces of paper that I could take home and peruse at leisure. After a bit of umming and ah-ing Leadbitter finally agreed to let me take home a floppy, provided I paid for the disk – and that's what I'd done.

'So you've got a disk and no computer,' said Steve.

'I thought I might ask Afsana to help me.' Afsana was our neighbour – a computer whizz kid who didn't despise computer idiots.

'Good idea.' The mere mention of computers makes his eyes glaze over.

We finished our lunch and parted outside the restaurant – Steve was going into town to meet a friend. I gave him a light kiss on the cheek.

'Thanks for coming to the gallery with me.'

'We didn't find out much.'

'It was useful anyway.'

'Have fun tonight,' he said with a wink. I snorted, gave his balding head a light tap and made my way back to the car.

Saturday afternoon, especially in the summer, is a quiet time in Acton. Most of the male population is either slumped in front of the telly watching the horse-racing or lurching, mildly pissed, out of the betting shop. Just off the High Street, there's a desultory market which fizzles out at about three o'clock. The only real sign of life is MacDonald's, packed with mums surrounded by kids and bags of shopping, nattering to each other and popping chips in the mouths of toddlers, half toppling out of the high chairs beside them. It's a low-key time, everyone waiting for Saturday night. Some people find the whole place depressing – not me. It's real – not pretty, but alive.

I'd decided to use the rest of the day to catch up on paperwork at the clinic and work on a paper I was due to give at an adolescent counselling conference in the autumn. I could look at Lyn's file at the same time. As I walked up to the front door of the clinic and turned my key in the lock, I knew immediately that something was wrong. The door opened too easily and there was a breeze blowing from the inside, which meant that someone had left the back door open. I hovered just inside the doorway, my ears straining for sounds of someone moving. From somewhere in the house, I could hear a high-pitched mechanical whine, like a computer in distress. I crept softly along the hall and peered into the reception area. 'Oh no!' I said it aloud. The scene was pure devastation – paper strewn everywhere, files littered over upturned chairs. Doreen's desk had been pushed over and the phone lay beside it on the floor – the source of the high-pitched squeal. I picked my way over to it and replaced the receiver in its cradle. I stood for a moment, trying to take it in. Scanning the room, I couldn't see anything obvious missing, just havoc wreaked deliberately and viciously. The computer lay on the floor beside Doreen's desk. The terminal had been deliberately smashed and its guts – wires, circuit board and tube – spilled out over a pile of appointment cards. Blind anger took over – what pointless destruction! What a pathetic way to get your kicks!

It was possible the person who'd done this was still in the house, but I guessed not. I left the room quickly and raced upstairs to my office. The door was open, just as I'd left it, and the room was completely untouched. I checked Clancy's and Robin's and Greg's, then came downstairs and looked in on Mel's – they were okay too. I went back to reception. The last time this happened, it turned out to be a fourteen-year-old boy trying to show us he could beat up a room at least as well as his father beat him. Was this another dissatisfied client trying to make a statement? We really ought to get a suggestions box, I thought, sarcastically, to save people all this trouble. Then I saw it. Pinned up on the notice board – a single piece of paper: 'YOU NEXT'.

I walked towards it slowly, peering at it, hoping it would yield some reassuring clue that it was not aimed at me. 'You next' – it could mean any of us, all of us – Mel, Clancy, Greg, Robin or me. It could mean nothing. I tried not to think about it in relation to Lyn or Caroline.

Leaving the paper where it was pinned, I clenched my jaw, took a deep breath and rang the police.

chapter eight

I tried hard, but I only managed to be five minutes late for my date with John. When it comes to meeting people, I'm compulsively punctual, even when I'd really prefer to be late. Quite apart from the etiquette – not wanting to appear too keen – I didn't want to sit alone in the pub for any length of time. Sleazy pick-ups I can deal with, but such is my sympathetic aura, if there's anyone within a five mile radius who's had a traumatic childhood and has a mind to tell their life history, they'll home in on me within seconds. 'The Plantaganet' is an upmarket Chiswick pub, full of media types. I bought myself a gin and tonic and sat down at a table in the corner which looked a safe bet from predatory life-story tellers. I felt smart and sexy in a black silk shirt and hip-hugging white jeans, my hair pulled up and back so only a few curled strands remained. I looked cool and controlled on the surface, but underneath I was rattled by the day's events and nervous about having to spend a whole evening with a total stranger.

As soon as I sat down, I spotted John buying a drink in the next bar. I controlled the urge to rush over and watched him for a moment. His neat hips and firm bum looked good from the side as he leaned on the bar, dressed in smooth pressed, light Levi jeans and a navy blouson jacket. As the barman pulled his pint, he adjusted his glasses and looked around – I was glad to see he looked about as nervous as I felt. He took a sip of his drink, then turned round and saw me. I smiled and waved and he smiled and waved back. As he walked over, my body chemistry registered his wide shoulders and smooth brown neck beneath a white denim shirt, done up with snappers. Control yourself, woman! When he got up to me, he smiled shyly and pushed up his glasses. I gurgled noiselessly; this man was seriously sexy and, even better, he didn't seem to know it.

'You okay for a drink?'

'Yes, thanks,' I motioned my gin and tonic, hardly tasted.

He put his pint on the table and sat down in front of it. 'Didn't see you sitting there.'

'I only just spotted you.' We grinned at each other like a couple of gawky teenagers.

He fiddled with his drink. 'So your kids have gone to stay with their father . . .?'

God. Was he already checking if I was free for the night? 'Yes,' I said with a slight frosty edge to my voice.

'I expect you're missing them,' he said kindly.

My voice resumed normal room temperature. 'Just a bit,' I admitted.

'Awful pub,' he said, looking around.

'Awful,' I agreed wholeheartedly.

There was an uneasy silence. I hate that kind of tension, when two people want to talk, but can't get started and I detest wasting time on small talk. I'm no good at it anyway. Giving a quick glance to the laughter lines round John's eyes, I decided to take a gamble on his sense of humour. I leaned forward and cupped my chin in my hand.

'So tell me about the first time you had sex,' I said, deadpan.

His mouth twitched with a ghost of a smile, but he held it in check and brought his voice down to almost a whisper. 'I was twelve years old,' he lied. 'And I made it in the back of a Mini with a friend of my grandmother's.' Sick humour – I love it. His face gave way to a merry grin and his eyes crinkled round the edges. 'How about you?'

I whispered too. 'Twenty-three, back of a motorbike, with a Hell's Angel from Milton Keynes.' We both roared with laughter. We were over the first hurdle – I knew I was going to enjoy the evening.

'Where shall we go for dinner?' I asked, feeling my nervousness starting to melt into pangs of ravenous hunger.

'I've booked a table at Chez Michel,' he offered calmly, 'But we can cancel if you'd prefer somewhere else.' I murmured appreciatively – escargots, smoked salmon mousse, duck in vermouth, flans worthy of the best French *pâtisserie*. I know the menus of virtually every restaurant in Chiswick even if I haven't eaten there and Chez Michel is the best I know. I tried not to think about the cost.

'Sounds good to me.' I smiled. We finished our drinks quickly and made for the door. He touched my arm as we left the pub, but we strolled the few streets to the restaurant walking self-consciously, a foot apart.

The subject of Caroline came up while we were still on the starter. I'd decided to forego the escargots in favour of langoustines dipped in a spicy dressing; John was tucking into a hearty onion soup. I'd been doing most of the talking up to then, telling him how I got into counselling, but once we started on Caroline, John sprang to life with a series of questions about how well I knew her and why I thought she'd committed suicide. I answered cautiously and wondered why he was so interested. Despite my initial resentment of Mel's warnings, I'd taken them to heart. I was determined that the combined effects of an attractive man and a heady, effervescent wine weren't going to lure me into indiscretion. Not that kind of indiscretion, anyway. I said I didn't know her that well, but I'd always thought of her as a vibrant, optimistic person and was surprised at her suicide. Then I turned the questions round and tried to draw out John on his friendship with James. Despite his apparent openness, I detected he was holding back too.

'He's a good bloke when you get to know him,' he said blandly. 'He must be a good architect too, he's made a packet.'

'Has he?'

John poured more wine into my glass. I motioned 'when' unconvincingly. 'House in Normandy, boat on the Thames . . . he's done all right.'

111

'He still works from home . . .'

John laughed incredulously. 'From home? That's just a bolt hole from the office. He employs about a dozen people – you should see their offices in Covent Garden!'

'What sort of things does he design?'

'Shopping malls, leisure centres . . . he did that great big office block on the Great West Road, for Tetron Pharmaceuticals.'

'Not the place with the chimneys and portholes that looks like an ocean liner?' I said, aghast. 'I nearly puke every time I pass it.'

'That's the one.' John grinned mischievously.

'Love it.' I added, pulling a disgusted face.

John laughed. 'It's different anyway.'

'Have you ever worked for him?' I asked him.

'Who, James? I've helped him out on occasions.' He sounded cagey. I tried to lure him into talking more about his work, but he wouldn't play. 'I hate talking about accountancy,' he complained. 'It's a job to earn money, that's all. I'm not that interested.'

'Why do it then?'

He shrugged. 'I couldn't think of anything else. I work long hours, but I earn a fair whack and when I come home I can switch off completely. It gives me a chance to do other things.'

'Like what?' I dipped a plump langoustine in the fiery sauce and took a bite, trying in vain to make it ladylike.

His eyes were merry. 'Like having dinner with interesting women.' He said it as if he meant it. I made a noise which sounded like 'harrum'.

'Can I taste your soup?' I asked, to cover my embarrassment.

As we charged forks and spoons and engaged in that mutual tasting of dishes which can seem as intimate as foreplay, my thoughts went back to James and I found my scepticism doing battle with the wish to be objective. I was prepared to allow that James might be a good architect, but clever he was not. A smart operator, likely to gain the confidence of big-league developers? No. He was a man with good connections and I was willing to bet that was the reason he'd got as far as he had.

'D'you know Edward Hunt?' asked John, as if reading my thoughts.

'I've spoken to him once or twice,' I said warily. 'Do you?'

'Only through James.'

'What do you think of him?'

He lifted his wine glass and regarded me thoughtfully over the top of it. 'I think he's sharp,' he said enigmatically and took a sip of wine. My heart sank. Edward Hunt may be a brilliant speaker, but I didn't care to get too intimate with someone who admired his politics.

'So you're all for traditional values are you?' I asked, trying to keep the serious edge out of my voice. 'The sanctity of marriage, a return to the nuclear family, lock up the women and put old people on the scrap heap?' John smiled, but I could see he was offended. I kicked myself mentally – me and my mouth.

'I didn't vote for him,' he said quietly.

'I'm sorry, I didn't mean –'

'I just think he's sharp. Clever. Gets what he wants.'

'I only know him by reputation.' I tried to back pedal. 'Though I've heard him speak.'

'He's a good speaker, don't you think?'

I felt perverse. 'If you can ignore what he's saying . . .'

'Which you can't.'

'Which I can't.'

John looked disapproving. I wondered if he, too, benefited from Hunt's connections. The waiter came and took our plates, creating a momentary diversion. There was an uncomfortable silence. I waited for John to make the next conversational move. He poured more wine, then said, 'So where do you fit in to the Hunt set?'

I met his eyes. 'I don't.'

He placed the wine bottle carefully back on the table. 'Nor do I.' He wanted me to know that.

'Did you go to the party – the night she died?'

He shook his head. 'Did you?' This was like twenty bloody questions.

'No.'

John smiled and raised his glass. 'Two outsiders,' he said, and took a sip of wine.

I didn't want to be tempted into an evening of speculation about Caroline and what had happened since her death, so I slipped into nosy counsellor mode and asked him about his childhood. He came from Leicester, the youngest of three children; his father pushed paper in a DHSS office and his mother worked in a shoe shop. He didn't offer any rosy childhood memories – he said he got away from home as soon as he could. His brother emigrated to Australia in the early seventies; his sister still lived in Leicester. As he talked, I did a bit of mental embroidery and pictured a stifling lower middle class family, bickering together in a box house. The father sounded like a pompous bully; the mother, intelligent, but downtrodden. John was the clever one of the family, did well at school, studied maths at Manchester, then moved to London and did accountancy. A couple more careful questions told me that his father regarded his success with mixed feelings, jealousy mingling with reflected glory. His mother was proud of him, but bereft, feeling that he had risen too far above her. He went on duty visits to Leicester twice a year and he felt like a stranger.

The duck in vermouth arrived and was as mouth-watering as I'd hoped. Since John had ordered fish, we compromised on a bottle of fruity *rosé* for the main course. My head was beginning to swim a little, but pleasantly. As soon as he finished talking, I detected that John was slightly alarmed that he'd revealed so much so quickly. To even up the confessional stakes, I told him the story of my father's parents coming over from Poland years ago, of my mother's family dying in Germany during the war and how at family gatherings, the pointless guilt of being survivors still hung on the air like the distant whine of enemy planes. I explained how my father's desire to become invisible as a Jew was always in conflict with his wish for his children to shine – hence the constant pressure not to draw attention

114

to ourselves in the petty private school he sent us to and yet the relentless exhortations for us to be the best in the class. John nodded knowingly. I told him how my older sister and I were like mirror images of each other – whatever she did, I did the opposite – but how, through therapy, I'd salvaged some valuable things from my Jewishness which had partially brought me back into the family fold. We sat in silence for a moment, both mulling over what the other had said. I liked him more for giving me an account of his background I could relate to. I savoured the last mouthful of the duck and tried not to imagine him undressed.

'Have you ever been to Ronnie Scott's?' he asked. I shook my head. I was looking at the menu again, convincing myself I was too full to contemplate dessert.

'Always wanted to.' I smiled inwardly. Going to Ronnie Scott's had been the subject of a huge argument between David and me. I'd wanted to go to the famous jazz club on my thirtieth birthday, but he'd flatly refused on the grounds that it would be expensive, smoky and would mean a late night. To me, his attitude signalled the beginnings of boring middle age; he felt I was just trying to make a point.

'You look thoughtful. How about it – or would you rather go home?'

I looked up to make sure he was serious. 'You mean – now?' I tried not to look aghast. A furtive glance at my watch told me it was twenty past eleven.

John smiled. 'Unless it's past your bedtime.' My first reaction was to cry off because of the babysitter – until I realised there wasn't one. I weighed up the options. I didn't want to go home alone; I didn't want to go home with John. I knew I'd regret it in the morning. I also knew that, sooner or later, I'd have to face up to what had happened at the clinic. I opted for later.

'Great.' I smiled and shrugged, as if going to jazz clubs was something I did most nights of the week. I love live music, but since the children were born, I've gone to films because they finish earlier.

John looked pleased, as if this was his way of saying he didn't want the evening to end so soon. We agreed wistfully that neither of us had room for dessert, so we downed a quick espresso and he asked for the bill. I offered to pay my half, but he refused graciously, saying it had been his invitation. We went by taxi, which took the Cromwell Road route into town. It was a treat not to be driving and to watch the city race by, twinkling with the soft-edged lights of a summer Saturday night.

It was past midnight when we went through the unprepossessing doorway in Frith Street. The place was packed. The guy at the desk was in his mid-fifties, with a pale, drawn face that rarely saw daylight, and his bushy beard spread apart to reveal a toothy smile when he saw us approach.

'How are you, mate? Haven't seen you here for a while. How's business?' Was it my imagination or did John shoot him a warning glance? He certainly hesitated before returning the smile.

'Nice to see you, Joe,' he returned crisply. 'Big night tonight?' Joe seemed to take the hint. He gave us our tickets and switched his attention from John to me. He rattled on about the Chilean band that was heading the bill, promising 'a real jump up' during the second set. I noticed that John was a member of the club – and that he seemed less relaxed than when we were at the restaurant.

Inside it was just as a jazz club should be – dark, fuggy, with small tables crowded together, yellowing table lamps illuminating the curling haze. A young black woman, dressed in a skimpy top and silky trousers, was easing her velvet voice round a blues number. I thrilled to the atmosphere and felt naughty and grown-up to be there. A woman in her forties came over to seat us. She smiled and kissed John lightly on the cheek – what was this, his fan club? – then showed us to a table at the far end of the room. I couldn't hear their chit chat above the singing, but it was more on her side than his. We moved the chairs so they were side by side, facing the stage and a waitress came straight over. I opted for a Perrier, John ordered a brandy and we sat back to absorb the scene.

The audience was younger than I'd imagined, a mixture of men and women in their twenties and early thirties. There was a low buzz of conversation beneath the singer's wailing blues, but most people were lost in the music. Within the gloom, patches of light fell on still faces, arms flung casually over chair backs, couples leaning together, heads resting on shoulders. A mellow, late-evening mood. I closed my eyes and let the slow notes seep into me. Beside me, John slid his arm across the back of my chair and gently rubbed my shoulder. I opened my eyes and smiled up at him and he answered the smile with a long penetrating kiss which would rate a 10 if I were crass enough to assess these things – which I am. I felt my resolve to go home alone melting at the edges. When we finally drew apart, we sipped our drinks in easy silence, letting the music flow between us. I couldn't help thinking how David would have felt the need to talk – analyse the setting, evaluate the music, intellectualise what should be a wordless pleasure. I wanted to sit back and absorb the atmosphere, lose myself in the pleasure of having no deadline to meet. John seemed to feel the same way.

When the woman finished her set, the mood changed abruptly. The main act was band of six men in their mid-twenties, dark haired, wild eyed and sizzling with energy even before they started playing. Their first number brought whoops of delight from the floor. When you hear Latin jazz for the first time, you suddenly understand the madness of Rio at party time – I could hardly keep still. During their second number, the whole band started to move round the room, storming the tables, inciting us to a frenzy of clapping, laughing and foot tapping. A few couples got up to dance. I drummed my fingers on John's left thigh and jiggled my feet; John tapped out the drum beat against my arm. As the band moved round the room, the confusion and activity stepped up, more people got up, moved around and danced, whooping and stomping. John squeezed me excitedly and I laughed aloud. As the number drew to a close and the band stomped their way back to the stage, I suddenly felt John go tense. I glanced up at him – he was looking in the direction of the bar, his face registering surprise and displeasure.

'What's the matter?' My voice made no impact over the noise, but

117

he got my drift, shook his head and mouthed 'Nothing.' The band started a slow romantic ballad, the kind of mournful lament you might expect to hear in a run-down bar in the back streets of a Chilean city. I love the sound of Spanish and the song touched me deeply, but the spell of the evening was somehow broken. I could sense that John was no longer enjoying himself. He drained his glass and shifted beside me restlessly. I looked at him enquiringly and asked if he wanted to leave. 'Not really, but it's pretty hot in here.' He flapped his hand in front of his face. Irritably, I finished my drink and indicated that I was ready to leave. He jumped up, anxious to be gone.

He weaved his way through the tables, keeping well away from the bar side of the room. As we neared the exit, I cottoned on – he'd seen someone he knew and didn't want to talk to them. Perhaps he didn't want to be seen with me. As we momentarily got separated in the crowd, I stopped and scanned the faces of the people at the bar. Subconsciously, I was looking for a woman who could be his ex-wife or a former girlfriend, but they were all men. At first, they all looked unfamiliar, then suddenly in a group at the far end, near the wall, I recognised a man leaning against the bar. It was Robert Winter, Caroline's lover. And he was staring straight at me.

'I'm sorry. I just felt claustrophobic.' We were standing on the dark, deserted pavement shivering in damp air. It was a lame excuse and John knew it. I went straight for the jugular.

'Why didn't you want Robert Winter to see us?'

'Who?' His voice was measured and controlled.

'Robert Winter. The man Caroline was having an affair with. I saw him at the bar.'

John shook his head slowly. I have a low tolerance for deception – my patience snapped. 'Skip it,' I said coolly. 'Thanks for a lovely evening. See you around.' I turned abruptly and starting walking down Frith Street, cursing the late hour and wondering where I could pick up a taxi.

'Sara – wait!' He caught me up. I stopped and folded my arms. His air of quiet confidence was gone, but he met my eye.

'You're right.' He took a deep breath. 'It was because Winter was there. I just didn't want to have to talk to him. I'm sorry.'

I inclined my head and looked enquiring. 'What's the problem?'

John thrust his hands in his pockets and scuffed one foot against the kerb.

'No problem. I just don't like the guy.'

'Because of his relationship with Caroline?'

'That and the fact that he's a pretentious twat.'

'He was hardly busting a gut to come over,' I argued.

'I assumed you knew him.'

'Why would you assume that?'

'I've said I'm sorry.'

I sighed. How could we be arguing already? We'd only just met.

'Look – if it's a problem that I'm a friend of Caroline and you're a friend of James, I can understand that. But surely you could have thought of it before you asked me out to dinner?'

'It's not a problem.'

Have it your own way, I thought peevishly. I bet your body's not that great anyway.

We stood on the pavement staring at each other in mutual mistrust. A car cruised up Frith Street, then disappeared in the direction of Tottenham Court Road. Night silence returned. A vagrant shifted and rustled in a doorway over the other side of the street. I had a sudden impulse to ask John a question. Some instinct which told me that if I asked now and caught him off balance I'd get the truth.

'John – do you know who killed Caroline?'

Sorry, Mel, it just happens.

John's head jerked up in surprise. Bingo! 'Killed her . . .?' His tone told me he knew, but he hadn't been sure if I knew. He gave me a long searching look, his face suddenly harder and more serious than it had been all evening. He paused for a second, then shook his head slowly.

'No. No, I don't.' We looked at each other guardedly.

'I think we'd better go home,' I said at last.

We travelled home in exhausted silence. The taxi dropped me at my door and we briefly kissed goodnight and made a vague arrangement to phone each other. I felt disappointed about how the evening had ended, but I had found out one thing – I wasn't the only person who knew Caroline died by someone else's hand.

chapter nine

The door to the clinic was open when Clancy and I got there on the Sunday morning. Standing just outside, we could hear the sound of hoovering and Greg's booming Yorkshire voice telling a complicated anecdote about Gary Lineker and a Spurs goal kick. Greg has a theory that men communicate through sport and he loses no opportunity to try and prove it.

We went straight in to survey the scene. Greg had organised two local lads with startling sinews and short haircuts to clear up the worst of the mess. Their T-shirts declared that they called themselves Spik 'n' Span and the 'communication through sport' theory didn't seem to be holding up above the noise of the hoover. Spik scowled at us from under the Lego table. Span's eyes lit up at the sight of two females and he stopped hoovering in order to strike what he hoped was an irresistibly sexy pose with the suction hose. Greg abandoned his story mid-gesture, like a player poised in a 'spot-the-ball' competition. I was pleased to see that the reception area was already looking almost back to normal, if you discounted Doreen's bare desk, where the computer used to be, and a gash in the seat of the sofa. Clancy gratified Span by hooting some ribald comment about size not being important. Feeling suddenly very weary, I motioned Greg and Clancy to come into the kitchen, so we could hear ourselves think.

'Great lads!' said Greg, beaming. 'Done a great job. Place was a tip.'

'It looks a lot better,' I agreed.

'Haven't found a single thing missing.' Clancy and Greg exchanged meaning looks.

121

'What about that note on the board?' They looked at me, clearly expecting me to launch into an energetic discussion about who had done it, and why, but I just couldn't face it. I filled the kettle, plugged it in and busied myself with making coffee to ease my clanging head. Let them draw their own conclusions. I knew Mel would be down on me like a ton of bricks at the staff meeting in the morning, quizzing me about whether I thought it had anything to do with my interest in Caroline's death. I didn't want a dress rehearsal with Clancy and Greg.

'It's lucky Doreen keeps the back-up files at home,' Greg was saying. It was something we'd learned from the last break-in. We keep our own case notes in our rooms; central records are kept in reception, but Doreen copies them each week and keeps the disks at home.

Greg had already started making a list of items for the insurance claim, so I gave them their coffee and left them to it. I wasn't in the mood for being efficient. I trod morosely up to my room feeling put upon and miserable. I put the coffee down on my desk, sank back into my chair and flung my feet on the desk on top of a pile of papers. I eased my head back and closed my eyes. Where to start? I'd been trying to avoid thinking about any of it since yesterday afternoon when I'd come in and found the clinic ransacked. I knew I had to face it, but I felt overwhelmed by the impossibility of piecing it all together. Despondency bore down on me like a juggernaut.

When depression threatens, action is the best course – don't think, just do something. With enormous effort, I eased my legs off the desk, trudged over to the filing cabinet and leafed slowly through the files. Hamman, Hardy . . .Hargreaves. I pulled out Lyn's file, took it back to the desk and turned to the notes I'd made on our first set of sessions, the year before. What was I looking for? Barry's hunch about blackmail – that's it, payments . . . someone was paying her and the payments stopped just before she died.

Immature affair with married man. Spend nights/afternoons

together. Violent father. Enjoys building up lover as mystery
figure.

That was my first entry – 25 February. It went on to outline some of
the difficulties Lyn presented when she first came – money, men,
anxiety, depression, low self-esteem.

9 March – pale and restless, depressed because he's too
busy to see her.

The case notes I write for myself are sometimes obscure, written in a
kind of shorthand. As well as straight facts, I also note down
psychological patterns, ideas, insights. It helps me remember, from
week to week, the themes clients are exploring and strands I want to
pursue. Accounts of Lyn's sessions were dominated by the symbol
'£=lve' – money equals love – a reference to my theory about her
penchant for rich men being a compensation for her withholding
father. Lyn always had money troubles. Money troubles and man
troubles – they seemed to go together. Back then, despite the fact
that she had a good job and a seriously wealthy boyfriend, she
seemed to be constantly in debt. Power was another recurring
theme; power over men and men having power over her. She
mentioned her father often –a big, charismatic man who was used to
getting his own way. Flirtation and seduction was the only way she
knew of getting hers. I scanned the sessions over two months in the
spring, piecing together a picture of a little girl trapped inside an
hourglass figure, tortured by an insatiable appetite for love, money
and power.

Another symbol I use is a black spot, to signify noticeable signs of
violence – a black eye, or a bruise. Lyn had quite a few of those. The
boyfriend never punched her in anger, it was all part of a weird
sexual game. I have a good memory for bizarre sexual practices – I
always think they may come in handy – but I must have blanked out
this one as distinctly lacking in fun. I scanned the notes and read a
few of the 'black spot' entries.

20 March Scarf to hide bruising on neck. Says it's just a game – she pretends to be an animal – horse, dog, etc. – he 'rides' her, with reins . . .

30 April . . . animal game getting more elaborate: chafing on neck (collar?). She has to wear skins. Tackled her on father's violence again . . .

4 May He left her in flat tied with up no clothes. Ptd out this was assault – had she thought of telling police? She refused.

'It's so out of character,' Lyn used to say, 'he's so classy' – that was her word, 'classy'. A 'classy' man with a 'classy' job. I heard her breathy, affected voice confide, 'he mixes with all the top people.' For some reason which I'd now forgotten, I hadn't believed her assessment; I'd imagined him to be like her father – a wide-boy made good. I scanned a few more pages. It was odd that I couldn't remember what he did for a living.

Then, suddenly, a name sprang out of the page at me from a September entry –

L. angry and upset – Edward says it's over.

I stared at the name in disbelief. Surely the man wasn't Edward Hunt? I shook my head – highly improbable – Edward wasn't that uncommon a name, although it's usually shortened to Eddy or Ted. In a flash, I remembered the session – it had been a major breakthrough. The boyfriend's threat of abandonment had triggered a childhood memory of an incident with her father when she was ten or so. It was the beginning of the school term and she was dreading going back to boarding school. She begged her father not to send her. Tired of trying to cajole her, her father lost his temper and hit her, telling her she was stupid and ungrateful. She became hysterical, weeping and pounding her fists against him. Suddenly furious, her father slapped her face so hard he fractured her jaw. The memory stirred up deep anger in Lyn – an unusual emotion for her to show

124

directly. This was the first – the only – time she ever seemed to get in touch with her bitterness at being rejected by her father and her response had been to say her lover's name over and over again, as if venting her anger by defying their strict rule of secrecy. The name hadn't stuck in my mind – only the force of her anger once it broke free.

Feeling suddenly excited, I scanned the rest of Lyn's notes.

> Did piece of work on jealousy, relating it to feelings for mother. Says she saw *him* on TV tonight – is this real, or a way of exaggerating his importance?

She never used his name. She told me it was to protect his identity – I told her it was to add to the mystery and subterfuge which was a big part of his attraction. 'He says we have to be careful . . .' she would say. 'It could mean an end to his career . . .' 'I don't want to break up his marriage . . .' 'He'd kill me if anyone found out . . .' I'd dismissed it all as typical of Lyn – dramatic and gullible. I wondered now if I'd been wrong. I scrabbled through more of the notes, scanning my appalling handwriting for another mention of the man's name, or clues about his identity. There wasn't one. Nothing to confirm it was Edward Hunt – but nothing to contradict it either. After the one lapse, Lyn was back to being discreet. Looking through the last of the sessions, I gathered that Lyn managed to start the relationship up again and was trying hard to please him. Psychologically, she was slipping back into old habits. A few weeks afterwards, she stopped coming to see me.

I stroked my cheek and thought about it. If it was Hunt – and it was a big 'if' – how could she have met him? Through Caroline? Or was it the other way round? Then I recalled that, around that time, Lyn's PR company represented a pressure group that was trying to lobby MPs on some issue and it was part of Lyn's job to arrange social functions to which MPs (and journalists) were invited. I remembered because a lot depended on it, she got very stressed and I had to ask her if I could talk to her GP about the amount of sleeping pills she was getting through.

I looked back at the notes and jumped around a few pages, trying to see if I could fit Hunt into the picture. Would such a man be attracted to Lyn? I couldn't see why not. She was the perfect contrast to Belinda. Soft, vulnerable and sexy – the ultimate mistress. Lyn was the harlot, willing to play the sado-masochistic games; Belinda the wife, queen of the parish fêtes and canapés. The best of both worlds – why not? If Hunt really had an affair with Lyn, it could also explain Belinda's hostility towards her. Yet Hunt was fiercely ambitious. A lover like Lyn would be a tremendous liability. The willing horse was also an erratic woman who was into drugs and worked dangerously close to the media. Would someone as clever as Hunt ever take such a risk?

'Hey!' Clancy's bark almost catapulted me out of my chair. I looked up at her, scowling.

'What?'

'We're going to the pub for some lunch – d'you want to come?'

I waved the file notes. 'No. I think I'll just –'

'Okay.' Clancy slammed the door shut, then opened it again and popped her head round. 'Are you moping?'

'No.'

Moping was a cardinal sin in Clancy's book. She hesitated in the doorway, but my frown dissuaded her from coming any further.

'We'll be at The George.' She half-turned and bellowed over her shoulder. 'Gre-eg!' I winced painfully. My late night had taken its toll – I had a pounding headache. 'The George – yeah?' There was a muffled reply from below. Clancy turned back into the room. 'Yeah, it's The George if you change your mind.'

'Fine.' She shut the door with a bang. I heard her mutter 'Shit!' as she bumped into the protruding bit of banister – she did it every time – and braced myself for the whole house to shudder as Clancy

slammed the front door. Vrrump! Their voices receded up the street.
I revelled in the silence.

Had Lyn Hargreaves dared to blackmail Sir Edward Hunt? She
certainly had a strong enough hand, but if he was as influential as
Clancy said, surely only a fool would attempt it? There was so much
at stake. Exposure of the affair in the Press would finish his political
career, based as it was on happy families and clean living. Just as he
was reaching the height of his powers, with the chance of a place in
the cabinet. And if Lyn also threatened to expose his sexual tastes ...
Hunt was ambitious and he was probably ruthless – so was his wife.
Lyn would have to be either brave or desperate to think she could get
away with it. Yet, the more I thought about it, the more credible it
seemed. Lyn as blackmailer – batting her eyelids, threatening and
cajoling by turns, craving his money when she couldn't have his love.
She probably couldn't believe her luck when the ploy worked –
power! And it would be quite in character for her to keep upping the
stakes, pushing him to the limit. But would Hunt really go as far as
killing someone for the sake of his career? Would Belinda? And
would either of them know how to find hoodlums who would do a
job like that without botching it, or running to the newspapers? I
could just about believe Hunt could fall prey to blackmail and that
Belinda could find out about it and still stick by him. What was
harder to credit was that either of them was sufficiently plugged into
the criminal world to know how to get someone to kill his lover. Mel,
I knew, would dismiss the idea as ridiculous.

I sighed heavily and wandered over to the window. The street was
deserted except for a little girl, about seven years old, playing a
solitary game by a garden wall. I felt a pang of loneliness and
wondered what the kids were doing. Things fitted, yet didn't fit –
spirals within spirals. I considered whether or not to tell Barry my
hunch about the blackmail, but I knew what he'd say – evidence,
Sara, I need evidence. Maybe I'd put the theory to Steve. I stayed by
the window long enough to watch the little girl skip off down the
road, then went back to the desk and gathered up the file. It was a

hunch, nothing more. As an afterthought, I pulled out a few of the 'black spot' pages, went into Greg's room and photocopied them. Then I took the notes downstairs, locked up carefully and stepped back into the dismal streets, wondering why I'd let Clancy steam-roller me into walking all the way to the clinic.

Dark clouds were gathering for the next shower and I was craving painfully my next cup of coffee. I started walking up towards Acton High Street. There had been a thunderstorm earlier and the day was grey and cloudy, a chilly wind scooping up the litter and dumping it in shop doorways. The uneven pavements were full of puddles and my shoes were soaked within the first five minutes. As I crossed Churchfield Road, empty except for a few Irish families making their way to mass in the High Street, I felt the cloud of depression returning. Why is life so complicated? You meet a nice guy, have a great evening, then he acts like a primadonna and you no longer know where you stand. Two women you know are dead, you want to know why and someone may have it in for you for being curious. Your children are away and you're missing them like hell. I kicked at an empty can, missed and cursed as I felt a twinge in my back. You're getting older too, I reflected gloomily.

A brooding paranoia settled in on top of the depression. If Edward Hunt got rid of people he didn't like, and if he found out I knew about his relationship with Lyn, he would be after me too. Was that what was meant by 'You next'? Belinda's voice came back to me with chilling clarity – 'My husband is an extremely powerful man, Ms Kingsley.' Perhaps Belinda had Lyn followed, found out where she went and whom she saw. My palms tingled with the sweat of anxiety – too many paths were leading back to me. Walking up the hill in the small side street, I thought I felt a presence behind me and glanced back quickly. Nothing. Just an old man shuffling along, peering into a rubbish bin beside the lamppost. I told myself not to be so stupid, pulled my sweatshirt sleeves over my chilly hands and started walking quickly. The feeling that I was being followed persisted all the way home, but I shrugged it off and made it into my street before the rain got heavy.

When I got up to where my car was parked I changed my mind about going home and knocked instead at a house three doors down. Afsana opened the door with her two-year-old clutching at her legs. I told her about the charity list and how I wanted to sift through it.

'It sounds pretty straightforward,' she said in her soft accent. 'Bring the disk and I'll show you how to pick out the data.' Normally I hate asking favours, but I didn't mind asking Afsana. She's the type of person who gives whatever she can, without making you feel guilty, and doesn't mind asking for help in return. I fetched the disk from the car and went back to the house. Her office overlooks the garden, like Jake's bedroom does in our house. I picked up Karim and pointed out a squirrel scurrying along the fence, while Afsana loaded the disk. She demonstrated which keys to press to choose a different part of the entry each time. Then she gently extracted Karim and left me to it.

I sat and stared blankly at the screen. I'd come to Afsana's on impulse, wanting to keep moving, wanting to hold the depression at bay; now I was here, I couldn't think of a single check to run. I tried Holmes-ian deduction, wishing Steve was beside me to be my Watson. If Caroline was investigating corruption in small charities – charities set up as tax shields – what would she look for? I didn't have a clue. I looked round the room in search of inspiration and became distracted by a photo of Afsana and Simon getting married. I wondered what her family thought of her marrying a white Englishman and what his family thought of their Pakistani daughter-in-law. They all looked quite happy about it in the photo. I forced my eyes back to the screen and tried to imagine I was a journalist, but all I got from that was a mental image of Harry Leadbitter with his bad breath and yellow teeth growling, 'Fuck off and just do it.'

Just for something to do, I pulled out a list of all the charities with expenditure of over £60,000 a year and flipped through a few at random. There were hundreds. Apart from marvelling at the amount of money people donate to clapped out horses and donkeys, I got nowhere. Distracted again, I had the bad taste to wonder if Edward

Hunt was a regular visitor to the Donkey Sanctuary, but the thought led inevitably to sex – and John – so I squashed it flat. My system was screaming out for a cup of coffee. Irritably, I pulled out entry after entry at random – hedgehogs, retired gentlefolk, Cambodian refugees – but I failed to see how Caroline had deduced anything at all from the list.

Before I gave up in disgust, I tried to look at it another way – that Caroline knew of a link between James and one particular charity and had discovered some irregularities in their dealings. Obvious. I blamed the hangover that I hadn't thought of it before. I put the cursor on to the field where it listed trustees and typed in the name James Blythe. I pressed 'search', the machine blinked and bleeped and there it was – I couldn't believe my eyes. Not only James' name, but Edward's too and – the biggest surprise – Robert D Winter. All three were trustees of a charity called SACA – South American Children's Aid. 'To help street children in South American cities by helping them to help themselves', went the blurb. Eureka! The 'current activities' section gave two projects as examples. In Rio, there were four volunteers who gave a small group of homeless children two hours of schooling a day, a decent meal and regular medical checks. In Buenos Aires, a doctor and a nun ran a hostel for pregnant teenagers – inviting repentance no doubt, but also showing the girls how to care for the babies and trying to get them reconciled with their families. All worthy stuff. The administrator was listed as a woman called Marjorie Martinez; she was the contact name for the charity's headquarters in Notting Hill. Income and expenditure seemed on the large side for such small-scale projects, but not outrageously so. I took down the address and telephone number, then went down to the kitchen to ask Afsana how to print out the page. A few minutes later, I was standing on the doorstep, thanking her profusely and feeling mighty pleased with myself. The charity seemed kosher from the outside, but I felt sure this was the missing link. I walked up to my house with a spring in my step, splashing my trainers deliberately into every puddle.

My answering machine was flashing like a maniac – three calls. First things first – I made myself a steaming cup of my best Italian coffee with hot frothy milk and took two or three grateful sips before going back to the sitting room to play back the messages. The first was a minute and a half of high-pitched voices giggling and whispering – 'This is Winnie the Poo-poo,' 'I can see your knickers tee hee hee.' This told me that David and Angie were having a Sunday morning lie-in, oblivious of the fact that Hannah had recently learned the art of dialling her own telephone number. I smiled indulgently, as a fond parent does who's not paying the phone bill and felt glad to have a good excuse to phone and tell them off. At least I'd hear their voices. The second message was Steve, saying he just wanted a chat (but really, I knew, wanting a blow by blow account of my night out with John). The third was from John asking me to call him. My stomach tightened; I hadn't expected to hear from him again so soon and I wondered what he wanted.

I phoned David first and asked to speak to the children. Hannah blamed Jake for the phone call.

'He said he wanted to tell you that you didn't pack his dinosaur T-shirt and he went on and on about it so much –'

'It was you!' Jake yelled in the background. 'You were crying!'

'One at time,' I said firmly. 'Were you crying, Hannah?'

'Yes,' said a tiny voice. We talked for a while, then I asked to speak to her father.

While she was fetching him, Jake picked up the receiver and wittered on for a minute or so about how he'd been up to Mars in his rocket, met a marshmallow and splatted it with his Coco Pops. I offered effusive congratulations and told him to put his father on. I asked David to let the children phone me at a pre-arranged time each day instead of haphazardly – Hannah clearly needed a more consistent link with home. He agreed without a murmur. That's one thing I appreciate about David – he defers to my judgement about Hannah and Jake, acknowledging that I know their needs better than he does. Most of the time, we manage to bury the bitterness and present them with a united front. I put down the phone and went to refill my coffee cup. David's a great father, I reflected – pity he turned out to be such a lousy husband.

Curiosity overcame me – I phoned John next.

'Sara! Thanks for calling back. Look, about last night . . .'

'Yes?' I said cautiously.

'I'm sorry it ended so . . . awkwardly. I acted daft. I suppose you wouldn't – er, are you free tonight?'

'Tonight?'

'Yes,' he said quickly. 'If you came over to my place, I could cook us some dinner and we could, you know, talk.'

I considered for an instant – I was knackered and I felt sure the relationship was a non-starter. But curiosity and sexual attraction are a potent mix.

'All right,' I said and took down the address. ('It's just to find out what he knows about Caroline,' I told myself defensively.)

When I came off the phone, I realised that I hadn't eaten a thing all day. I swallowed the last of my coffee, then boiled myself a couple of eggs with two slices of wholemeal toast. I wolfed the lot in a couple of minutes and felt a lot better. Nibbling a third piece of toast I phoned Steve, updated him on my findings and told him about the rapid exit from Ronnie Scott's to avoid Winter. I remained non-committal about my feelings for John despite a thorough interrogation.

'Is he your usual type?' persisted Steve. 'Does he have a beard and wear baggy cords?'

'He wears designer suits and he's probably never read a work of literature in his life,' I boasted. 'So there!'

'Mazeltov,' said Steve, laughing.

When I finished chatting to Steve I glanced at my watch. Four o'clock. Just time for a long bath and a glance at the paper. I realised guiltily that I hadn't even thought about the seminar for the adolescent conference. I promised myself I'd make a start during the week.

John lived in the ground-floor flat of a terraced red-brick house, just off Fulham Palace Road. It's a busy area and I had trouble parking. The evening was gloomy, with a light drizzle and a chilly wind. I got out of the car and turned up the collar of my leather jacket, wondering what had happened to the sweltering summer. As I stood at the front door, clutching a bottle of Australian Chardonnay, I found myself glancing nervously over my shoulder looking for – who knows what? I must stop this paranoid behaviour, I told myself. In one of the houses opposite, a net curtain was lifted slightly, then dropped again; a blue Ford Escort, which had been behind me since Hammersmith, was still edging up the street looking for somewhere to park. None of it could be called suspicious, but I still felt uneasy.

I heard quick footsteps in response to my ring and John opened the door.

'Hi.'

'Hello.'

'Come in.' We looked each other up and down for an instant, then he smiled. Such merry eyes. I grabbed my doubts by the scruff of the neck and tossed them over my shoulder into the road. I stepped inside and John shut the door. I held out the wine and grinned awkwardly.

'Thanks.' He took it and put it on the hall table, then took a step towards me and tentatively laid his hands on my arms. I moved towards him and we kissed once, twice, then long, luxuriously, searchingly. He pulled my body close and placed his hands firmly on my back.

'I wanted to do this last night,' he breathed.

'So did I.' We kissed again. 'Let's do it now,' I suggested.

We undressed in the hall, unable to part long enough to make it to the bedroom. We made love hungrily, urgently, like clandestine lovers alone for the first time. Some bodies are made to find each other. Two strangers can find a primal rhythm which eludes couples who have been together for decades. Each movement sparks its perfect reply, each touch a countertouch, like two creatures performing a predetermined dance.

Afterwards, as I lay on the bed with my head on his shoulder, feeling the rise and fall of his chest return to its normal pace, I grappled with a dawning thought. Something was wrong about his flat. I hadn't seen much of it – only the hall and the bedroom – but it wasn't what I'd expected. John was supposed to be a friend of James Blythe. James was rich, golfy, materialistic – John's flat was a modest conversion, with books in the bedroom. He was divorced, with a child and presumably had to pay alimony; even so, he and James seemed poles apart. Were they really friends, or were they doing business together? The thought unsettled me. John stirred, as if sensing my mistrust, drew me closer and kissed my ear. I rolled over and looked him in the eye.

'If you knew Caroline was murdered, why didn't you talk to the police?'

John groaned and pulled the sheet over his head. 'Can't we leave Caroline out of it tonight?'

I pulled the sheet down. 'No.'

John sighed. I climbed on top of him and pinned his arms above his head, swinging my breasts across his chest. I felt the muscles in his shoulders go taut as he tried to raise his mouth towards the left nipple. I pushed him down again.

'Tell!'

His eyes looked wary. 'Why?'

I licked his nose. 'Because I want to know.'

He sighed again, then pushed up his arms effortlessly and gently rolled me off him.

'I'll get the dinner first. It's just pizza and salad. We can eat it in bed.' Playing for time. I lay back for a moment and stretched luxuriously. As John banged about in the kitchen, I leaned out of bed and reached for my sweater. Pulling it on, I padded over to check the bookshelves in the corner of the room. I don't know what I thought I'd find, but it wasn't these: Steven Hawking's *A Brief History of Time*; Tolkien; Brecht, some nineteenth-century classics and a slim volume of medieval poetry. An intellectual. Shit. How would I ever live it down with Steve?

'Wine?' called a voice from the kitchen.

'Please!' I called back. I walked over to the bed, flung myself across it and picked up his current reading, a couple of books lying open on the bedside table. One was a biography of Tolstoy, the size of a brick, the other a trashy spy thriller. I was glad to see he took some time off. There was a photo in a frame on the bedside table – his son, aged about four, I would guess. He was laughing, head thrown back, sitting on a tricycle. He had the same eyes as his father.

I hopped back into bed just as John came back, still naked, bearing two plates and two glasses on a tray. I gazed at his body appreciatively. He handed me a plate with a large slice of pizza and crisp green salad, then got back into bed beside me. We ate in silence. When I'd finished, I took a sip of wine and nudged his elbow.

'Tell me,' I demanded.

'You don't give up, do you?'

I grinned in reply.

He swallowed his mouthful of pizza. 'Okay. I'm not sure she was murdered, I just wouldn't be surprised, that's all.'

'Why?'

He took another bite of pizza and chewed meditatively. 'Because James moves in a big league and Caroline interfered in some deal which was worth a lot of money – or so I heard.' He turned his grey eyes on me with an intent gaze. 'D'you know anything about that?'

I shook my head. 'Who killed her?' I asked him.

'I don't know.'

'What was this deal she interfered in?'

'I don't know that either.'

I pulled a face in disbelief. 'Aw, come on. His accountant . . .?'

'I've told you, I'm not his accountant. I give occasional financial advice, that's all. But his goodwill is worth a fair bit to me – he puts business my way. Sara –'

'Yes?'

'You really should keep out of this. When there's a lot of money at stake – things can get nasty.'

I made a face. 'Terrific. The boys are playing boys' games, so the girls should keep out.'

John frowned. 'When boys like this are playing, girls can get hurt, or worse. So can some of the boys, come to that.'

'Are you one of the boys, John?'

He flushed. 'And to finish answering your question, I didn't go to the police because I've nothing to tell them. If you know something, you should go. Though you may not get very far because James doesn't want an investigation.'

'I bet he doesn't,' I said acidly.

'D'you know who did it?' he asked, a little too casually.

'Not yet.'

He shook his head. 'If you've got evidence, go to the police. If you haven't, steer clear. Please.'

'Why should I?'

He touched my face. 'Because you might get hurt.'

'Use your influence, then maybe I won't,' I said cunningly.

'I don't have any influence.'

'I'm glad to hear it.' The silence dangled between us like a hangman's noose. John finished his meal, put the empty plate on the bedside table, then turned to face me and put his hands on my shoulders.

'Look, Sara ...' His face was serious. 'It's going to be difficult for me ... for us to see each other if you don't stop hounding people about Caroline.'

I stared at him, incredulous. 'What?'

He massaged my shoulders. 'James is my client.'

'And Caroline was mine!'

He looked up sharply. 'So you were her counsellor?'

Silly mistake. It was my turn to blush. 'That's irrelevant. What are you trying to say?'

'I'm saying it makes things difficult – for you and for me.' His voice softened. 'I'm trying to warn you.'

I was cut by the phrase. 'I think I'll go.' I started to get out of bed. He caught my arm.

'Not again. Please. Let's talk about it.' I looked at his face – calm, humorous, open. Appearances can be deceptive, I reminded myself. Even so, I let him draw me back into the bed.

'I ... find you ... attractive. I'd ... like us ...' He stumbled for the words. 'You know, I don't want this just to be ... I don't want to chuck it away before it's started.' I felt bewildered, confused. Who's side was he on? John reached out his hand to my cheek and turned my face towards him. Slowly, he placed his lips on mine. His tongue traced an arc inside my mouth. We lay back against the pillows and his hands moved down onto my back and thighs, stroking persuasively in slow circles. Sod it, I wanted him again. He pulled back for a moment.

'Trust me,' he whispered.

I pulled him towards me again, yearning for his touch.

chapter ten

The following afternoon, I was sitting on an eastbound Central Line train, wondering if the day could possibly get any worse. A drunk had just rolled into the nearly empty carriage and chosen to sit beside me. I'd already moved carriages once to avoid an ex-client. The afternoon sun glared through the windows, assaulting my tired eyes; it was a relief when the train went underground at Shepherd's Bush.

Mel had been distinctly frosty at the morning staff meeting. Outwardly, she was gentle and supportive, but I knew her well enough to read the coded messages. She said she was concerned for my safety, but her steely eyes chastised me with the accusation of stubbornness: 'Endanger yourself if you must', they said, 'but keep the clinic out of it.' I was adamant that I'd done nothing to provoke an attack on the clinic – it was true. But it was also true that the break-in had made me more, rather than less, determined to find Caroline's killer. Mel sensed it and issued her silent reproach; I stubbornly battened down the hatches.

Terry O'Reilly, a local beat officer, was waiting to see us when we got out of the meeting – they had caught Tracey shoplifting on two separate occasions on the Saturday and both store managers wanted to prosecute. Terry knew Tracey's history, so he came to the clinic. I was grateful to him, but I felt deflated – naïvely, I'd believed her when she told me she hadn't wanted to nick a thing for weeks. I asked Terry to wait while I consulted with Clancy, who phoned the mother. It turned out that she'd thrown Tracey out of the house on

Friday night for 'making eyes' at her boyfriend. We all knew what that meant – the old greaseball had tried to on with the child once before. We agreed with Terry that I'd try and find Tracey and then ring the store managers to see if I could get a stay of execution.

Late morning, I had an appointment with my least favourite client – a charmless middle-class bully from the local high school. Alex was smug, conceited and loud, but I had to believe that somewhere underneath the brash exterior was a sensitive soul struggling to emerge. The trick was knowing how to uncover it – like trying to excavate a dinosaur's bone from underneath a tower block. Materially, he had everything going for him, yet he expressed his zest for life by beating up eleven-year olds. Tracey had nothing, but she was still trying to love and be loved. The contrast between them was enough to convert me to genetic determinism – some people are just born bloody-minded.

I slipped out of the clinic at four o'clock, muttering vaguely about an appointment in town. I asked Doreen to take messages and relay anything important to my answerphone at home. Earlier in the day, I'd phoned Marjorie Martinez at South American Children's Aid and told her I was organising the NCT's Autumn Fair and that we wanted to donate some of the money to an appropriate charity She twittered hopefully. I asked if I could come and have a chat about what the charity did and she practically swallowed the mouthpiece with excitement. I guessed she wasn't used to people taking much of an interest. She sounded sixtyish, earnest and gushing. I'd probed to find a 'quiet time' at the charity, trying to make sure no one else would be there – especially the esteemed trustees.

'I'm afraid it's always quiet here, except when the trustees meet,' she said, with disarming candour. 'Sir Edward' (she said the name with hushed reverence) 'drops in now and then, but it's usually Mr Blythe who sees to the paperwork and so on and he's a bit tied up with personal affairs at present.' I ummed knowingly. Late afternoon was the only time I had free, so I arranged to be at the charity at five.

As the train rattled into Holland Park station, the drunk beside me suddenly started to snore. Clouds of alcohol fumes wafted under my nose and his head lolled perilously close to my shoulder. I tried not to take it personally, but I felt persecuted. I got up out of my seat, intending to stand by the doors until the train reached Notting Hill. Then I noticed that a man at the far end of the carriage mirrored my move. He was in his late twenties, well built, wearing a white T-shirt and black jeans and there was nothing unusual about him, except that I'd first noticed him in the carriage I'd skipped out of at East Acton. I felt a cold stab of fear – was he following me? The carriage doors opened; I stayed put and so did he. Without glancing in my direction, he thrust his hands in his pockets and leaned casually against the glass partition at the end of the row of seats. He didn't appear to notice me, but I couldn't shake off the idea that it was odd that he'd changed carriages when I did.

We drew into Notting Hill to find a crowd of schoolkids gathered on the platform. I jumped out among the throng then looked back to the carriage; I was pleased to see the guy with the black jeans was still standing calmly against the glass partition. I fought my way towards the exit through the kids, who were surging forward towards the train and chattering excitedly in Italian. Just before I turned into the tunnel marked 'Way Out', I turned back once more to check my carriage. He was gone. I looked around nervously, but I couldn't see him. Forget it, I told myself. Your imagination's working overtime.

'SACA, 1st floor' – it was a small discreet sign beside a door, nestling between an up-and-coming little gallery and a junk shop, in a street off the Portobello Road. The property must be worth a fair bit because of the location, but the place itself looked tatty. I rang the bell and Marjorie's voice quavered over the intercom.

'Hellooo?'

'It's Sara Kingsley, from the NCT.' I glanced tentatively up and down the street for the guy in the black jeans, but there was no sign of him. The door buzzed; I pushed it open and climbed the bare stairs to the first floor.

Marjorie shook my hand warmly and started bustling about with the kettle to make a cup of tea. She was very much as I'd imagined her – the archetypal Tory woman volunteer, busy and well meaning. Her fine white hair was set into fluffy Barbara Cartland curls. She was wearing the proverbial twin-set, but she'd skipped the pearls in favour of a necklace made of wooden beads – a concession, perhaps, to working for an 'ethnic' charity. She must have detected my therapist aura because she started on her life history before the kettle even whispered.

'My late husband was from Buenos Aires you see, that's what first got me interested. Would you like a biscuit, dear? I think I have some in the cupboard.'

'Well if –'

'My mother died only two months ago, bless her soul. She wasn't awfully keen on Freddie and I must say she was absolutely right because he turned out to be a bit of a ruffian, but we lived in Brazil for a while and I used to see these poor little mites sleeping on the pavement and I thought "Surely something can be done?"'

As she gushed on about the living conditions of the street urchins of Buenos Aires, I tried to give the appearance of listening attentively whilst taking in the office. It was just one small room with a desk, a filing cabinet and a phone. Marjorie was stamped all over it – the neatly potted busy lizzies on the window sill, the 'country cottage' style tray with bone china cups and saucers. There was a computer wearing a new looking plastic cover; I wondered if Marjorie had ever used it.

'How long have you worked here?' I asked her when she paused for breath. I could see it would be hard to get a word in edgeways.

'Five years – since SACA started actually,' she replied, pronouncing it 'saw-ca' and pouring the water into the teapot. 'You see –' Marjorie held the teapot in one hand and leaned forward to breathe the name reverentially, 'Sir Edward Hunt was a rather good friend of Freddie's. He heard I was looking for a job – mother said I needed some sort of hobby – and he asked me if I'd be interested in helping until he found someone permanent. I organised one or two rather successful fêtes and a ball and I suppose I rather took the cause to heart,

141

because here I am, five years later, still holding the fort!' She smiled gaily. 'Sugar?'

'No, thanks."

She put the wafer-thin china cup on the desk beside me. 'Now, I expect you want to hear exactly what we do.'

'D'you have any literature I could –'

'Silly me! The annual ball!' Marjorie trotted over to the desk, arms flapping, and picked up a neat pile of papers. She reminded me of Jemima Puddleduck, from one of those odiously twee Beatrix Potter books. 'It's next Saturday, 25 July, at Richmond Hill Hotel. We always have it at the end of July,' – she leaned towards me over the desk and breathed conspiratorially, 'Sir Edward finds it's the only time he can *almost* guarantee his attendance. Perhaps some of your members would like to buy tickets? Where is it you're from, dear, the NCB?'

'NCT,' I corrected her, 'National Childbirth Trust.'

She nodded blankly. 'Lovely.'

I should have said the KGB.

I took the fliers, murmured non committally and glanced at the price. £50 minimum, with further donations invited. I cursed inwardly. It might be useful to go, but it was a lot to pay, especially when you weren't sure where the money was going. Marjorie sat down and sipped her tea, holding the cup correctly, her little finger waggling free.

'It's been most enjoyable in previous years,' she confided. 'The fun starts at eight-thirty p.m. and goes on, oh, well past midnight. Quite a few people stay at the hotel. It's become quite an event!' I promised I'd ask around to see if I could sell a few tickets.

I asked her to tell me a bit about the charity's history. She reminded me that Sir Edward was originally from Argentina. Before he became an MP, he travelled widely on business in South America and was moved by the plight of the children he saw. In his first term as MP, he set up the charity. They had a mailing list of donors all over the country. Hunt himself chose the projects, on visits to Buenos Aires and Rio; James took care of the business side and Marjorie dealt with day-to-day enquiries and donations. Robert Winter seemed only nominally involved.

'Such busy men, yet they give so much time,' twittered Marjorie, admiringly. 'Have you ever heard Sir Edward speak? Marvellous speaker! He always says a few words at the ball.'

We chatted for a while and drank our tea in lady-like sips, but when she started repeating a story she'd told me ten minutes earlier, I felt I had heard enough. I told her I must be going and asked if she had any bumph on the charity I could take away with me. She gave me a slim leaflet and a glossy annual report.

'Lovely to meet you. Do drop by any time.' She patted my arm and leaned towards me. 'You have such a nice face, dear. I could chat to you for hours.' I smiled wanly. Just doin' my job, ma'am. I stood up and moved towards the door.

'We're looking at one or two other charities . . .' I told her. 'I'll let you know as soon as we decide.'

'Hope to see you at the ball,' she said, her button eyes shining. She hadn't even asked for my phone number.

I was relieved to get out of the stifling cosiness of her office and back onto the street. I felt guilty about lying and oppressed by Marjorie's loneliness. I started walking towards Notting Hill, my head full of her voice, unclear about what I'd gained from going there. I was falling into a tired reverie when a sudden sharp pain in my back made me jump. I let out a short involuntary cry and a hand gripped my left arm from behind.

'Keep walking. I've got a knife. Scream and you're dead.' I half turned and saw a white T-shirt and a pair of black jeans. I felt a thin trickle of blood down my lower back. My whole body started shaking. In a film, I would have kicked him in the balls and run for it. In real life, at six o'clock on a Monday evening on a quiet street off Notting Hill, I fought back the tears and kept walking.

We walked a few yards, slowly. My breath came in short gasps; every step was an effort. I saw an old man pass on the other side of the street and I turned my eyes towards him imploringly, hoping he would understand what was happening, but he didn't spare us a glance. My mind cleared. Reality seemed heightened – the sun extra bright, each sound distinct through the rushing of blood in my head. I remembered a wise social worker, with thirty years' experience, who once advised me – if you're ever attacked, keep talking. Never mind what you say, just keep talking.

'You're making a big mistake.' My voice sounded odd, small. 'I don't know what you want, but you've got the wrong person. I'm from the NCT, I'm a mother. I've got two kids waiting for me at home.' I couldn't tell how I was doing, but I knew I wasn't dead yet. I could feel the knife in my back, piercing the skin with each contact. I knew it should hurt, but terror is a great anaesthetic. 'Have you got kids?' I continued. 'Hannah and Jake, mine are called. Seven and four. They'll be wondering where I am. I hope your boss won't mind that you've got the wrong person.' I hoped he had a boss. I hoped he wasn't just a maniac picking randomly on the first lone woman he saw. I could feel his breath on my neck and his thick fingers tightened their grip on my arm. Was I making him nervous? 'Have you ever been inside? You'll go down for years over this. My father's a high court judge. I wouldn't bank on anyone getting you off. Fifteen, twenty years . . . your kids'll be grown up. How old are they now?'

'Shut up.' His voice was gruff, and cockney. We crossed the road in slow motion. We seemed to be making towards a small mews at the end of the street. I tried not to think of what he'd do when we got there. Why wasn't there anyone around? I wasn't convinced talking was a good idea, but now I'd started, I couldn't stop.

'Are you going to kill me?' I babbled. 'I think you should tell me because I'd like to phone Hannah and Jake to say goodbye. Are you going to kill me?'

'Keep walking,' he hissed and prodded me again with the knife. I gasped. I felt it that time – a searing pain as the knife nicked my flesh. 'Don't scream. Just keep walking.'

I was beginning to feel faint. I concentrated on putting one foot in front of the other. The blood was seeping through my trousers at the back. We were almost at the mews. I could see the uneven

144

brickwork, cast in shadow, grey and cold. A miserable place to die. My eyes were swimming and my mind wandered. I thought I saw a figure lurking in the shadows. Who was it? Lyn. I thought I could see Lyn's face, contorted with terror, peering out from a hole in the wall. Was she really there, or was it a vision of her face the split second before she was crushed under the wheels of a train? I blacked out for a second, then swam back towards consciousness and realised I'd slumped in his arms. I couldn't feel the knife; he was half pushing, half dragging me towards the mews.

'Lyn? Lyn?' I mumbled to the apparition as we approached. 'She died a few days ago,' I said, by way of explanation to my attacker. 'She was pushed under a train.'

'What?' He jerked me to my feet and pinned me against the wall. The knife was against my stomach now. With my head held rigid against the wall, I could just see the long thin blade – one short thrust and I'd be finished. 'What're you talking about?' I looked into his face. He has pasty skin, drawn over high cheekbones and tight mouth, set in a cruel line. His eyes were blue, empty and stupid. Perhaps he was the one who pushed Lyn. I closed my eyes and leaned against the wall, forcing myself to think.

'My friend saw you,' I lied, opening my eyes with sudden inspiration. 'He's got a photo; he's going to take it to the police.' I could almost hear his brain clicking as he took that in. A flicker of anxiety passed over his face. He must be the one who pushed her.

'That's a fuckin' lie.'

'He's a dodgy press photographer. He just happened to be standing there. He's been trying to find you to see how much you'd give him for it.'

He grabbed my chin, squeezed it hard and jerked his face into mine: 'Where's he live? What's his name?'

'I – I'll show you. I can get it for you if you like. I know where he keeps the negatives.' I couldn't believe the stupidity of the lie, yet he hesitated. He couldn't decide if I was telling the truth or not. His jaws twitched as he worked through the options, his mouth working silently, his eyes flicking from side to side. My perceptions were strangely clear now, as if my mind was detached from my body. I noted the scar running right across his left eyebrow; the slightly darker roots of his hair beneath the ash blond. I glanced over his shoulder. Only ten yards further on was Notting Hill, bustling with people.

'It's not far from here,' I said quickly. 'It's in the street by the Gate cinema. We could go there now.' Part of me couldn't believe he'd even consider it. He still couldn't decide. He looked quickly over his shoulder, then turned back to me and clenching his huge fist, punched me squarely in the stomach. I doubled up, retching. The hideous pain of the wound in my back made me groan involuntarily. He clamped his hand over my mouth. Where was everyone? Surely someone would pass by soon?

'If you're fuckin' lying,' he whispered, 'I'm gonna rip your guts out.'

'Mm, mm!' I made emphatic noises through his hand. He seemed suddenly convinced. He removed his hand from my mouth and relaxed his grip. In that split second, summoning up all my strength, I pushed him to one side and ran blindly into the street.

'Aaaaargh!' In nightmares, you open your mouth and no sound comes. Not in real life. My scream tore through the silence of the quiet summer afternoon; I knew it was my only chance of staying alive. Then, smack! Running wildly, I hit what appeared to be a huge moving black plastic sack, which dropped to the ground and spilled its guts all over the road. The rest was pure farce.

'Oy!' The man's face was a parody of a surprise – saucer eyes, dropped jaw, mouth framed in a big 'o'. I swivelled round; my attacker was right behind me, knife drawn, poised to grab me.

'Wot's up, Dave?' I swivelled back. Two other men had appeared behind the first. I've never been so glad to see a group of dustmen.

'He's got a knife!' I pointed to black jeans, but he was already half way down the mews. One of the dustmen ran after him.

The man I'd bumped into noticed me swaying slightly and caught my arm.

'You awright, love?'

'I'm fine,' I said serenely – and promptly passed out into the pile of rubbish on the road.

The hospital wanted to keep me in overnight. They said the wound was superficial, but I was in shock and ought to be sedated. I protested that I felt okay, mildly shaken – I was desperate to get home – and told them politely where to put their sedation. Luckily, one of the nurses in casualty was Gail, a mate of Clancy's and I managed to convince her to find a doctor willing to discharge me. They needed the bed anyway. Shock is a strange state. You don't know you're in until you start to come out of it. I realised I'd been a little hasty when I started sobbing uncontrollably into Steve's jacket in the mini-cab. Steve, friend that he is, had abandoned a dinner to come and fetch me – the hospital wouldn't let me go alone.

I'd already told my story once to the police at the hospital. When I went through it all again for Steve, over a brandy at two o'clock in the morning, the full horror of what could have been hit me like a bombshell. My life had been saved by a thin thread of chance. A man wanted to kill me, *would have* killed me if I hadn't said what I'd said, hadn't pushed him away at just that moment, if I hadn't run slap bang into a group of dustmen who just happened to be passing.

'I could be dead,' I kept repeating to Steve. 'I could be dead and Hannah and Jake would be without a mum.' Strange how the maternal bond is so bound up with survival. It also struck home that he hadn't tried to rob me, or rape me – he just wanted to kill me. Confronting the awfulness of the nightmare seemed somehow to defuse it. After trembling and sobbing for a while onto Steve's shoulder, the shock receded and I began to feel better. I was alive. I'd escaped with just a minor wound. I felt lucky.

Barry arrived at Steve's flat at six o'clock, just as the street was waking up. We were still sitting in his front room wrapped up in sleeping bags, clutching large cups of steaming coffee. I'd half-heartedly offered to go home at four o'clock, but Steve wouldn't hear of it. He's a night person – he doesn't mind losing sleep – and I was

147

grateful not to have to face the empty house. I felt desperately anxious that I'd missed my seven-thirty phonecall to the children the night before and I was waiting for a decent time so I could ring. Barry looked uncharacteristically rumpled, his face still clouded by sleep. He accepted Steve's offer of tea, sat down and scrutinised me closely, as if checking that all the bits were there.

'You're a lucky lady.'

'Not luck,' I answered chirpily. 'Skill.'

'So I heard. Told him his mother was over-protective, did you?'

'Something like that.'

'We've got him, you know.'

I gaped in disbelief. 'You haven't!'

'It was a good description, especially the scar. We picked him up at closing time at a pub in Wood Green. I'm going to have to ask you to come with me to identify him.' I leapt out of the sleeping bag, wincing with the pain of my sore back, and unceremoniously planted a kiss on Barry's cheek.

'Steve!' I said excitedly as he came in with the tray. 'They've got him!'

Steve glanced at Barry. 'That was quick.'

Barry shrugged nonchalantly. I took a piece of toast from the plate Steve handed me and bit into it. I had a sudden satisfying fantasy of stabbing 'black jeans' over and over again while his arms were held by two strong coppers – but my natural decency intervened. Maybe I'd just punch him. Barry leaned over and pulled me back to reality.

'If you could bear to go over it once more. I'd like to hear exactly what happened.'

I sat down, took a large gulp of coffee, then launched into the story all over again. Like a painful birth, it helped to relive it. This time I added all the bits I'd left out with the detective at the hospital – the connection I'd discovered between Blythe, Hunt and Winter and a charity on Caroline's list; the image of Lyn's face which led me to make the connection between her attacker and mine; my pathetic lie about a photograph which drew my attacker's half-admission that

148

he'd pushed Lyn in front of the train and miraculously saved my life. I even added the possible affair between Lyn and Edward Hunt. Barry took it all in, frowning with concentration.

'So who's the guy?' I asked, still half expecting to hear that he was a random mugger.

'He's a trained hit man. A good one,' said Barry. 'You should have been an easy target, but I suppose he's used to fighters, not talkers.'

'Who would hire him?' asked Steve, fascinated.

'It varies. Lately, it's been drug barons sending him after big-time dealers.'

Steve and I exchanged perplexed looks.

'We'll try and use this story about the photo to get him to talk,' said Barry, reading our looks. 'But I somehow doubt he'll be that stupid.' He looked from me to Steve and back again. 'We'll ask around, find out where he's been, who he's been seen with. Wood Green'll be on to it already. They've probably talked to National Drugs Intelligence too, to see if they know anything.'

'Could it be Hunt?'

Barry shrugged and looked doubtful. Then he turned to me with a serious air.

'Whoever it is, you're going to have to be careful. They obviously think you know more than you do. I'd advise you to stay somewhere else for a few days and not to go out alone.'

I gaped. 'Not go out alone? What am I s'posed to do – get a minder?'

'You could stay here,' said Steve, doubtfully. Barry shook his head.

'It's too near her home. Isn't there anyone else you could stay with?' As if on cue, the doorbell rang and a shining brown face with a fierce frown appeared at the window.

'Oh, God.' I suddenly felt exhausted.

Steve went to let Clancy in.

Clancy enfolded me in a vice like hug and patted my back.

'Ouch!'

'I couldn't believe it when Gail called me. What the hell've you been doing, you silly bitch?' Clancy released me, but left her arm protectively round my shoulder and glared at Barry and Steve, as if they were partially responsible for what happened. 'I think I'd better take her home.'

Barry repeated the edict about not going out alone.

Clancy tightened her grip on my shoulder. 'She can stay with me for a while.'

'Now wait a minute –' I protested limply.

'Where do you live?' asked Barry.

'I couldn't possibly –'

'Shepherd's Bush.'

'Ideal,' said Barry approvingly.

I shot him a death-glance. 'It's very kind of you Clancy, but –'

'You have to go somewhere, Sara. Some fucker comes to get you at my place, they'll have me to contend with.'

There was some truth in that. Getting past Clancy's six-foot frame and rapid fire mouth would not be easy.

'Well?' said Clancy, releasing me and folding her arms. I hesitated, picking at the sleeping bag. Clancy was warm and kind and her big presence was reassuring. I didn't want to stay with anyone, but I also didn't want to be a sitting duck, waiting for someone to take a pot-shot. The only stumbling block was Clancy's inveterate bossiness, but knowing her, she'd lose interest in the minder role after a few hours and leave me to come and go as I pleased.

'Okay. Thanks, Clancy.' I said, as graciously as I could. Steve raised his eyebrows. He's heard all my Clancy stories and his eyes twinkled with amusement at the thought of my staying with her.

We agreed that I'd go with Barry to identify the monster, then we'd pick up Clancy at the clinic and come back to my house so I could pack some clothes. First, I pulled on a loose shirt and shorts of Steve's – my clothes had gone straight into the dustbin – and rang the children. I thought carefully about what to say to David about why I hadn't phoned the night before – in my eyes, there was no good excuse except the real one – but I needn't have bothered. He said they'd been out at seven thirty and assumed they'd missed my call. Between gritted teeth, I told him I'd be at Clancy's a lot over the next few days as we were working on a paper and that the children could reach me there. He yawned, grunted and hung up.

The identity parade was almost Gothic. One's image of these things comes entirely from TV soaps, so when it happens in real life you have the overwhelming sense of acting a part in a play. There they all were, behind a glass partition – the off-duty coppers and one dim-witted criminal, sticking out like a sore thumb. 'Cut!' I felt like saying. 'Get that man off the set and find someone who looks less clichéd.' I stood and stared at him for a moment, wanting to imprint his face on my mind, so I could stick pins of revenge in him at a later date. You animal. Mentally I spat in his face, wishing he could see me, my fury and disdain. He looked evil, mindless and strong – I shuddered and the horror flooded back. I pointed him out, pressing my finger against the glass.

'That's him.' The policewoman beside me sensed my trembling and gently led me out of the room.

It all took longer than I'd anticipated, because I had to go through my statement again for the detective sergeant at Wood Green. The rules are tight about which officers are allowed to be present at a line-up, so Barry had gone off with a mate of his 'to chat about one or two things'. When Barry came back I could tell his chat had been fruitful. I waited until we got back into his car.

'What did you find out?'

Barry pursed his lips. 'We-ell,' he said slowly, 'one or two things are beginning to tie up.'

'Like, what?'

'They've found two witnesses who say they saw your friend on the platform when the Hargreaves girl was pushed, so we've definitely got a link there. And our drugs people know about him – apparently, they've been keeping a close eye on his bosses.'

'Have they found any connection with Blythe or Hunt?'

'It's early days. Give them a chance.'

I tried to get more out of him, but couldn't. Infuriatingly, he kept shaking his head and clicking his tongue.

'This could be a big one,' he kept repeating enigmatically.

Barry saw Clancy and me into my house, then left saying he'd be in touch. It seemed like weeks since I'd left to go to John's on the Sunday night. The house still felt empty and silent without the children, yet I was grateful they'd been spared the terror of their mother not turning up to collect them, and the anxiety of hearing I was in hospital. John had left a message on my answering machine, saying nothing in particular, asking me to call when I got a chance. I made a mental note to phone him later – I couldn't face talking to him now. I realised I was in desperate need of a shower, or, in deference to the dressing on my back, an all-over wash. Clancy seemed quite happy to wait.

'Mel says not to worry,' she said, waving her arm in a gesture of abandon. 'She agrees I should stick close to you for a while. And she's getting you into a victim support group – starts Wednesday.' I growled non-committally. That sounded like a real busman's holiday.

I felt better once I had washed and changed into my own clothes. Clancy was lounging on my bed with a headset on, moving her head from side to side and humming snatches of a tune, so I had a few moments to think. As I rounded up a few things to pack into a hold-all, I started piecing together what I knew. Caroline came to see me because she wanted me to warn Lyn about a man. It suddenly occurred to me that the man she meant must have been Edward Hunt, not James Blythe. Maybe Caroline knew about the blackmail, knew that Edward and Belinda Hunt would only tolerate so much, so she decided to relay a threat from them in order to keep Lyn away from her husband as well as Hunt. Lyn heard the warning, but wouldn't heed it. She continued to see Blythe and she upped the price of keeping quiet about Hunt. She pushed the ambitious Hunts too far and they hired someone to get rid of her. It was a far-fetched explanation, but not impossible.

But what about Caroline? I felt sure that Caroline's death had something to do with her curiosity about SACA. She must have discovered something so damaging that the person implicated had to kill her to stop her talking. I realised then that Lyn's death might have another explanation. If Caroline told Lyn what she had found out about the charity, they would want her dead too. It suddenly dawned on me how much I had put myself in danger. It was partly unwitting – Lyn, who was playing for high stakes with an influential politician, just happened to be my client – but I had also walked into it with my inveterate nosiness. I had gone out of my way to portray myself as Caroline's confidante, whereas in fact, I knew next to nothing about the trouble she was in. I had been digging into the same charity story as Caroline – I had even visited the place. Clearly, someone had tried to kill me because they thought I knew too much.

'What's the information I'm supposed to have?' I said it aloud, mostly to myself.

Clancy yanked off the headset. 'What?'

'Is it that I know Caroline was murdered? Barry knows it – so does John – but they're not stalking them round the streets of Acton.'

'They're men.'

I shook my head emphatically. 'It's not just that. It must be something to do with the charity, something that Caroline might have told me before she died . . .'

Clancy was uncharacteristically silent as I pondered, then she came out with one of her lightning insights:

'Blythe's the weak link. Let's go and scare him.'

I looked up from my packing and stared at her. 'What do you mean?'

'Confront him. Ask him what he knows. We can't get near Hunt, or his wife, even if they're involved. Blythe's the only one who'll talk.'

I shook my head slowly. 'He'll probably refuse to see us.'

Clancy sat up ramrod straight, crossed her legs and waggled a finger at me. 'Stop playing the victim, Sara. You have a right to know why you were attacked. You have a right to know why two of your clients died within two weeks of each other.'

I nodded, chastised. 'Someone wants you *dead*, babe. We have to find them, before *they* find *you*.'

I swallowed. 'Thank you for putting it so directly, Clancy. Okay – how do we get Blythe to see us?'

Clancy sprang off the bed and knocked over my table lamp. 'Shit!' I watched wanly as she picked it up and set it back on the bedside table. I was glad she wasn't staying at my house.

'Leave it to me,' she said. 'Where's his office?'

I tried to think through a fog of tiredness. 'Covent Garden, I think. "James Blythe, Architect". Maybe we should make an appointment.'

'If he's there, he'll see us.' Clancy promised.

I finished packing the bag, picked it up and walked slowly to the top of the stairs. Watching me struggle, Clancy suddenly remembered she was supposed to be playing Florence Nightingale.

'Here, let me take it. Are you sure you want to do this? We can go see him tomorrow if you like.'

I shook my head. 'Ring his office and see if he's in.'

While she found the number, I sat down and closed my eyes. My back hurt, I had a headache and I felt light-headed from lack of sleep. But I felt sure Clancy's idea of seeing James was a good one. Her words rang in my ears. 'Blythe's the weak link.' If anyone could be made to spill the beans about what was going on, it was James. James was no hardened criminal. If he had played any role in the death of Caroline and Lyn, he was probably scared shitless. If he really knew nothing, there was no reason to resent our interest – we could offer our sympathy and leave.

Clancy has this wonderful confidence which allows her to walk into a sparkling all-metal-and-glass Covent Garden office, crawling with expensively dressed, languidly sophisticated young women and look as if she has more right to be there than they have. I limped along behind her feeling like the cat's breakfast. Perhaps it also has something to do with her being so tall. Dressed in a man's shirt and hip-hugging black bicycle shorts, she marched up to the black matt reception counter behind which sat two pouting beauties, answering gently purring phones, and demanded loudly, 'Mr Blythe, please.'

One of them looked up and assumed a plastic smile. 'Certainly. What name?'

'Clancy Jackson and Sara Kingsley.' Clancy drummed her fingers on the counter and sprayed the reception area with a scatter gun stare. Several people ducked. We'd agreed on a strategy in the taxi – she'd get us in, then I'd do the talking. The first young woman scanned a piece of paper in front of her.

'Do you have an appointment?'

Clancy smiled dangerously. 'Mr Blythe said we could pop in and see him any time.'

'Oh.'

Exchanging glances with her clone, the young woman lifted the phone with her fingertips, pressed a few buttons and crooned into it through painted red lips. With obvious satisfaction, she replaced it in less than thirty seconds.

'I'm afraid Mr Blythe's secretary doesn't have a note of your names. And Mr Blythe is busy at the moment.'

Clancy turned to me, laughing. 'James is busy!'

I nodded stupidly, not quite seeing the joke, and tried to resist the temptation to tug Clancy's sleeve and make a dash for the street.

She turned back to the receptionist. 'Would you call Mr Blythe, please. I'd like to speak to him.'

The big blue eyes blinked with annoyance. 'He's busy.'

Clancy smiled sweetly. 'Then un-busy him.'

The receptionist's false posh accent started to slip into Saff Landan. 'I told you – 'e can't see you,' she snapped. 'You'll 'ave to ring his secretary this afternoon.'

'Let me speak to his secretary,' said Clancy patiently.

The blue eyes narrowed. 'You're not on 'er list!'

Clancy rested her elbows on the counter and leaned forward and lowered her voice threateningly. 'Listen, sweetheart – Maggie Thatcher ain't on the list, the Pope ain't on the list, and I ain't on the fuckin' list, but if you wanna keep your job – call her!' I nestled against a large, exotic plant to the side of the reception desk in the vain hope of being mistaken for a branch. Both receptionists flushed, turned to each other again with pursed lips and exchanged silent glances of mincing disapproval. They reminded me of synchro swimmers. Reluctantly, the first receptionist picked up the phone and stabbed out a number, then she passed it to Clancy. Clancy's voice turned to thick honey.

'Oh, hello, yes this is Clancy Jackson from the Acton Counselling Centre. I'm here with my colleague Sara Kingsley and we need to see Mr Blythe *very* urgently.' The receptionists and I stared at each other in the pause.

'I understand that, but if you would just tell Mr Blythe that Ms Kingsley has some important information to give him about Mrs Blythe, I think he'll appreciate the urgency. Thank you.' Clancy drummed her fingers on the counter again, then stopped abruptly. 'Yep. We'll be right up.' Without even a glance at the receptionists, Clancy grabbed my arm, extracted me from the foliage and propelled me towards the lift. 'Second floor. Let's go.'

James stood up when we walked into his office.

'What's all this about?' It was a glass room, light and airy, partitioned off from the rest of the floor. Outside it, several artistic-looking men were staring with deep concentration at high-tech drawing boards; one or two of them glanced up discreetly as we came into view. James' office was like a goldfish bowl – you couldn't pick your nose without the whole floor being aware of it. Clancy moved forward and offered her hand – James shook it gingerly.

'Clancy Jackson. Pleased to meet to you, Mr Blythe.'

'Right.' James blinked nervously. 'I'm pretty busy you know –'

'I'm sorry to intrude like this,' I said, 'but I need to talk to you.'

He glanced at Clancy, noting her height – and her colour.

'So who's this – your sister?' He laughed feebly. I was glad he said it; his flippant tone gave me a rush of anger.

'I think you've got some explaining to do.'

'Sorry?'

I walked up to the desk and faced him across it. 'Ever since I've

156

been showing an interest in how Caroline died, I've been somewhat accident prone. The clinic has been ransacked and, yesterday, a man tried to kill me with a knife. You wouldn't happen to know anything about that, would you?' I thrust my face just a little too near his for comfort – he blinked, taken aback. He moved back a step and combed his hair back with his fingers.

'Bad luck. Sorry to hear that. But why come to me? Matter for the police, surely?'

'Just checking to see if you can give them any short cuts.'

He looked from me to Clancy and back again, then glanced nervously out to the main office. 'Er, why don't you sit down? Coffee?'

'What a good idea,' grinned Clancy, drawing up a chair that looked like an Aztec birthing stool. While James dialled his secretary, I pulled up another of the black wooden chairs and flinched as my back touched the hard, nobbly wood. James sat down behind the desk and blew air slowly out of his pink cheeks. I tried to hold on to my rage, not to let it dissipate into polite chit chat. I pulled the tortuous chair closer to the desk.

'You know, of course, that Lyn Hargreaves was my client?'

His complexion turned from pink to red to white. He didn't know. 'W-who?'

I turned to Clancy and jerked my head in James' direction. 'What a memory! Lyn Hargreaves,' I repeated. 'The woman you were having an affair with.'

His jaw twitched.

'And the woman Edward Hunt had an affair with before you.' I added. He coloured again, leaned forward and placed his hands down on to the black desk.

'What on earth are you talking about?' He looked shocked.

I left an empty silence, then said quietly, 'Lyn was Edward's lover – didn't you know?'

'That's ridiculous.'

He sat back in his chair, his boyish looks suddenly ageing.

'I was Lyn's counsellor. She spoke about you a good deal.' Subtext: I know all about you, Jimbo.

'All right, I knew her. But the affair was over. On my side anyway.'

'She came to see me on the Friday after Caroline died. Like Caroline, she didn't show any signs of being suicidal. But the following Saturday, after going out with you, she was attacked. The men who beat her up said it was a warning – what d'you make of that?'

James swallowed hard. The strategy was working. He'd been put on the spot and he wasn't a quick thinker. He fiddled nervously with a pen on the desk. 'I don't know.'

'Did you know about the attack?'

'She told me she'd been mugged. Told her to go to the police. She didn't want to. You know she . . . she took drugs.'

I nodded and resisted saying he seemed to drive 'em to it. 'When was the last time you saw her?'

'Wednesday.' The day before Caroline's funeral. He rubbed his forehead which was shining with sweat. 'Face was a mess, arm in a sling. She said the men were dealers.' That figured. She got the idea from me. James shrugged defensively. 'It was a part of her life I knew nothing about.'

The door opened and a woman came in with three cups on a tray. She was smart and middle aged and looked like a walking advertisement for Country Casuals. She set down James' coffee with maternal care.

'Thank you, Jean.' As he busied himself with the sugar, Jean gave us each our coffees with an accusing air which seemed to say, 'I hope you're not upsetting my boy.' I wondered what it was that made women want to mother him – I must be missing a hormone. When his secretary had gone, James pulled down his cuffs nervously and picked an invisible speck of dirt from his shirt.

'What exactly d'you want?'

My fury was still on the boil. 'I want know why Lyn died so soon after Caroline. I want to know why you don't want a murder investigation. I want to know why someone is trying to kill me.'

He paused for a moment, then thrust his fingers through his hair again. His eyes darted to the outer office, aware that we were being watched. 'Haven't a clue why someone is trying to kill you – if they are. Sounds like paranoia to me.'

I gave him a cold stare. He squirmed a little in his executive chair and made a helpless gesture. 'Look – Caroline committed suicide. D'you think I'm happy about that? D'you think I haven't got regrets? Course I have. Thought of nothing else. Shouldn't have carried on with Lyn, should have ended it sooner and so on and so forth. I've thought of nothing else. So don't come in here telling me –'

'I'm not telling you anything, I'm *asking* you – do you really believe that Caroline committed suicide . . .?'

He couldn't meet my gaze. 'Loved my wife, you know. She was a clever lady. Too clever, perhaps.' He shook his head sadly. 'Shouldn't have carried on with Lyn – should've ended it after that first time – but you know how it is when two people – well, maybe you don't. Infatuation, I suppose you'd call it.'

I looked at his weak flabby face, blotched with emotion. Pity grappled with disgust. 'I'm tempted to say that *one* death can be regarded as a misfortune, *two* looks like carelessness.'

His face flushed with anger. 'If you've got proof –'

I dismissed him with an impatient wave. I was tired. I wanted answers. 'Did you know about Lyn and Edward?'

'I –' He caught my warning look. No more lies, James.

He shook his head. 'Knew my sister had it in for her – didn't know why.'

'I think she was blackmailing him.'

James' jaw dropped. Clancy let out a low whistle. 'Lyn? Blackmailing Edward?' James was aghast.

'Maybe that's why they had her killed.' I shouldn't have said it, but I felt reckless and I wanted a reaction. James got up abruptly and walked to the window, turning his back to the room. Clancy caught my eye and nodded encouragingly for me to carry on. There wasn't a lot more I could say – it was all guesswork and dangerous guesswork at that.

'Didn't she talk about her previous boyfriend?' I asked.

'Said he was an old fart,' muttered James wonderingly. 'A fool and his money . . .' He spun round and faced me. 'You're making an extremely serious allegation, young lady. I hope you have evidence to back it up because Sir Edward is going to take a fairly dim view of someone who marches around calling him a murderer.'

I gave a short laugh. 'Who's going to tell him? If you tell him that, I'll tell him you've told me all about the charity – SACA.'

James tried gamely to disguise his horror but his face said it all. He took a sip of coffee and his hand trembled. 'W-what about it?'

I stood up and went over and sat on the desk. I could feel the eyes from the outer office burning a hole in my back. 'You tell me.'

James leaned over to replace his cup, but he set it down too hard and it fell on its side, spilling coffee over the desk. He grabbed a couple of tissues and mopped it up.

'You're up to your neck in this, aren't you James?'

James' fresh complexion flushed with anger. 'You bitch.' He took a step towards me and I heard Clancy spring out of her chair. I didn't move. Something within me had turned to steel. My voice lowered almost to a whisper.

'We're in the same boat, James, you and me. We both know more than they want us to know. Isn't that right? Tell me about it. Tell me about SACA. What's it for? Why didn't they want Caroline to find out about it?'

He clenched and unclenched his fists and looked anxiously over my shoulder into the office. 'I don't know what you're talking about. You keep your nose out of that. It's – just a charity.'

I moved closer. I've never been a bully, but I felt like one now. I wanted to hit back. Harder and harder. I'd been attacked. James was an unfaithful man. A man who didn't care how many women he hurt as long as he got what he wanted. He deserved everything he got.

160

'How safe is Harriet, James?' I whispered. 'Will she be next if you step out of line?' I'd said too much. He raised his clenched fist and I raised mine but we were both too chicken to use them.

'Take it easy.' Clancy put one hand on each of our shoulders. I swayed and felt sick. The door of the fish tank opened.

'Everything okay, old man?'

James forced a hooting laugh. 'Fine, fine.' He smoothed back his hair and went over to the young man in red braces standing by the door. 'These ladies are . . . not too happy about the Gifford Street redevelopment.' Then *sotto voce*. 'I can handle it. Thanks Toby.' He shut the door and went back to his chair. Clancy and I did the same. We sat for a moment in tense silence. Clancy broke the deadlock.

'This is going to take a lot longer if you two don't talk to each other.'

'Why was I attacked?' I demanded.

James looked exasperated. 'I haven't a clue why you were bloody attacked. Ask the police.'

'Who was behind it? Hunt. Winter? Someone else?'

'I don't know!'

'Your wife takes an overdose when she's never injected before in her life. Your lover mysteriously falls under a train the week after – and you don't suspect a thing. Oh, tell me another, for Christ's sake!'

'Lyn should've told me about Edward,' he sighed. Then slowly, he asked me, 'D'you really believe Caroline was murdered?'

He knew it too, but he couldn't face it until this moment. He looked pitiful. For him, Lyn dying was a mixed blessing; Caroline dying was a tragedy. I suddenly glimpsed his grief, his guilt, his hopelessness, his despair. He was a podgy schoolboy – not bright, but well-meaning – who'd made some weak decisions and was now paying an exorbitant price.

I had never doubted that he knew Caroline had been murdered. Suicide is such a hostile act – when a person chooses deliberately to leave their child, their parents, the people who love them – that you look for almost any other explanation to avoid it, including murder.

161

James pretended he believed in Caroline's suicide because he was scared to look at the alternatives. Now he seemed to confront the idea for the first time.

'It's that bastard Winter!' he burst out suddenly. 'He was the last one to see her alive!'

'You mean, he saw her after the party?'

'Yes! He went back to the house!'

'How d'you know?'

James shrugged awkwardly. 'Didn't go straight to bed, you see. Went back home to see Caroline. Wanted to try and straighten things out – have a talk. I saw Winter's car parked in the next street, so I turned round and went back.' So they left the party together, had sex, and not long after that she was dead.

'Did you tell the police?'

He shook his head.

'Ring them now.'

'No.'

'Then I'll do it.' I sprang towards the phone.

James clamped his hand over it. 'I'll deny I ever said it.' I stared at him.

He met my eyes. He looked scared. 'She's dead. It won't bring her back.'

'You really hate women, don't you, Mr Blythe?' put in Clancy irrelevantly.

James looked anxiously towards the outer office again. Several heads ducked down as he did so.

'I'm still going to tell them,' I said firmly.

He gave a mirthless laugh. 'Good luck. I hope you manage to live. Now if you've finished –'

I checked quickly with Clancy and her nod told me she thought it was time to go. I stood up. With visible relief, James walked round to our side of the desk and held out his hand. It was a gesture made for the benefit of our outer audience – I ignored it.

'You have my number if your memory improves,' I said coldly.

'It won't.'

He opened the door to let us out. Several pairs of eyes peeped out from behind their drawing boards.

'Er, well, thanks for coming.'

Just outside the lift, Clancy stood for a moment and undid the top button of her shirt. I hoped to God she wasn't about to do something outrageous like whip out a breast – she's capable of doing anything if she thinks it'll further a good cause. Instead she hauled out a small black box which had been hanging round her neck, hidden in her voluminous bosom. She dangled it in front of James' nose for a second.

'Don't worry if you forget anything you said, Mr Blythe,' she said loudly and cheerfully, 'I got it all on tape.'

James blanched. Clancy swept me in front of her into the lift and the doors closed. I looked at her wonderingly.

'Have you really –?'

She winked delightedly. 'Certainly have.'

We giggled like schoolgirls all the way down and made a V sign to the receptionists as we passed.

chapter eleven

Initially, Marjorie Martinez did not give us a five-star welcome. She kept Clancy and me waiting in the street for five minutes or so and I wondered if she was checking with one of the trustees as to whether or not she should see us. It had been only two days since the attack and I felt nervous standing so near to where it had happened. Clancy stood close to me, her head constantly moving as she scanned the street, like a royal bodyguard. Then the door buzzer sounded and we went up.

Once we were in the office, Marjorie gave us a twinkling smile and put on the kettle.

'Sorry to keep you waiting. The office was such a mess! I'm not used to visitors – people usually phone.'

We muttered an apology.

'Perfectly all right. Now make yourselves comfortable and I'll be with you in a minute.' She waved to us two chintz-covered chairs and started arranging cups and saucers and a plate of biscuits on a tray. We chatted about the weather until the tea was made and we were all sitting cosily.

'What can I do for you?'

We repeated what we had said over the intercom – that the NCT definitely wanted to make a donation, but we had one or two questions to ask about the charity. She nodded, only half listening and beamed at me.

'Haven't I seen you before?'

I was completely taken aback. Her blue eyes sparkled innocently.

'I – I came to see you two days ago.' I faltered.

'Of course, of course.' She gave a trill of laughter.

Clancy and I glanced at each other uncertainly. Either she had a serious short-term memory problem or she was over-doing the dotty old lady act.

Clancy took over. 'We like the idea of donating to SACA, but we hadn't realised you were so closely connected to one of our members, who has just died.'

'Caroline Blythe was quite active in the NCT,' I explained, 'and we were thinking of organising a fund-raising event in her memory. Was she very much involved?'

'Oh, goodness me, no.' Marjorie shook her head and took a sip of tea, finger waggling out to the side. 'Mrs Blythe was a well-known journalist, as I'm sure you know. She was too busy for charity work.' Was there some snide intent in that remark?

'But didn't she help in the office, or do any fundraising?' I persisted. Caroline must have got her information on the charity from somewhere.

The tissue-paper skin around Marjorie's mouth tightened. 'I'm afraid Sir Edward is rather strict about the office. Mrs Blythe did stand in for me once or twice, just after mother passed away, but I'm afraid Sir Edward was not too pleased about it.'

'When was that? I'm sorry, how long ago did you say your mother died?'

'Two months.' Marjorie's lips quivered. 'She was ninety-two, but it was still quite a shock.'

'I'm sure.' So Caroline was left alone in the office two months ago. Nothing to stop her giving it a good going over. 'So you wouldn't have any objection to us raising funds in her name?'

Marjorie offered us the plate of biscuits. We both took one.

'I'd have to ask the trustees about it, but I'm sure Mr Blythe would have no objection. In fact, I'm sure he'd be delighted.' She looked from me to Clancy and her eyes filled with tears. 'Poor man,' she whispered. 'What must he be going through?'

Clancy shifted impatiently in her chair. 'Can we get in touch with

165

any of your local groups, Mrs Martinez?' she asked brusquely. 'To get a few fundraising ideas?'

Marjorie shook her head. 'Donations come mainly by post.' She dabbed her eyes, self-consciously. 'We don't do much locally. But I have a book on fundraising if you'd like to have a look?'

'I can get one at the library, thanks,' said Clancy. 'Well . . .?' She looked at me meaningfully. I stood up and put out my hand towards Marjorie.

'That's all we wanted to know. Thank you for your time.' She squeezed it with her dry fingers.

'Not at all, dear,' she said. 'I shall be hearing from you, then?'

'Our committee meets next week. I'll give you a ring after that.'

'Have I given you a leaflet about the fundraising ball? Only £50 and all in a good cause!'

'You mentioned it last time.'

She laughed. 'Aren't I a nag? Still, pass the word around.' She saw us to the door and said a cheery goodbye. As before, she didn't ask for a phone number where she could reach me.

Clancy exploded as soon as we hit the street.

'Shit! What an act.'

'You think so?' I turned to her curiously.

'"Haven't I seen you before, dear?"' mimicked Clancy. '"Mother was ninety-two but it was still such a shock." I've met that type before. She's no more senile than I am.' I filed that insight away for future use.

'At least she told us what we wanted to know. Caroline did come into the office and Edward Hunt was none too happy about it.'

'Okay. Can we go and do some work now?'

'Absolutely.'

We drew up outside the clinic and Clancy opened her door; I stayed put.

'Aren't you coming in?'

I shook my head. 'I've got one or two things to do –'

She folded her arms. 'Like what?'

166

'I want to see a friend. Talk things over.'

She looked sceptical.

'Clancy, it's daylight. I'm going to keep on the move and I'll see you back here in two hours.'

'Victim support's at the Priory Centre at six.'

I nodded vaguely.

'Call me at five.'

'I appreciate your concern Clancy, but –'

'Call me.'

'All right.'

She slammed the door with superhuman force, making the car shudder from side to side. I watched her lope up the path to the front door and breathed a sigh of relief. Alone at last! I hadn't realised how claustrophobic I was feeling after two days of continuous minding. I could feel my body tense as I took over responsibility for myself. It felt good. My back wasn't so painful now and my brain was sharper for a good night's sleep.

Clancy and I had taken the tape to Barry as soon as we left James Blythe's office – I didn't want to take any chances. Clancy, not trusting Barry, took the precaution of copying it first. Barry was cautiously impressed and immediately dispatched someone to re-interview Blythe, Winter and some of the other people who'd been at the party. I felt the net was closing, but that until the big fish were in it, my life was on a knife-edge. Someone wanted me dead. I wasn't ready to die yet. I wanted to see my children grow into adults, to watch their lives unfold. I wanted to see different places, meet different people, bask in the freedom it had taken me so long to claim as my own.

I put the car into gear and headed for my street. I parked a couple of roads away on a busy short-cut between the Uxbridge Road and Horn Lane and, checking carefully to make sure I wasn't being followed, walked quickly down to Afsana's house. She was in, working. Karim was at the childminder's.

'Afsana, have you got a moment?'

167

'Sara! Come in. How are you? Steve told me about the attack. Terrible. Some mad person, I suppose.'

I followed her into the kitchen, but refused the offer of a cup of tea.

'I'm sorry to disturb your work, Afsana.'

'No problem.'

'I just have a quick question. That printout . . . I've looked at it again and again but it doesn't seem to tell me anything. I sort of expected more details. I just wondered . . . there's no way of getting more information from the list is there?'

Afsana frowned. 'Yes and no.'

I looked at her questioningly.

'What you have is a 'cardbox' list of several hundred entries. Each charity is listed as a separate file. The first page has basic information, but behind that, on subsequent pages, there's space to put more detailed information.'

'Aha!'

'But I checked on several entries to see if the second page had been used – and it hadn't. It hadn't even been set up. It was just the list.'

'What about the charity I was interested in – did you check that second page?'

'No,' she admitted. 'But –'

'Maybe that was the only one used.'

'Maybe,' she said doubtfully.

'Could you check?' I persisted.

'Do you have the disk with you?'

As it happened, I did. I'd been thinking of little else but this damn charity list since I was attacked. I'd come to the conclusion that unless the SACA entry was written in some kind of code, there was nothing incriminating about it at all. I was sure there must be something else. I carried the disk with me in the hope that the missing link would leap out at me, or that I might get the chance to ask Afsana.

She tapped the keyboard with deft movements. I tried to look knowledgeable, but I felt like a spare prick at a wedding. She found the SACA entry in the index, then pressed a few keys to get into the second page. I peered at the screen anxiously, not quite understanding what she was doing. Then, as if by magic, a list of numbers appeared.

'You're right,' said Afsana, calmly. 'There is more data here.' We both stared at the list for a moment. It was short, all one on page – about twenty or thirty lines, each containing two six-figure numbers.

'What is it?' I wondered.

Afsana looked up at me. 'Bank accounts,' she said, as if it were obvious.

'How d'you know?' I asked, sceptically.

'Haven't you noticed numbers like this on your cheque book? The one on the left is a bank code, the one on the right is the account number.'

'Oh.' I puzzled over them for a moment. Whose bank accounts? And what did they have to do with SACA?

'Shall I print it out?' asked Afsana. She was getting impatient. She had work to do.

'Sorry. Yes, please, Afsana.' The printer buzzed for a few seconds. She passed me the numbers and the disk and I slipped them back into my bag. Was this the information that was putting me in the firing line? It seemed singularly unexciting. I thanked Afsana for her time and said I'd let myself out.

'Take care of yourself,' she said gently.

'I will.'

I walked briskly back to the car, anxiously aware of every doorway, every footstep, every other person on the street. I resented my jumpiness – I'd never been afraid to walk in these streets before, particularly during the day. I tried to walk the way I'd been taught in self-defence class – big strides, chest pushed out, butch expression – but I got such pitying looks from the people I passed, I decided it wasn't worth it. I was relieved to get inside the car and lock the door. I glanced at the clock on the dashboard: four fifteen. I started up the engine, then cruised round the block and started to weave my way through the back streets towards the Uxbridge Road. I was just composing a witty remark for Clancy on how she ought to offer her services as a professional minder when I noticed, in the rear-view mirror, a white Ford Orion pursuing the same eccentric route as me. I felt a knot in my stomach tighten. I slowed down and screwed up my eyes to try to get a better view of the driver – all I could make out was that it was a lone man wearing mirror shades. I'd been on the lookout all day for someone following me and just as I'd convinced myself I was imagining the whole thing, a car seemed to be tailing me.

I like driving – especially in London – and I know the streets around my house inside out. If this guy was following me, I felt sure I could lose him by taking a complicated route. I went past Steve's flat and turned left without indicating. I looked in the mirror – he was still there. I turned left again, then right, then left into a street that leads up to the Westway, our overcrowded motorway into Central London. The white Orion stayed with me – one, then two cars behind. Discreet, but persistent. I decided to try something more radical. I indicated left, checked that there was no oncoming traffic, then made a sharp U-turn, right back towards Acton. The cars behind me honked furiously. I saw surprise register on the Ford driver's face as I shot past him going the opposite way. I smiled to myself. But when I got to the traffic lights just before Sainsbury's, there he was again, several cars behind, easing into the lane beside me. I gritted my teeth. I had to shake him off. I had more people to see and I didn't want company.

The traffic lights changed and I suddenly had a brainwave. Sainsbury's car park looks as if it has only one way in and out, but people who shop there regularly know that you can get out of the car park a different way by cutting through a lorry bay at the side. I prayed my shadow was an Asda shopper. I turned into the car park and slowly cruised around as if looking for somewhere to park. I stopped beside a car where a woman was loading her shopping together with twin babies and a toddler. I knew she'd take hours getting that lot into the car. The Orion driver knew it too. He carried on round the car park and nestled into a space which gave him a good view of the exit. Pretending to get impatient, I moved off slowly towards the supermarket entrance, still apparently looking for a space, then, when another car shielded me from view, I nipped through the lorry bay and out the other side. Heart pounding, I checked in the mirror. I'd lost him. I pressed my foot on the accelerator, turned back on to the High Street and made my way down to Chiswick.

I couldn't remember the number, but I thought I'd know the house. It seemed like weeks instead of days since I came to visit Helen Marchment, thinking she might be the friend that Caroline wanted me to see. I was banking on the fact that four thirty is a good time to catch someone at home with children – they've usually got them parked in front of the telly so they can make the tea in peace. Chiswick mums don't always conform, because they ferry their darlings to and from ballet classes, music lessons and gym. Fortunately, Helen proved to be of the couch potato school of mothering – I could hear the familiar quacking inanities of the Count Duckula cartoon as I pressed the bell beside the solid oak front door.

I wouldn't say Helen looked pleased to see me, but she didn't shut the door in my face.

'Yes?'

'I came to see you a couple of weeks ago – Sara Kingsley, Caroline Blythe's friend?'

'I remember.' But, clearly, it hadn't been the high spot of her week.

'I'm sorry to call round unannounced like this, but could you spare me a minute or so?'

She seemed reluctant, but she was too polite to turn me away. 'All right. Come in.'

'Who is it, Mummee? Is it Daddy, Mummmeeee, is it? Is it?' The Count Duckula fan rushed into view, a strapping blond, blue-eyed four-year-old, dressed up as Superman.

'Hiya, Superman.'

'Pow! pow! pow! You're dead!'

Helen smiled wanly and gave me a 'Why are little boys so revolting?' look.

'Thank you, Charles. Run back to the television room now.'

I returned Helen's smile. She called into the kitchen.

'Rosetta, could you keep an eye on Charles for a moment, while I talk to this lady?' Rosetta emerged slowly, a beautiful, feline adolescent with long black hair, clad in tight jeans and a halter neck. Having an au pair like that in the house must be like living with a time bomb. Helen led me into the sitting room, where we had sat over coffee the last time. It still looked pristine, with plump, puffed up sofas, seemingly untouched by human forms. Helen motioned for me to sit. We both sank down, making deep indents into the virgin cushions. Helen raised her eyebrows coolly.

'Well – what can I do for you?'

I took a deep breath. 'Helen – I don't believe Caroline committed suicide – I think she was murdered.'

Helen blanched slightly, but her expression remained unchanged. 'Murdered?' She repeated the word slowly as if trying it out for size.

'She'd been investigating a story about charities which led her to something involving James. Her interest upset some dangerous people. I think they killed her.' I leaned forward and sought her eyes. 'And I think you can help me find out who did it.'

She stared at me for a moment, then stood up abruptly, walked over to the bureau and opened one of the drawers. For one absurd moment, I thought she was pulling out a gun. Instead, she picked up a packet of More cigarettes, lit one and inhaled deeply. She took an ashtray and nervously flicked invisible ash into it.

'Aren't the police looking into it?' she asked. Her sharp features were clenched into a guarded and slightly puzzled frown.

'The police are looking at new evidence. But they're hampered by some influential people who don't want them to find the truth.' Naming no names. Helen raised her eyebrows – she knew who I meant.

I told her briefly about the clinic being ransacked and the man

172

with the knife. She listened, still with the same expression – reserved, perplexed, but not exactly surprised . . .

'What makes you think I know anything?' she asked.

'Caroline had no one to talk to, no one she could really trust. Her husband's a shit, her best friend betrayed her by becoming his lover. I think she trusted you. I think she told you what was going on.'

Helen's hard gaze softened slightly. 'Did you know Caroline well?' she asked.

I shook my head. 'Not really.'

Helen pressed her hand against her chest. 'My first reaction when I heard how she died was disappointment. I didn't think she was the type to take her own life. She was too . . .' she flapped her hand, casting around for the right word '. . . plucky. She was jolly good fun.' Helen took another deep drag on the cigarette. Absently, she stood up and moved to a chair some distance away. I knew she was unsure about whether or not to trust me.

'How can I help?' she asked, warily.

I sat forward, eager to draw her out.

'Think back to the weeks before she died. How did she seem? What was happening in her life? What did she tell you about the story she was investigating?'

Helen puffed meditatively on her cigarette. 'She was preoccupied. Frankly, she was becoming a bit of a bore about it.' She paused and scrutinised me carefully.

'Some of our chats were fairly confidential.'

Discretion – an over-rated upper-class virtue if you ask me, but I nodded to show I appreciated her dilemma. She crossed her long legs.

'I'm not sure how relevant any of it is,' she said doubtfully. 'I've been over it all with the police. She didn't tell me anything that would give someone a reason to kill her.'

'Don't worry about the relevance,' I said, my impatience growing. 'Just tell me what she said.'

Helen carried on frowning. She was a slow thinker. I forced myself to get a grip on my impatience. I let the silence grow, giving her the space to decide whether to talk or not. Helen inhaled deeply and blew the smoke out in a slow stream.

'About three months ago, Caroline came round in tears because she'd found out who James was having an affair with.' Her voice was slow, almost a drawl. 'She'd suspected for ages that there was someone else, but she didn't know who it was. Then a friend happened to make some joky remark about how terribly trusting she was to let husband wine and dine her best friend and she put two and two together.'

'She must have been furious.'

'I've never seen anyone so angry. She was beside herself. She didn't know what to do.'

I nodded – tell me about it.

'She talked about leaving him, she talked about whether or not she should have it out with Lyn. She said she was going to take Harriet and go to her mother's – but she'd said that before. We had a few drinks, she went home and things seemed to go on much as before. Most of their friends knew what was going on. Then, not long afterwards, Caroline phoned me to say she was desperate to have lunch because she had so much to tell me. I thought she was going to tell me she'd left him.'

Helen stood up, walked over to the ashtray again and flicked ash off the cigarette. I envied her cool, effortless elegance and the way her clothes seemed to hang just right.

'I met her at Bibendum – the Terence Conran place – and she had three amazing bits of news. The first was that she'd heard that Edward Hunt had an affair with Lyn before she met James and she was using it to get money out of him. Caroline suspected that was how Lyn financed her habit.'

'You told this to the police?'

'Actually, no. Not this part. I didn't think it was appropriate.'

How discreet of her. Nothing like the Establishment looking after their own.

'How did Caroline find out?'

'Belinda told her.'

'So Belinda knew?' I had guessed as much.

'Oh, yes,' said Helen nonchalantly. 'Belinda and Edward's marriage is just a sham – all Belinda wants is to choose the curtains at Number Ten and all Edward wants is a presentable wife. Belinda plays it perfectly – she's terribly ambitious.'

'I see.' I said, shocked, but determined not to show it.

Helen drew once more on her cigarette, then put it out. She went over and opened a window and shook the curtains in an attempt to eradicate any trace of smoke.

'Rupert hates me smoking,' she smiled apologetically. She came and sat on a low armchair nearer the sofa where I sat. 'Caroline was afraid Lyn might try to get money out of James, but I told her I didn't think she need worry.' She shot me a confidential glance. 'James is *appallingly* mean about money.'

'Did James know about Lyn and Edward?' If he did, he made a good show of being shocked when I told him. Helen made an open gesture.

'That's what I said to her – why don't you tell him? But that was Caroline. She said she wasn't going to tell him because he wouldn't believe her, but I think she was waiting for the right time – to use it to get him back.'

'She wanted him back, then?'

'We all have our little weaknesses,' she said cattily. 'James was Caroline's.'

I was warming to Helen by the minute.

'What was the next piece of news?'

'Oh, this story about charities. She'd been working on an article about corruption in small charities and that gave her the idea of using the South American children's charity as a case study. She didn't want to ask James about it, so she managed to persuade the woman who runs the charity to let her work in the office for a few days. She got a copy of the accounts and a few contact names. But when she tried to follow them up, she couldn't get anyone to see her.'

'Why not?'

Helen frowned. 'Well, although money was coming in from the local groups, no one had heard of any of the contacts.'

'So she thought it was a cover?'

'She thought it was odd, so she told James about it and he went mad. He told her if she didn't stop meddling he'd leave her and take Hattie with him. He was so shirty about it, Caroline was convinced Edward and Robert had got him into some big business deal and that he'd make a hash of it and lose lots of money, so she was determined to find out what it was. But the really big news over that lunch was that she and Robert Winter had started a relationship.'

This was like a TV mini-series set in Chiswick. 'Quite a lunch,' I remarked.

Helen laughed. It was the first time I'd seen her tight face relax. She had perfect teeth and the laugh lit up her eyes.

'I told her quite plainly I was delighted she'd found someone else.'

'What's Robert Winter like?'

I had my own opinion but I wanted to hear hers.

'Stunning. He's an art dealer. Very well off. Lovely little flat in South Ken.'

I tried a little old school tie trick. 'Winter . . .' I fudged. 'Would he be related to . . .?' She took the bait.

'Oh, no. He's not related to anyone. He came from Croydon or somewhere. He's done awfully well. He trained at the Slade and then just met the right people.'

So he didn't inherit money, he made it. Was the art market really that buoyant? 'Was the relationship still going on when Caroline died?'

Helen considered. 'Yes. I think so. But . . .'

I sat forward on my seat. 'Yes?'

Helen considered. 'She . . . she said recently that she had this feeling that Robert was just using her. They seemed a bit distant at the party the night before she died. He's very charming – and terribly bright – but I know he was keen for her to drop the charity story too. He's a trustee, of course. She was never quite sure if he had some ulterior motive.' It did seem an odd coincidence that Winter should initiate an affair with her just at the time she was getting interested in SACA.

'I didn't see Caroline for a while after that, but she kept in touch by phone. By this time she was becoming obsessed by the charity and its accounts. Her latest theory was that it was some kind of tax shield for Edward. She was worried about James being caught up in it. James is so stupid about business, Caroline thought he was quite capable of getting himself up to his eyes in something without really understanding the implications. She still loved him, you see. She was convinced that Edward was – how shall I put it? – not as honest as he should be.'

'Do *you* think he's honest?'

Helen smiled and smoothed the cover on the arm of her chair.

'As honest as a politician can be.'

Good answer – ten points for tact. I smiled appreciatively and motioned her to go on.

'Then a week or so later, Caroline phoned me in a terrible state. She said she'd found out that Edward Hunt and Robert Winter were involved in something dreadful and that they'd forced James in on it too because of all the favours Edward had done for him. She said she didn't know what to do. She couldn't possibly expose the story because of James.'

I looked at Helen. Her face told me this was also something she'd kept back from the police. She was taking a risk in telling me. 'Do you know what it was?'

She shook her head. I believed her. What a charming lot they were . . .

Helen leaned back in her chair.

'That's all I know – I told you it isn't much.'

It seemed quite a bit to me. 'It's helpful. Thank you.' I felt I wanted to keep moving. I noticed the clock on the mantelpiece – five thirty. Damn. Clancy would be getting worried.

'May I use your phone?'

177

'Of course. It's in the hall.'

While Helen went into the television room to check on Superman and his minder, I dialled the clinic and asked Doreen to give Clancy a message. She refused point blank.

'She asked me to put you through as soon as you rang,' said Doreen. I started to protest, but she put me through anyway.

'Where the helluv you been?' yelled Clancy.

'I couldn't get to a phone,' I said curtly. 'I'm fine, but I'm busy. I can't make victim support this week, but I'll be back at your place by ten thirty – okay?'

'No. Not okay. Look Sara, I'm supposed to be –'

'Sorry Clancy, have to go. If I'm not back at ten thirty, call Barry.' I clicked down the receiver and dialled again, glancing at my watch to recheck the time. I expected to get an answerphone, but John answered the phone himself.

'Hello?'

'It's Sara – how come you're not at work?'

'I worked at home today. Where've you been? I've left no end of messages.'

'I've been a bit tied up. I wondered if I could pop over and see you.'

'Great!'

I felt a warm glow from his tone.

'How soon can you be here?'

'Oh, in about . . . half an hour.' The traffic would be bad.

'I'll cook a meal.' His concern for food impressed me.

'Good. See you soon.' I put down the phone, gathered up my things and poked my head into the television room on the right.

'Thanks, I'm off now.'

Helen came into the hall to see me out. 'Do let me know if there are any developments.'

'I will.' I held out my hand and she shook it languidly. She said goodbye and clicked the door behind me. I stood for a second in the doorway, looking round to see if the coast was clear. No sign of the white Orion. No strangers lurking on the street. I walked quickly to the car and shot off quickly to brave the rush hour crowds.

When you've been without a man for a while, it's the cuddles you miss as much as the sex. The kisses on the stairs as you pass, holding hands in the street, curling up together on the sofa. When I arrived at John's, as if by mutual consent we played house – me coming home, him cooking a meal, hugging each other casually in the kitchen instead of leaping into bed. I had my first glass of wine, then I told him about the attack. He was full of concern and wanted to know every detail. He made me pull up my jumper to show him the wound – it was healing nicely by now. I snuggled into his chest and sniffed his neck – a pleasing, male scent. He stroked my upper back.

'You should be more careful,' he said. 'You're lucky to be alive. At least you'll leave meddling in this Caroline business now, won't you?'

I extracted myself from his arms. 'What d'you mean, stop meddling? I'm in this up to my eyeballs. What shall I do – put a sign outside my house saying "Sara's given up, fellas, knock it off"?'

'Haven't the police offered you any protection?'

'No.' I said, sulkily. 'I'm staying with a friend and they've told me not to go out alone.'

John looked exasperated. 'Then why did you come out alone?'

'Did you *want* me to bring a friend?'

'Yes,' he said firmly.

'Into threesomes, eh?'

A smile played around his eyes. 'You're a stubborn bugger, aren't you?'

I grinned and gave his shoulder a playful punch. 'Known for it, sonny.'

He went back to preparing the dinner.

I sipped my wine, leaned against the fridge and watched him cook. It says a lot about a person, how they cook. He was preparing a mouth-watering mixture of garlic, rosemary, anchovies and wine vinegar to add to some lamb chops, sizzling in a pan. I'm the kind of cook who confidently throws everything together in double quick time, making a huge mess in the kitchen, which I then have to clear up. I learned to cook by watching my mother, so I work fast and rarely look at books. I'm usually cooking for two hungry children who want to eat immediately. John's style was more painstaking. He put each ingredient in the bowl in a meticulous, almost studious, way. He didn't actually measure anything, but he assessed the amount carefully and washed the utensil as soon as he'd used it.

'Who taught you to cook?'

'I taught myself.'

'Are you always this tidy?'

'Does that mean something psychologically?'

I made a vague gesture. 'Premature potty training. Nothing to worry about.' He chuckled. His hands were large, but his fingers tapered slightly at the tips, giving him a delicate touch. He sliced the anchovies into slivers and used the same slicing action with the fresh rosemary. I was fascinated by his fastidiousness.

We ate in the kitchen, sitting at a small table overlooking the garden, chatting as we savoured each mouthful, the mood low key and restful. The phone rang twice, but John let the answerphone take it. We kept off the subject of Caroline, suicides and murders, choosing instead to pull apart a film we'd both seen and found interesting. It was as if we'd fast-forwarded through the usual agonies and arguments to a time when you feel completely at ease in other's company. I liked the fact that we were able to talk pleasantly as two people, rather than being locked into communicating as lovers.

We moved into the sitting room with our coffee and I told him I had to leave soon. I felt guilty about Clancy and wanted to be back on time. At the back of my mind, I was debating whether or not to show John the list of bank account numbers – if I was honest, that was the main reason I'd come over to see him. On the one hand, I was eager to know what he made of it. On the other, I wasn't sure I trusted him where James Blythe was concerned – I wished I knew exactly where he stood. It was nine thirty – I'd have to introduce the subject quickly or not at all. John put on some music – Billie Holliday. I reached over to my bag.

'I want you to take a look at something.'

He came and sat down on the floor beside me and put his arm round my shoulders.

'Have you heard of South American Children's Aid?' I felt, rather than saw him, tense.

His voice was still relaxed. 'It's a charity, isn't it? James has invited me to a fundraising do this Saturday. I think he's a trustee.'

'Do you handle the accounts, by any chance?'

John sighed. 'Here we go again. No, Sara, I don't handle the accounts because I'm not James' bloody accountant. What about it, anyway?'

I handed him the paper with the numbers on. He looked at it, scanned down the list slowly and then looked up at me. He disguised it admirably, but my years of experience have taught me to read faces like books – he clearly saw something in the list I didn't.

'What's this?' he asked. The casual tone was forced.

'I was hoping you might tell me.'

'It just looks like a list of numbers to me.' Afsana knew it was a list of bank accounts, and she's not even an accountant. He tried to keep his tone light. 'Where did you get it?'

'You tell me what it is and I'll tell you where I got it.'

He looked at the list again and shrugged. 'Search me.'

I took back the paper and stood up.

'Never mind,' I said brightly. 'Worth a try.' I took back the paper, gulped down my coffee and stood up. 'I must be going now.'

'Wait a minute!' I've never seen a grown man leap up so fast. 'Let me look at it again.'

'Another time. I've got to go –'

'Please –' He put his hand and I snatched the paper away. He grabbed my wrist – I raised my chin and coldly met his eyes. We froze in that position. He wanted the list – he wanted it badly – but he couldn't bring himself to fight me for it. He let go of my wrist. I put the paper back in my bag.

'I'll give you a ring,' I said casually.

He went to grab his jacket from the back of a chair. He seemed agitated.

'I'll drive you back to your friend's.'

'No thanks.'

'All right, you drive and I'll follow you in my car.'

'No.'

His face flushed. 'You're in danger,' he said, almost angrily. 'Can't you understand that?'

'Thanks for telling me.' I said calmly. 'I'll bear it in mind.'

He followed me to the front door. 'Be careful.'

'You too.' I walked briskly to the car, got in and started the engine. John waved briefly from the doorway and shut the door. I felt a leaden sense of apprehension. What was it about that list which made John so nervous? Why didn't he come clean and tell me about it? I sighed with disappointment. It wouldn't matter if John wasn't so attractive – so apparently honest, such good company. Why was he lying through his back teeth over his relationship with Blythe and Hunt?

I forced John out of my mind and told myself to concentrate on the road. I glanced in the mirror. Oh, no! The white Orion again. I slowed down for the traffic lights before Hammersmith bridge and squinted at the driver in the dim half-light – a lone man again, maybe the same one, but definitely the same car. This time, fired by anger, I acted quickly. As soon as the lights went green, I roared off over the bridge. Traffic was flowing smoothly right up to Hammersmith Broadway. The Broadway isn't exactly a roundabout, it's three lanes of fast-moving traffic with buildings in the middle. Cutting into the flow of traffic, especially at night, is an art. I took a calculated risk and darted forward. The Orion behind me couldn't follow without hitting something and had to wait for the next break. I tore round the Broadway, took the second exit – King Street – then turned right into another approach road back to the Broadway. Not being able to see me, the Orion would have had to gamble on an exit – probably King Street – and the one thing he wouldn't expect would be that I'd go round the Broadway a second time. This time, I took the Shepherd's Bush Road and drove straight to Clancy's. I'd managed to shake him

182

off again – I hoped he felt a proper fool. But a cold chill in the pit of my stomach turned itself into an uncomfortable question – the Orion driver had definitely not followed me there, so how did he know I was at John's in the first place?

I parked the car right outside Clancy's flat, dead on ten thirty. I suddenly realised how tired I was. I climbed the stairs heavily and let myself in with my key.

'Hi, Mom, I'm home!' I called, in a mock American accent. Clancy appeared in the doorway of the sitting room and stared at me mutely. I stepped back in surprise – I expected her to be sitting crossly, arms folded, ready to tell me off. Her eyes were on fire.

'Clancy! What's the matter?'

She took a deep breath. 'Don't panic, Sara,' she said, her voice faltering with emotion. 'David phoned and – Hannah's gone missing.'

chapter twelve

'What do you mean – missing?' It was like the sound of fabric ripping, like the deadly crunch of one car smashing into another. I reeled back as if from a blow. Not Hannah. Not my baby.

Clancy started to explain, but I couldn't take it in. My brain was roaring self-reproach – I shouldn't have got involved in Caroline's death; I shouldn't have let Hannah go to David's; I should have told David to watch the children extra-carefully; I should have –

'. . . and Hannah went off to look inside the milking tent with all these cows milling around and somehow they lost her –'

'What? What cows? What are you talking about?'

'Sit down, Sara!' ordered Clancy.

I sat down.

Clancy mouthed the words slowly, 'Hannah got lost at an agricultural fair late this afternoon. But it's okay, she'll turn up, they're going to find her.'

'What happened? Where is she?' I was still trying to grasp it.

'David wants you to ring him.' Clancy got the phone and I dialled his number with shaking hands. He answered after the first ring. His voice was only just holding.

'I took them to a fair this afternoon, near Leominster – Angie stayed at home. Hannah was rushing about everywhere looking at all the animals. I kept telling her not to wander off –' His voice cracked. 'I'm sorry Sara, I'm so sorry . . .'

'It's not your fault. Just tell me what happened.'

'Hannah wanted to go inside this marquee where they were giving a milking demonstration, but Jake wanted to watch the ferret racing,

184

so I said okay, you go and watch the milking and meet me here in ten minutes.' He left her in the tent! He left my baby all alone! Stupid, stupid man. 'When I went back to the tent she wasn't there.'

I had a vivid image of Hannah's beaming, toothy smile and shining eyes and my arms ached to hold her.

'What did you do?'

'It was late by this time – six o'clock. I went to see the organisers, checked the lost children's tent and so on. A couple ȯf people said they'd seen her just outside the tent, talking to an elderly lady with three spaniels, but no one could remember seeing her after that. We waited and waited – Jake asking every five seconds "Where's Hannah, Daddy?" "Isn't she coming home with us?" and other helpful remarks.'

'Oh, God.'

'I phoned Angie on the off-chance that Hannah phoned her, but she hadn't. Then we called the police.'

'What are they doing?'

'Everything they can. One of the people who saw Hannah was very helpful and stayed around until the police came. He gave a description of the old lady, so they're looking into that. One good thing is that everyone knows each other round here – the police have put out public appeals and they're hoping someone will have noticed something.'

My heart was pounding wildly, but my mind was clear. I looked at my watch – ten forty-five. I could be there by one thirty. 'I'm coming down there. I'll leave now.'

'No!' said David sharply. 'The police say it's important for us to stay by the phone. Go back to your house. Hannah knows both our phone numbers, so if she's just lost –'

'– or if someone has taken her –'

'We can't think about that. We can only hope –' He didn't finish the sentence.

'David – a client of mine . . .' I felt torn between unreasonable blame and desperate guilt. I had to tell David something but I didn't know where to start. This was my fault. I got us into this – my curiosity, my stupidity, my arrogance.

'It's . . . it's a long story, but someone has been after me, trying to . . . to kill me. I was attacked in the street by a guy with a knife – that's why I've been staying at Clancy's. I just hope this isn't . . . anything to do with that.'

He hesitated – he didn't know what to say.

'These people,' I continued, 'The ones who are after me – they seem to have . . . a lot of contacts, a lot of influence. I wouldn't put anything past them. I . . . I think I should tell the police about it – the ones who are looking for her.'

It took him a few seconds to take in what I was saying. 'You mean – you think these people might try to get at you through Hannah?'

'Yes.'

'Why didn't you tell me you were attacked?'

'I should have done. I'm sorry.'

He was silent for a moment, probably thinking 'stupid, stupid woman.'

'The only important thing is to get her back,' he said.

'Yes.'

We returned to practicalities. 'Go back to your house. I'll give you the name and number of the police who are dealing with it.' He gave me a number in Leominster.

'Obviously, if either of us hears anything –'

'Yes.'

'And David . . .'

'Yes?'

'I'm sure it'll be okay.'

'Yes,' he said doubtfully. 'Yes, I'm sure it will.' We hung up.

Clancy offered me a drink, but I refused. I wanted to keep my head clear and sharp. I started to pack up some things.

'Are we going back to your place?' asked Clancy.

'I am. You stay here and get some sleep.'

'No. I'll come.' I blessed her, silently. We hurried down the stairs

186

and got into the car, all my tiredness having melted away as the adrenalin started to flow. I felt alert in the way you do when you're trapped in a nightmare and all your senses are focused on escaping from it. As we drove along the Uxbridge Road, still bustling with people wandering home from the pub, Clancy read my thoughts.

'Stop blaming yourself. None of them knows where David lives –'

'They could find out.'

'You're paranoid.'

'She knows she mustn't go with strangers, Clancy – God knows, I've told her a million times – they must have taken her by force.'

'She's a bright kid. She wouldn't do anything stupid.'

'What about the old lady?'

'It could've been anyone.'

'They can't have just disappeared – someone must have seen them.'

Clancy didn't answer. I knew she feared the worst.

When we got to my house the first thing I did after checking the answering machine was to call Barry. He was brisk and efficient.

'Have you had any notes, threats, phone calls?'

'No.'

'Good. Did you mention to anyone connected with Caroline where David lives? Blythe? Hunt? Lyn Hargreaves? Think carefully.'

'No. I'm sure I didn't. Caroline might possibly have known ... but I doubt it.'

'Okay. I'll get on to the local lads and see what I can find out. They'll probably want to talk to you.'

They did. I spent an hour and a half retelling the Caroline story. You could tell the officer in Leominster thought it a likely yarn – a typical, over-dramatic tale of London folk.

Barry phoned again when I'd finished and tried to reassure me. 'Don't jump to conclusions. Plenty of kids run away and you find them a few hours later playing detectives in a garden shed. She'll turn up.'

'Not Hannah. But I hope you're right.'

187

'I think it's highly unlikely to be connected to the Blythe case, but if anyone contacts you, ring me straight away.'

'Okay. Thanks, Barry.'

I paced up and down staring at the phone, willing it to ring. But the phone was maddeningly silent. Steve saw lights on at the house and came straight over. He was shocked and upset when I broke the news, but he still managed to radiate a quite confidence. The three of us sat, staring at the phone, talking out various possibilities of what might have happened, desperately trying to persuade ourselves, and each other, that it would all turn out well in the end. When Steve went home, Clancy went off to sleep in my bed while I curled up in a duvet downstairs by the phone.

It was a long night. Every time I closed my eyes, I saw Hannah's face, Hannah's smile, heard her voice telling some tale from school or a never-ending story, plucked from her imagination. Or singing a song in the car in a high, wobbly voice. My fitful sleep was peppered by horrifying dreams of pain and fear and the sound of the phone ringing, which launched me onto my feet, but turned out, cruelly, to be fake. Each time I woke up, I remembered anew that the nightmare was real, repeated to myself what was too awful to face: 'Hannah's missing. Hannah's gone. I may never see Hannah again.' I tried to reach her telepathically, to think of her so strongly that my thoughts must reach her. I got such a vivid picture of her that way, I convinced myself she wasn't dead. She couldn't appear to me so real, so solid and yet be lying somewhere cold and lifeless. I even prayed. I made bargains with God, made promises I swore I'd keep if only Hannah could be safe. Another truth hit me in the midst of all the dread – that through all the harassment and drudgery of looking after small children, it's vital to savour the sheer joy of caring for them. Only when you think they might be gone – for ever – do you realise how much your life's pleasure comes from them, how they make the world bright and fresh. Without their energy, their eagerness, everything is grey and drab and meaningless.

At seven a.m. the phone rang. I snatched it up –

'Yes?'

'Sara – it's John.'

'Oh!' It was a sound of pure frustration and disappointment.

He went right past it. 'I've got something to tell you –'

'Is it Hannah?' I asked breathlessly. He sounded puzzled.

'What?'

'Hannah – my daughter – she's disappeared. Do you know anything?'

'No, I'm sorry. That's terrible. What happened?'

I gabbled the story, then added, 'Just tell me one thing, John. I don't care what you know or don't know about Caroline's death or Blythe or the charity, or anything. Just tell me this one thing – is Hunt behind all this? Is it him – or his wife, or Winter? Who's doing this to me?'

'I don't know,' he said flatly.

My voice rose a notch higher. All the pent-up emotion of the night was ready to burst. 'For Christ's sake, my daughter is missing! She could be dead. At least tell me if it's Hunt or not.'

'I think – I don't know – I think . . . Hunt might have been the one who sent that chap after you, but –'

'That's all I need to know.'

'But –'

I slammed the phone back on to the receiver. I thought of Hunt's suave arrogance and thought how easily I could kill him. John was irrelevant. Blythe was irrelevant. They were both working for that power-hungry bastard. I had only one thought now – I must go and see Hunt.

I phoned David just to be sure he hadn't heard anything. Nothing. I talked to Jake briefly and told him we were all very worried, but we were sure Hannah would be home soon.

'What if she isn't, Mummy? Where is she?'

I refused to be drawn. 'I don't know where she is, Jake, but the police are looking everywhere for her. They'll find her.'

All the time, at the back of my mind, I was mulling over how I could get to see Hunt. Where would he be at this time? At his house in Surrey? Who could give me a short-cut to him? Not James. Not Belinda. Helen! On impulse, despite the early hour, I dialled her number. Her husband answered and I asked to speak to her.

'I'm afraid she's still asleep.'

'I'm sorry, but please could you wake her. It's terribly urgent.'

'Who is this?'

'Sara Kingsley.'

'Wait a minute.'

Helen came on the line sounding croaky and annoyed.

'Hello?'

'I'm sorry to wake you up Helen, but I had some dreadful news late last night. My daughter Hannah's disappeared – she's just seven – and I'm afraid she might have been kidnapped. I think it may be to do with – what we were talking about yesterday.'

'Oh, dear.'

'I want to talk to Edward Hunt.'

She didn't respond.

'I want to talk to him, but I don't have his number or his address.'

'Can't you get him at the House of Commons?'

'I need to see him now, Helen. Now. This morning. I think he may know where Hannah is. Please. Have you got his private address?' I sat in agony as she slowly took in what I wanted.

After a pause she said, 'Wait a minute.' She covered the phone and I heard muffled talking.

'I don't have it, but my husband does. What day is it? Friday. He stays in town during the week . . .' There was some shuffling in the background.

'Thanks, darling,' she said. 'Right – have you got a pen?' I took down a phone number and the address of a place in Belgravia. I thanked her gratefully and hung up.

Hands trembling, I rang the number. A man answered, his words slightly slurred with sleep – but I recognised the sonorous voice.

It was definitely him. I clicked down the receiver without saying a word. He was there right now. If I was quick, I could catch him. I raced upstairs, splashed some water on my face and pulled on some fresh clothes. I made an attempt to comb my hair without a great deal of success. It felt good to have a sense of purpose to be actually doing something instead of waiting by an interminably silent phone.

In the kitchen, Clancy was making coffee, clad in a huge Bob Marley T-shirt. She looked up anxiously. 'Any news?'

'No.' I grabbed my bag, checked to make sure the computer disk was there, then extracted the printout.

'Where are you going?'

'To see Hunt.' Clancy opened her mouth to protest, but I held up my hand to cut her short. 'Clancy – listen. Call Steve and ask him to make several copies of this list – at least three. Tell him to keep one at his flat and post one to you at your address and fax one to Barry Graham at Chiswick police station, with a note explaining how I got it. You stay by the phone until I get back . . . I mean – *please*, Clancy, *would* you stay by the phone?' I stood up on tiptoe and kissed her cheek. 'You're a pal, Clancy. Thanks.'

She narrowed her eyes. 'Cut the charm, it makes me nervous. Leave Hunt's address and number by the phone. If you're not back in two hours, I'll send a search party.'

'Okay.'

I left Hunt's details by the phone and went to the front door, then I changed my mind. What if Orion man was conducting a dawn vigil? I went back through the kitchen and left by the back door. I picked my way across the dewy grass of our pocket-handkerchief garden, hoisted myself up on to the fence and dropped into the tiny passage which runs along the terrace. (Hardly even a passage – more of a jungle path.) Wet with dew, I emerged on Churchfield Road and went straight to A1 Cars to order a minicab. The sun was already warm – it was going to be a beautiful day, but all I could think of as I walked along was my sweet, chubby Hannah. Every step was laced with dread and half formed images of where she might be and how she might be feeling. But I was driven on by one clear idea – that if Hunt was behind this I would get Hannah back by using every possible means. Hunt could have everything I possessed – including my life – in return for Hannah's safety.

The cab was a battered old Volkswagen estate, driven by an Egyptian who had been up all night and was very keen to share his thoughts on the current state of the Egyptian economy. The journey seemed to take hours and I was anxious Hunt would be gone by the time I got there. Every traffic light seemed to be against us. At seven forty-five, I spotted the right number in an elegant Georgian terrace a few streets away from Belgrave Square and interrupted the driver's diatribe on Egypt's foreign policy to get him to stop. I leaped out, paid him, then strode up to the door and pressed the shiny buzzer of the intercom.

'Yes?' It was a woman's voice.

'Sara Kingsley. I need to see Sir Edward Hunt. Very urgently.'

'One moment, please.' I waited for two or three minutes, expecting refusal, planning how I would insist. Then to my surprise, the door was opened and a middle aged woman ushered me inside.

She was obviously the housekeeper. A woman of forty or so, probably Filipino, dressed not exactly in a maid's uniform, but in a black skirt and white blouse which amounted to the same thing. The door opened into a grand entrance hall with a polished granite floor, covered by an exquisite, richly coloured Eastern rug – silk, no doubt. Straight ahead was a gracefully sweeping staircase. Despite my agitated state, I was struck by how beautiful and well-proportioned everything looked in a Georgian house which had not been chopped up and converted to offices or flats.

The woman led me into a room off to the left – a kind of study-cum-library, with a desk, a leather sofa and chairs and glass bookcases. She betrayed no surprise at my arrival so early in the morning and gave no indication of how Hunt would receive me.

'Sir Edward will see you in a moment,' she said in a monotone. 'Wait here, please.' She indicated a chair for me to sit in, then strode

192

out and shut the door. I paced anxiously round the room, unable to sit still. I peered out on to the street through the heavily curtained window, then scanned the bookcases absently. They were mostly leather-bound volumes, history and politics, some of them in Spanish. The room was sparsely furnished, but what was there was worth having – an antique walnut occasional table, a large leather-topped desk with elaborately carved legs, a crystal whisky decanter. Hunt wasn't short of either taste or cash. I felt nervous, but determined. The mere fact that Hunt was seeing me meant that I had something to bargain with. The trick would be to know what it was and how to use it. Was it knowledge of Lyn's affair, or the bank numbers, or both? Whichever it was, I was going to have to bullshit my way to getting Hannah back.

A moment or so later, the door opened and the man himself stepped quietly into the room. Even at this time of day, at such short notice, Hunt looked immaculate. Closely shaven, besuited, his grey-flecked hair, carefully combed. His left eyebrow was, as usual, raised higher than the right giving him an expression of mild amusement.

'Miss Kingsley,' he said calmly. 'What can I do for you? Do sit down.' He waved a hand graciously in the direction of a chair.

I remained standing and stared at him.

'Where's Hannah?'

'I beg your pardon?'

'My daughter, Hannah. Just tell me where she is and what you want.'

He sat down on a high leather wing-backed chair, crossed his legs, placed his long, well-manicured fingers together and put them to his lips. 'I take it your daughter is missing.'

The detached tone cut right through me. I had difficulty restraining myself from smacking him in the mouth. 'You know she's missing.' I hissed between gritted teeth.

'My dear Miss Kingsley,' he said sharply. 'I can see you are distressed, but please will you sit down. How old is she?'

I sat down, clasping my hands together to stop them shaking.

'She's seven,' I said, controlling my voice with effort. 'Too young to be used as barter for a set of bank account numbers.'

He frowned. 'What on earth are you talking about?'

'You know what I'm talking about.' I said, almost shouting. 'I have the numbers of SACA's bank accounts. One disk here – copies in other places. If you don't give me Hannah, I'll take them straight to the police.' Slightly calmer I added, 'Return her unharmed and all the disks will be destroyed.' My heart was pounding.

Hunt seemed unmoved. 'What a vivid imagination you have, Miss Kingsley.' Hunt remarked. Slowly, he uncrossed his legs, rested one elbow on the arm of his chair and placed a finger on his cheek. 'You are suggesting that I have kidnapped your daughter in order to procure a set of bank numbers.' He paused and looked thoughtful for a moment. 'That's an extraordinary and, I might add, serious accusation. Have you gone out of your mind?' I was impressed by his cool, but not daunted. I knew enough about Hunt now not to trust the young statesman exterior. This was one elegant gentleman who had some pretty sordid connections.

I gave way to a surge of impatience. 'All right, how about this. You've had Hannah kidnapped in order to stop me releasing to the tabloids details of your extramarital affair with Lyn Hargreaves, a drug addict.' He continued to stare at me impassively.

'A great story for the right paper,' I continued. '"Sir Edward Hunt's kinky love life". Or perhaps it should be "Minister Linked to Woman's Murder"?' I quavered inwardly at the accusation and tried to think only of Hannah. Hunt, still perfectly composed, brought his hand down and rested it loosely on the arms of the chair. The counsellor in me was intrigued by his body language. It was uncannily studied and controlled. His voice was low and measured.

'Are you threatening me, Miss Kingsley?'

I leaned towards him and met his stare head on, spitting the words into his face. 'Just give me my daughter back and I'll forget I ever knew Lyn Hargreaves.'

A nervous blink betrayed a chink in his sentient mask. But his tone remained flat. 'Your insinuations are frankly as disgusting as they are untrue. You have no evidence whatsoever of this alleged affair. Not even the lowliest tabloid would take such a story.'

'What about a serialisation of the dead woman's diary? Would that be evidence enough?'

He sat very still, pressed his lips tightly together and raised one eyebrow interrogatively.

'Lyn Hargreaves kept a detailed diary the whole time. She gave it to me for safe keeping about two weeks ago. I've lodged it with someone I can trust.' I was pleased with that lie, thought up on the spur of the moment.

'You expect me to believe this?'

The thought of Hannah made me reckless and familiar. 'Come on, Hunt, you know what Lyn was like – always out for the main chance. It wasn't just the money. She knew you'd get her, sooner or later. She just wanted to bring you down with her.' My words hung on the hushed air, mingling with the heavy smell of leather and wax polish. The classical formality of the room seemed menacing, like an invisible force surrounding me, ready to strike. Then the tense silence was shattered by the piercing whirr of a telephone. Only I jumped. Hunt reached out an arm to answer it. 'Edward Hunt.'

He listened for a moment and then held out the receiver.

'It's for you.'

My stomach lurched. I jumped up and grabbed it from his hand. I was full of trepidation.

'Yes?'

'She's okay, Sara!' Clancy yelled. 'She's okay! They've found her!' My head swam. Initial puzzlement gave way to utter relief. My eyes filled with tears. I glanced over at Hunt, watching impassively through half-closed eyes.

'Thank God,' I whispered, trying to hold back the tears. Then, taking my voice under control, I asked roughly. 'Where was she?'

'With the crazy old lady. She told Hannah she had a spaniel puppy for her, back at her house. She took her out to a farm. She gave Hannah the puppy, then told her it was too late to go home. The guy from the next farm saw her in the morning and called the police.'

I was speechless – I couldn't trust myself to utter a word without breaking down.

'Are you still there, Sara?'

'Yes.' I gulped. 'Tell them – I'll drive down this afternoon.'

'They're coming home. David's bringing them as soon as Hannah has finished with the police.'

'Is she . . . okay?'

'She's fine – can't understand what all the fuss is about.'

'Thanks for telling me, Clancy.'

I put down the phone and stared at Hunt.

'It wasn't you.'

He laughed. 'No, it wasn't me.' For one wild moment I wondered how I had got there. What the hell was I doing in an MP's flat at eight o'clock in the morning, threatening to expose him to the tabloids with a fake diary? I had two options. I could plead insanity, make my excuses and think about what it all meant later, or I could stay, use the leverage and find out what I could. If Hunt was as innocent as he claimed, he was being mighty patient. Why hadn't he called the police immediately and had me thrown out?

'I apologise.'

He nodded graciously and started to get up. 'I'm sure you want to go back to your daughter.'

I raised my hand. 'One moment.'

He sighed wearily and glanced at his watch.

'Miss Kingsley, I have to be at the Commons at nine. I take it you retract your threats and accusations. We both know them to be pure fabrication.'

'Do we?' I tried the eyebrow trick, not entirely successfully. I stood up and walked behind my chair and stroked the satin back with my hands. 'Sir Edward, I have not had a good week. On Saturday, the clinic where I work was vandalised. On Monday, someone tried to kill me. On Tuesday, my daughter disappears. Before that, two women who came to me for counselling died in mysterious circumstances. For someone who leads a fairly uneventful life, this is too much excitement all at once.'

'Get to the point.'

I gripped the chair back. 'The point is, I still think I have something you want. Two things,' I corrected myself. 'Lyn Hargreaves' diary, and the list of SACA's bank accounts. I have no personal vendetta against you – I won't give the diary to the media. But I do want to know the truth about who killed Caroline and Lyn. It's too late to stop me now – the list of bank accounts has already been sent to the police. And this time, they're taking it seriously.' I hoped that would turn out to be true. The way Hunt was sitting reminded me of a jaguar – a coiled spring of bristling energy, waiting to pounce. But nothing I said seemed to unleash him. Hunt pulled down his cuffs and swept a fleck of dust off his lapel. He stood up.

'I'm afraid you're out of your depth, Miss Kingsley,' he said enigmatically. He opened the door of the study and stood there waiting for me to go through. As I passed in front of him I caught the damp, spicy fragrance of expensive aftershave.

'Given your interest in SACA,' he said to my back, 'one hopes you will be supporting our function tomorrow night.'

I swivelled to face him. 'Will you be announcing your retirement?' I asked sweetly.

He countered with a sardonic smile. 'I would certainly advise you to hear my speech before going to the police.'

My stomach flipped over. Was this a trap? Did Hunt want me at the dinner so he could kill me, or get at Hannah and Jake, or was he really going to reveal something important? The housekeeper appeared from nowhere to show me out.

'I'll think about it,' I said coldly.

Hunt headed for the stairs. 'I do hope your week improves.' It was a laconic, throwaway line, tossed over his shoulder as the housekeeper saw me to the door. It was the nearest a man like Hunt could get to bravado.

I shouted at Hannah mercilessly when I saw her. Yelled all the pent up fear and relief until we both burst into tears, then I pulled her into my arms and showered her with kisses, hugged her, stroked her, felt each one of her precious limbs until she begged me, giggling, to set her free. Jake, feeling left out, threw himself into the scrum and I slobbered over them as much as they would let me. I found myself following them from room to room. It was bliss to have Hannah and Jacob back in the house again, to fill the empty spaces with their rapid movements and high-pitched voices. When everyone had gone – David, Angie, Clancy and Steve – I sat the children down and got Hannah to tell me exactly why she had gone with the old lady and why she had ignored my warnings about talking to strangers.

'You said *men*, Mum. Don't talk to strange men.' She was right, of course. 'And you said if I was ever in trouble to go to a *woman* and I *was* in trouble, I was lost, so I asked this nice old lady and she said she had a spaniel puppy she'd been saving just for me not far from the show – I thought she was Daddy's *friend*.' Her lower lip started to quiver again. I gave her a cuddle and decided to leave it, for the time being, at a reformulated warning about strangers, with extensive subclauses to cover women of all ages, martians, cows, and dogs of every breed.

I was surprised not to hear from Barry. I tried to call him at intervals during the day, wanting to thank him for the part he played in finding Hannah and also to find out whether he had any more on Caroline's killer. But each time I called, they told me he was unavailable. As the day progressed, I started to feel paranoid. Was Barry avoiding me? Had Hunt gone to his friend the Chief Superintendent again? Barry seemed my only hope of ending the nightmare. If I could convince him the bank account numbers were significant, if he could drag up enough evidence to recommend a murder investigation against Hunt's wishes, then the heat would surely be taken off me. If the police had as much information as I did and were committed to doing something about it, the murderer would surely have no other motive to kill me but revenge. I felt alone and vulnerable, and obsessively protective of Hannah and Jake. I hardly slept again that night, getting up at intervals to check that they were still safe and sleeping.

I finally got hold of Barry Saturday lunchtime, at his home. My fear was confirmed when it was clear he didn't want to talk.

'I told you Hannah would turn up, didn't I? Anyway, I'm just in the middle of something so I'd better –'

'Wait a minute Barry. Did you find out anything from Winter? Was he the last one to see Caroline alive?'

'I can't comment on that, I'm afraid.' His tone was final.

I knew better than to argue, so I changed tack. 'Did you get the list of numbers I faxed you?'

'Yes.' Just 'yes'?

'D'you know what they are?' I asked impatiently.

'Could be bank accounts,' he said warily. 'We're looking into it. Now, Sara, I've got to go. I'll ring you next week.'

'Barry –!' He wasn't going to get rid of me that easily.

'What?'

'I saw Hunt yesterday and he suggested I should go to the SACA dinner in Richmond tonight – said he'd be making an important speech.'

'Did he now?' It was the first flicker of interest Barry had shown.

'What do you think – shall I go?'

Barry hesitated. 'I'm not sure I can advise you about that.'

'Oh, loosen up, Barry!' I found his PC Plod tone intensely irritating. 'Do you think it's safe to go, or not?'

'I don't see why not,' he said stiffly. Then, in his normal voice, he added, 'But don't go in your own car and get a reliable babysitter for the kids.'

Babysitter? I snarled inwardly – I was planning an armed guard.

The SACA fundraising dinner was held at a secluded hotel just off Richmond Hill, overlooking the river – so modest and well hidden I had some trouble finding it from Richmond Station. I gave my coat in at the hotel cloakroom and went straight to the loo. I love posh hotel loos, with their gilt and velvet chairs, bottles of cologne and moisturiser, and crisp, clean towels. They seem to me the essence of luxury. I stood in front of the sparkling full-length mirror and checked my appearance. The ticket for the dinner hadn't specified a dress code, so I'd opted for a short, slinky black velvet dress studded with tiny pearls – one of the few truly expensive dresses I own. I'd bought it for a friend's wedding a couple of years ago and hadn't worn it since. My hair was up, the frizzy curls held in place by two black combs which set off nicely the two drop pearl earrings. I frowned into the mirror – my dark eyeshadow seemed to go all round. There were dark rings underneath my eyes from stress and lack of sleep and somehow they made my nose look bigger. I wished I were tucked up in bed at home, preferably in the same room as the children. I tried to shake off anxious thoughts about leaving Hannah and Jake for the evening. I'd asked Clancy and Steve to babysit together and begged them not to let the children out of their hearing. I'd spent half an hour before I left issuing strict instructions about not answering the door or the phone, unless it was me, in which case I'd give four rings first.

The dining room was to the rear of the hotel, overlooking the river. There were windows on three sides, providing a marvellous view of the graceful curve of the river as it sweeps away to Hampton Court. I took a glass of sparkling wine from a tray offered by a waiter and went to admire the view. The lush trees at the river's edge were becoming silhouettes against the reddening sky. A pair of scullers sped along, their backs see-sawing like a metronome; the last pleasure boat bumped and bobbed against the landing stage, spewing out its cargo of tourists and plodding families.

Turning back to the room, I saw it was starting to fill up. Hectoring, ruddy-faced men were exchanging handshakes and hearty greetings. Their wives hung back, or else pretended to examine the pictures dotted about the room, in an effort to cover their early-evening embarrassment. I stood to the side watching wearily, too tired to make the effort to mingle. There was an artistic contingent – two well-known actors, married to each other and known supporters of the Conservative Party, talking to a someone I vaguely recognised, probably a children's television presenter. The others were an assortment of Tory councillors, businessmen – some of whom looked South American – and Rotarians. Marjorie was bustling around fluttering her hands and kissing the air beside people's cheeks. I looked around for Hunt but he was nowhere to be seen. James was there, laughing with a group of buddies. And I spotted Robert Winter managing to look both chic and rebellious in a cream suit, black tie and a panama hat. Typically, he was leaning against a wall, looking utterly bored, while two near-naked young women vied for his attention. He caught me looking at him and returned my scrutiny with a cold stare, but showed no sign of recognition. I turned away quickly, my anxiety level shooting up.

There were about thirty round tables in the dining room, each elegantly set with pale pink table linen, heavy duty cutlery and crystal glasses, eight settings to a table. I wandered between the tables, surreptitiously looking at the name cards to see who I'd be sitting with. When I found my name tag, I registered with a jolt that someone had thoughtfully placed me next to John. John Miller. A good way of keeping an eye on me, I reflected cynically. I considered swapping the tab, but by now everyone was milling round the tables looking for their place and it was clear that some people had gone through complex political manoeuvres to secure the place they wanted. I wasn't willing to brave the wrath of a portly councillor, deprived of his place beside the head of the finance committee. Marjorie and John appeared at the table from different directions, at exactly the same moment.

'So glad you could come, dear,' gushed Marjorie, shaking my hand with her cold, dry paw.

'Hello, Mrs Martinez.'

'Marjorie, *please*. Why, Mr Miller . . . how delightful.' She lowered her voice to a mock whisper. 'As you see, I managed to seat you beside Miss . . . from the NBC.' At least he had the grace to blush.

Marjorie beamed at us both briefly, then put a bejewelled hand on each of our arms.

'Hope you enjoy it!' she laughed gaily. And she bustled off, like a buzzing bee determined to visit, however briefly, each flower in the room.

'We . . . need to talk,' said John in a low voice.

'I don't think so,' I said, staring past him to the group which was approaching our table.

'Maybe this isn't the best place.'

'Maybe there's nothing to say.'

He looked quite different in a suit. I was glad, because it made it easier to see him for what he was – the employee of a corrupt politician. Pity he was such a good lay. I wondered how on earth he'd got caught up in it all – was it the money? The vicarious sense of power?

'I heard about Hannah,' he said eagerly.

I nodded curtly – from Hunt, no doubt.

'That's very good news. Did they arrest the woman?'

'Yes. Hannah won't be left alone for a minute from now on,' I said darkly.

'You feel that way now,' he said, easily. 'But you'll probably let up in a week or two.'

I stared at him, appalled – was this a veiled threat from Hunt?

'I don't think so,' I said icily.

I felt ashamed of having allowed myself to fall for him; that I had been so reluctant to pass up a possible relationship that I gave him the benefit of the doubt, when I knew he was lying through his teeth. Why didn't I let him go after that first night? I felt there must be some unconscious force at work which was impelling me to seek out deceivers, to prove, perhaps, that deception was all one could expect from men. How could I have been so wrong about someone? I made another rash decision – to go to Mel, cap in hand, and admit she was right about my being obsessed with men and deception. Maybe I did need help.

The other people at our table took their places and the waiters served the first course. The meal tasted like ashes in my mouth. I kept craning my neck anxiously in order to get a view of the top table. Neither Hunt nor his wife was there. I could just make out James, Winter, Marjorie between them, and then next to James, just one empty chair. Presumably, Belinda wasn't coming. The chair was intended for Hunt, the great philanthropist, whenever he deigned to turn up. Where was he? I was relying on him being there. I tried not to expect anything dramatic from his speech. But I felt my time was running out – unless I could convince Barry to act on the information I had, my life, and the lives of my children, would remain at risk.

John made a few desultory attempts to open a conversation, then lapsed into silence when he realised I wouldn't play ball. We both tried to talk to the rest of the table, but they all seemed to know each other intimately, as well as each other's children, holiday desti-nations and house decorating plans, so John and I were condemned to eat in uncomfortable proximity, in almost total silence. When the first course had been taken away, I couldn't resist interrupting the man on my left, to ask, 'Isn't Sir Edward Hunt supposed to be here?'

'That's right. Apparently, he was on his way, but he was called to an urgent meeting.'

My heart sank. 'Is he still coming?'

'Oh, yes, I'm sure he is. Sir Edward said he'd be here in time for pudding, didn't he darling?'

'It was a phone call from the Prime Minister, I believe,' breathed his wife with awe. I could tell John was also watching and waiting for Hunt. We continued eating side by side in tense mutual mistrust.

By the time the main course came, I was finding the tension unbearable. If Hunt wasn't coming, I may as well go home. Just as I was contemplating giving up and pleading illness, there was a flurry of activity near the door of the dining room. Several men appeared and stood discreetly against the back wall. I thought at first it was Hunt making his grand late entrance, preceded by his minders. Then another grey-haired man came in and made his way to the top table. He spoke first to Robert Winter, then James Blythe and Marjorie, then moved back down the table to talk to Winter again. The grey-haired man gestured towards the door, as if asking him to step outside for a moment, but Winter was shaking his head and gesticulating. James leaned across Marjorie and joined in the discussion. Winter started to argue with the grey-haired man, getting more and more heated, the sound of his voice rising above the burble of the dinner table talk. I could only make out one or two words –

'. . . ridiculous! . . . demand to see my solicitor . . .' One or two people turned to stare. The man placed a heavy hand on his shoulder. All of a sudden, Winter stood up, grabbed the edge of the table and flung it back with a resounding crash. The room fell silent, then everything happened at once. Winter leaped over the table and started to thread his way through the seated diners towards the window. A voice yelled, 'Stop! Police!' at Winter's back and several of the men pulled out guns.

John sprang up, 'Where the hell's Hunt?'

The initial burble of curiosity and surprise rose rapidly towards hysteria; one or two of the women screamed and were hustled under the table by their menfolk. Three officers hurtled across the room after Winter, leaping on to tables, sending food, glasses and crockery flying. Winter was several tables ahead of them, thrusting chairs aside and shattering glasses in his wake. People watched him, open mouthed, cowering as he pushed past them. I suddenly grasped what he was doing – a few more feet and he'd be able to leap out into the garden and run for the bushes by the river.

'Stop him!' I sprang out of my seat and grabbed an empty wine bottle.

'Sara – no!'

Ignoring John's cry, I scrambled over a couple of chairs, sat down heavily on an empty chair and shot out my foot in his path – bingo! Winter was spread-eagled on the floor, cursing loudly. I raised the wine bottle, ready to bring it down on his head.

'Hold it!' A hand grabbed my wrist from behind and pushed me to the floor, while another policeman hurled himself on top of Winter. The two men rolled over between the chairs, Winter struggling

204

wildly, howling guttural curses. His cream suit was crushed and stained with red wine. He was such an unlikely contrast to the languid stylish figure of an hour ago, that for one stupid moment I wondered if this was some kind of performance art laid on as entertainment. When a second policeman joined the fray, I tossed the thought aside. The struggle looked real enough. The two officers grappled with Winter for a second, then hauled him up between them, gripping one arm each. Winter raised his head and tossed a lock of hair out of his face. I stood up shakily, still holding the wine bottle which had dripped red wine onto my legs and shoes. Our eyes met. His were dark pools of pure hatred. As one of the officers clicked on the handcuffs, Winter contorted his features into a grotesque grimace and spat vigorously into my face. I gasped with horror and instinctively slapped him. The policemen tightened their grip.

'Out of the way, miss. C'mon, mate, move it.' They started to half push, half drag him out of the room. I wiped my face with a napkin and looked back towards the top table. James Blythe, looking dazed, was quietly submitting to the indignity of being handcuffed. Marjorie, also handcuffed, was weeping copiously between two women police officers. I recognised Barry among the figures standing by the wall near the door, talking earnestly into a police radio.

Barry started to push his way through the throng towards where I was standing. John intercepted him just before he reached me.

'Where's Hunt?' he yelled at Barry, raising his voice to be heard above the din.

'On the plane to Argentina.'

'Oh, for fuck's sake! What happened?'

'Your boys lost him, that's what happened.'

'Jesus.' John looked devastated.

'Will someone tell me what's going on?' I shouted.

They both looked at me.

'We've got them,' Barry said, smiling smugly. 'It's all over.'

'All except for Hunt,' growled John.

'I thought you were working for Hunt,' I said to John. My head was muddled.

Barry laughed. 'This is John Miller, Sara – Customs and Excise.'

'What?' I turned to him. Our eyes met for a moment. He was the first to turn away.

'I'm sorry. I'll explain later.' He made off into the throng.

I stared incredulously, and wondered if I'd heard him right. Customs and Excise? A customs officer? I couldn't decide whether to laugh or cry. I'd been going out with a bloody customs officer! It wasn't as bad as being Hunt's right-hand man, but it wouldn't be the career of choice for the man with whom I shared my bed. Barry came and stood beside me.

'It's a drugs operation. They've been watching Hunt for months. Miller was working under cover. You know him, do you?'

I cleared my throat. 'Uh, vaguely,' I replied.

Barry was buzzing. 'The charity's a money-laundering operation. You can be quite proud of yourself – those bank account numbers were all they needed to link the operation to Hunt. He must have known the game was up – he scarpered to South America in the early hours of this morning.'

'Can you get him back?' I asked.

'Maybe,' said Barry. 'That's not my department. First thing is to get these two murder investigations under way.'

At last! I hardly dared ask the next question. 'Did Hunt kill Caroline?'

Barry shook his head. 'Miller reckons Hunt put Winter up to it. Caroline was getting too near to finding out how SACA operated. They warned her, but she wouldn't play. What I couldn't tell you yesterday was that we've now got some good forensic on Winter – semen and fabric samples that put him at the scene, and several witnesses, including James Blythe, who saw his car near the house, at, or after, the time of death.'

'He killed her after they made love?'

Barry looked uncomfortable. 'One theory is that he followed her

206

home, killed her, and then – couldn't resist. He's a bit of a sicko by all accounts.'

It might help explain his taste in art. 'What about Lyn?'

'That was more of a routine elimination from what I can gather.'

'A routine –?'

'You don't make millions out of importing cocaine without squashing a few people. Lyn gets greedy, Hunt's under pressure because people are starting to talk, so he decides she has to go. Bit stupid of him so soon after Caroline, but maybe he was getting panicky. Politicians, drug barons – the buggers have always got their weak spots.' Barry rubbed his hands with glee. 'Not often you get a politician who's a drug baron, though. What a scandal, eh?' I shook my head to try and clear it, unable to take it all in.

A few minutes later John came back and offered to drive me home. I suddenly felt utterly and overwhelmingly exhausted. I wasn't sure I was up to being in the same car as him, talking to him, but curiosity got the better of me. I wanted to hear his side of the story. I nodded my acceptance. Barry was busy punching a number into a portable phone.

'We'll be hours yet,' he said happily. 'Got to get this lot out.' He indicated the roomful of confused diners, all standing around in stunned groups, asking each other questions. 'I'll probably send someone round to get a statement from you tomorrow. Hello . . .? Mike – it's Barry.'

The grey-haired man was trying to mollify groups of angry diners. Hotel staff were running round, trying to clear up the mess. The noise of people talking and crockery crashing into bin bags was deafening. John and I pushed our way through the crowd to the door – a word to the policeman on duty there, and we were out. I fetched my coat and we stepped out into the car park to breathe the cool, refreshing air. The smell of the river hung on the night, damp and heavy. The noise and blazing lights of the hotel started to recede as we walked towards his car, our feet crunching on the gravel.

'So you thought I was working for Hunt?'

'Not really,' I lied. 'You had "customs officer" written all over you.'

'We've been watching Hunt for the last year,' said John, as we cruised through the near empty streets of Richmond. 'We knew he was running a massive, worldwide drugs operation, but we couldn't definitely connect him to any single network. Then we started investigating James Blythe, Hunt's brother-in-law, doing incredibly well from contracts handed to him by Hunt –'

'Why did Hunt help him so much?'

'That's what we wanted to know. We knew there must be a pay-off and we thought Blythe was probably laundering the money through the building projects. It was my job to get in with Blythe and try to get access to the accounts of some of his joint ventures with Hunt.'

'Did you find anything?'

'Nope. Not a thing. It all seemed to go one way – from Hunt to Blythe. When Blythe's wife was killed, we found out about the story she was working on and guessed, like you, that it must have been because of her interest in SACA. Ideal for laundering drugs money, charities – I'm surprised it isn't done more often. But we still didn't have any hard evidence. Then I met you and I thought you might have it.'

'So you decided to screw it out of me – literally.'

'No!' protested John. 'That part was unintentional.'

'Terrific.'

'I don't mean it like that. I mean – I liked you, I wanted to get to know you. When I asked you out, I justified it to myself by telling myself you knew something I didn't. It almost cost my job, if that makes you feel any better.'

'It doesn't.'

'When Winter saw us at Ronnie Scott's that night – if he'd told James I was seeing you, I could've kissed goodbye to all the trust I'd spent months building up. All those fucking golf matches.'

'Don't you like golf?'

'I hate it. Football's my game.'

Well there's a blessing. Customs Officer he might be, but at least he wasn't a golfer!

208

'I thought Winter was the most likely suspect from the beginning,' John continued. 'The way he seemed to suddenly muscle in on Caroline just as she got interested in the charity. What a sleazeball.'

'How come you knew she was murdered?'

'I didn't know, I guessed. But I didn't have anything to tell the police that would let them call it a murder, especially with Hunt putting the squeeze on. Winter did a neat job too – except for staying too long at the scene.'

I let that pass. It was too disgusting to talk about. 'What about Marjorie Martinez – was she in on it?'

John laughed. 'Up to her eyeballs! Her husband Freddie was a major player in the network – killed by a hit man in Rio, probably on Hunt's orders. Cutting her into SACA was a way of shutting her up.'

I couldn't wait to tell Clancy her instinct about Marjorie was right.

I wondered what would become of our relationship now. I felt ambivalent. I hated the fact that he'd lied to me. I didn't like his job. And yet, he was intelligent, funny, sexy . . .

'What happens now you're not working under cover?'

'Back to the office – that's my bit of excitement for the next ten years. They don't let you do it that often because you get recognised.'

We sat thinking our separate thoughts for a minute or so. I found myself wondering how far his deception went – and how much it mattered.

'Is John Miller your real name – from Leicester and everything?'

'Course it is – everything I told you was true.'

'Except you're not an accountant.'

'I am, but I work for Customs and Excise.'

'Who was the guy in the white Orion?'

John smiled sheepishly. 'Sorry about that. He was one of ours.'

'He's bloody hopeless.'

John smiled. 'I'll tell him you said so.' His voice became serious again. He stole a glance at me as he drove. 'If you don't want to see me again – I can understand that. But I want you to know, from my point of view – I'd like us to . . . you know, to carry on . . . to start again.

I don't know about you, but – I like being with you . . .' His words hung on the air. They sounded true – I thought they were true – but who could tell? I thought for a while before replying.

'I'll have to think about it. I've got one or two things to sort out first.'

I let myself into the house quietly and shut the door. I stood still, just inside the hall, and listened for a moment. I could hear the reassuring rise and fall of Jake's snoring in the room at the top of the stairs. I opened the sitting room door to find Clancy and Steve sitting on the floor, bickering over a game of Scrabble. They both jumped when I opened the door, looked up and waited for me to speak. I had an overpowering desire to giggle.

'It's over,' I said, sinking into a chair and grinning like an idiot. There was an expectant silence.

'What happened?' It was Steve who spoke.

'He was a customs officer!' I burst out.

Clancy and Steve looked blank.

I threw back my head and laughed, for the sheer joy of being alive.

The Women's Press is Britain's leading women's publishing house. Established in 1978, we publish high-quality fiction and non-fiction from outstanding women writers worldwide. Our exciting and diverse list includes literary fiction, detective novels, biography and autobiography, health, women's studies, handbooks, literary criticism, psychology and self help, the arts, our popular Livewire Books series for young women and the best-selling annual *Women Artists Diary* featuring beautiful colour and black-and-white illustrations from the best in contemporary women's art.

If you would like more information about our books, please send an A5 sae for our latest catalogue and complete list to:

The Sales Department
The Women's Press Ltd
34 Great Sutton Street
London EC1V 0DX
Tel: 0171 251 3007
Fax: 0171 608 1938

Also of interest:

Hannah Wakefield
Cruel April
A Dee Street mystery

Dee Street doesn't want to fall out with her old friend, Janey
Riordan. After all, Janey has just found her a key defence witness
for an upcoming murder trial. But Janey still owes Dee's law firm
a lot of money and no amount of favours can replace the cash.
Now Janey's refusing to pay and, even worse, is risking their
friendship with a nasty, and very public, argument.

Then Janey is found murdered – and all the evidence points to
Dee . . .

'Excellent and original.' *Daily Telegraph*

'An engaging first-person heroine with real depth and a
distinctive voice.' *Time Out*

'Lively, entertaining and legally accurate.' *Guardian*

'Riveting.' Patricia Craig, *London Review of Books*

Crime Fiction £5.99
ISBN 0 7043 4475 0

Marcia Muller
A Wild and Lonely Place
A Sharon McCone mystery

Sharon McCone. Private Investigator. Determined. Decisive.
Daring. Now drawn into a world of international crime . . .

A series of diplomats have been the targets of a vicious bombing
campaign. Reluctantly, Sharon McCone agrees to help a security
firm protect their client and, behind a wall of diplomatic
immunity, uncovers a sinister web of intrigue, corruption and
murder. Now a child's life is in peril and, as McCone's trail leads
back to those she's been hired to defend, she finds herself in the
sights of a ruthless and cold-blooded killer . . .

**'Marcia Muller and her private investigator, Sharon
McCone, hold hands and jump off the deep end . . . The
professional risks pay off all round.'** *New York Times*

**'Muller produces the sort of thrillers that enthusiasts
always hope for but rarely get.'** *Sunday Times*

'Excitement amplified.' *Literary Review*

Crime Fiction £5.99
ISBN 0 7043 4454 8

Meg O'Brien
A Bright Flamingo Shroud
A Jesse James mystery

Jesse James has learnt never to rely on the men in her life. When the going gets tough, they're sure to leave. Just like the grandfather she never knew. But now her grandfather is back – if the man who knocked on her door is who he claims to be.

He's a down-and-out conman, a liar and a thief, but he needs Jesse's help. 'Gramps' has swindled a dangerous man and is in hiding for his life. Against her better judgement, Jesse allows herself to get involved. But once the man who claims to be her relative is safe, Jesse herself becomes the target of a vicious, cold-blooded rage . . .

'**A wise-cracking, street-smart heroine in the V I Warshawski mould . . . Fast-moving, feisty and fun.**' *Sunday Times*

'**A verve and naturalness unmatched since Sue Grafton teamed up with a Gatling gun.**' *Clues*

'**Meg O'Brien is a real find. Credible characters, wonderful dialogue. A bestseller.**' Ted Allbeury

Crime Fiction £5.99
ISBN 0 7043 4463 7